SIX TALES OF THE JAZZ AGE AND OTHER STORIES

BY F. SCOTT FITZGERALD

NOVELS

THE LAST TYCOON *(unfinished)*
with a foreword by Edmund Wilson and notes by the author
TENDER IS THE NIGHT
THE GREAT GATSBY
THE BEAUTIFUL AND DAMNED
THIS SIDE OF PARADISE

STORIES

BITS OF PARADISE
uncollected stories by Scott and Zelda Fitzgerald
THE BASIL AND JOSEPHINE STORIES
edited with an introduction by Jackson R. Bryer and John Kuehl
THE PAT HOBBY STORIES
with an introduction by Arnold Gingrich
TAPS AT REVEILLE
SIX TALES OF THE JAZZ AGE AND OTHER STORIES
with an introduction by Frances Fitzgerald Smith
FLAPPERS AND PHILOSOPHERS
with an introduction by Arthur Mizener
THE STORIES OF F. SCOTT FITZGERALD
a selection of 28 stories, with an introduction by Malcolm Cowley
BABYLON REVISITED AND OTHER STORIES

STORIES AND ESSAYS

AFTERNOON OF AN AUTHOR
with an introduction and notes by Arthur Mizener
THE FITZGERALD READER
with an introduction by Arthur Mizener

LETTERS

THE LETTERS OF F. SCOTT FITZGERALD
with an introduction by Andrew Turnbull
LETTERS TO HIS DAUGHTER
with an introduction by Frances Fitzgerald Smith
DEAR SCOTT/DEAR MAX
edited by John Kuehl and Jackson Bryer

AND A COMEDY

THE VEGETABLE
with an introduction by Charles Scribner III

SIX TALES OF THE JAZZ AGE

AND OTHER STORIES

By F. SCOTT FITZGERALD

CHARLES SCRIBNER'S SONS, *New York*

Charles Scribner's Sons
Macmillan Publishing Company
866 Third Avenue, New York, N.Y. 10022
Collier Macmillan Canada, Inc.

Library of Congress Catalog Card Number 60-6410
ISBN 0-684-71762-X

20 19 18 17 16

Printed in the United States of America

INTRODUCTION

Of all the things which have been said and written about my father since he died nearly twenty years ago, I think he would be most flattered by the following entry in Number 7 of the "Fitzgerald Newsletter," a publication edited by Matthew Bruccoli and printed by the University of Virginia Press.

"The FN," says the Fitzgerald Newsletter, "has long regarded with distaste the liberties taken with the author's wife. It is clearly impudent for writers who never knew her to refer to Mrs. Fitzgerald as 'Zelda'—just plain 'Zelda.' It does not seem to us that this is a mark of affection. Rather it appears to carry a sanctimonious snicker . . . the same familiarities have long been taken with Fitzgerald, of course, but we *were* startled when he turned up as 'Scott' in a Ph.D. dissertation which presumably had been approved by a board of scholars."

I cite this as an example of what the daughter of a cult is up against when she thinks of writing about her father—even the daughterly prerogative of registering occasional indignation has been pre-empted by others. Over the past ten years since the "revival" began, he's had his admirers, detractors, protectors, disciples, imitators, and sociological and economic dissectors (see "F. Scott Fitzgerald and the Communist Society," or "The Meaning of the Work of F. Scott Fitzgerald in Relation to Psychoanalytic Principles"). Everybody, as Dorothy Parker said in her *Esquire* review of *Beloved Infidel,* has dug up the bones of F. Scott Fitzgerald, and some, to use her own delicate phrase, have even gnawed on them. What am I to add, who can scarcely distinguish any longer between the real and the unreal, what I've read or heard somewhere and what I actually remember—and without even one of Proust's famous *madeleines* to bring the past tumbling back with vivid images and sharp impressions?

I recall mostly that my father was always sitting at his desk in a bathrobe and slippers, writing, or reading Keats or Shelley—although there was often a faint aroma of gin in the air to dispel too romantic a picture. And there is just one clear recollection that I know is mine and which I bring up because there are so many occasions when I'm reminded of it. It's the trick of how to remember the kings of England.

"Daddy, you're crazy," I told him when he insisted on sitting me down one night, lecturing me on the virtues of having a trained mind, and making me memorize the pyramid he'd devised.

"This will be the most useful thing you ever learned," he said sternly. "This and Jiu-Jitsu, which I plan to have you learn someday so you can defend yourself under any circumstances. Now say after me in a sort of sing-song, because that's the only way to learn it:

William William Henry Stephen
Henry Richard John Henry

"Now the next lines you'll never forget as long as you live because they form a pattern:

Edward Edward Edward Richard Henry Henry Henry
Edward Edward Richard Henry Henry
Edward Mary Elizabeth
James Charles Cromwell Cromwell Charles James
George George George George
William Victoria
Edward George Edward George

"Then," he said, "you simply memorize half a dozen key dates, like 1066 and 1215 and 1620, and associate them in your mind with that particular king. After that, you always have a frame of reference to start with."

He struggled for years with a similar trick for remembering the American presidents, but never was able to invent the perfect formula. It wasn't just kings and presidents, but ancestors, that we were forced to hear about (though I was an only child, there were always other children like Andrew Turnbull, our neighbor, or my childhood friend Peaches Finney, to share these horrors). On the wall of his writing-room as far back as I can remember hung one of those striped charts of the history of man in snake-like parallels.

"Do you children have any idea," he would ask, "what your great-great-grandfather did?"

The answer was an awe-stricken "no," of course.

"He raised potatoes in Ireland," he would say triumphantly, having looked it all up ahead of time, or, "He was a hired soldier in Germany. Now—do you know what your great-great-great-great-great-great grandfather probably did?"

Again an anxious silence.

"He lived in a cave, probably. He lived by spearing fish, and he probably carried a big club." I realize now what the objective was—to give the young and foolish a sense of history, which he had himself in such abundance. Malcolm Cowley has made this point before, in his *New Yorker* review of Edmund Wilson's labor of love, *The Crack-Up*—but I think it's important because it accounts for so much of the special, unique flavor of his writing, and even to some extent for the miseries he suffered in his later years. He was like a surgeon performing an operation upon himself, hurting terribly but watching the process with a fascinated detachment. He was a historian by nature, and the era which he recorded happened to be the Jazz Age, but in my opinion he was not "the historian of the Jazz Age," in the sense that it was his identification with the Jazz Age which gave him his extraordinary popularity in the twenties and early thirties and again today. To me this volume, appropriately named *Six Tales of the Jazz Age and Other Stories,* serves to reinforce this point.

It combines stories from *Tales of the Jazz Age,* published in 1922 following his second novel, *The Beautiful and Damned,* with stories from his third collection, *All the Sad Young Men,* which followed his third novel, *The Great Gatsby*. During these same years he also wrote other stories, which are not reprinted here because Malcolm Cowley has included them in his earlier collection: some of the best known are "May Day" and "The Diamond As Big As the Ritz," which were in the original *Tales of the Jazz Age,* and "The Rich Boy" and "Winter Dreams," which were included in *All the Sad Young Men.* A few short pieces in the original collections have been left out, for the very reason that they are "pieces" rather than stories proper.

Except for these few omissions, the "tales" in this volume represent the best of my father's short stories—in his own unusually accurate judgment of these matters—between the years of 1920, when he turned 24, and 1924, when he hit the ripe old age of 28. He actually wrote at least twice this number of stories, but they were uncollected and could now only be found in the back files of such magazines as *Redbook* or *Cosmopolitan.* In his ledger—he documented his life with lists and scrapbooks and photographs in a remarkably careful way for a man so restlessly romantic, but there, no doubt, was the historian again—he listed most of these as "Stripped and Permanently Buried," which meant that he had plucked the best thoughts for deep-freezing in his notebooks, and discarded the carcasses as unworthy of preservation for posterity.

Monthly Expenditure 1923

TAXES---	200.00
RENT----	300.00
FOOD----	200 00
COAL + WOOD	35 00
ICE----	8 50
GAS----	27.00
LIGHT---	14 50
PHONE---	25 00
WATER---	5 00
SERVANTS---	295.00
DOCTORS---	42 50
DRUG STORE--	32 50
CLUB-----	105 50
NEWSPAPERS--	5 00
BOOKS----	14 50
FLOWERS----	9 00
AUTO------	23 00
PLUMBER----	13 50
ELECTRIC---	1 50
COMUTATION---	4 00
SCOTT'S CLOTHES	33 00
Zelda's CLOTHES	1.00 00
BABY'S CLOTHES	2.5 00
HOUSEHOLD--- AND MISSCLANEUS CHARGES	81 00
TYPING-----	12 00
	1620 40

TRIPS, PLEASURE + PARTIES

House Liquor	80 00	(apportioned per 1 mo)
PLAZA	26 50	"
ALABAMA	33 00	"
ATLANTIC CITY	10 00	"
THEATRE	20 00	"
BARBER	10 00	"
HAIR DRESSING	15 00	"
CHARITY	4 00	"
WILD PARTIES	100 00	"
Taxis	15 00	"
Gambling	33 00	"
LUNCHES (N.Y.)	25 00	"
SUBWAY (ect)	29 00	"
Miscelaeneous Cash	276 00	"
	785 60	
	1620.40	
	2396.00	

COURTESY OF FRANCES FITZGERALD LANAHAN

The earliest stories, like "The Camel's Back," brought $500 from *The Saturday Evening Post*—and it is a tangible measure of my father's remarkable and rapid success that for one of the last ones in this volume, "The Adjuster," he was paid $2,000 by *Redbook*. I bring up these vulgar material matters because I am always impressed by the amount of work my father turned out in his brief lifetime. During these years, he consistently made somewhere between $20,000 and $25,000 dollars a year—and a typical year's output would include half a dozen or more short stories, at least half a novel, a movie scenario or two, four or five articles, several book reviews, and possibly part of a play.

This is hardly relevant, but while I was preparing myself to write this introduction by going through mountains of old clippings and letters, I came across his actual list of how he spent that money, painstakingly printed in his own hand, complete with characteristic misspellings. This is for the year 1923, the same year in which he wrote many of the stories in this volume.

The struggling young author of today may marvel at such riches, but I wonder even more at such productivity, considering the amount of income and the gusto with which it was put into circulation. Judging by my own experience, I've often wondered how there was a moment left for the bathtub gin and the splashing in the Plaza fountain. Somehow, there must have been 48 hours a day in that Golden Era, so that against the thought that it was wasteful that he died so young I have always been able to comfortingly weigh the fact that he packed at least two lives into those 44 years.

Even more puzzling to me—and I assume to all readers who were born too late to remember the Jazz Age—is how my father came to be a symbol of it at all (except much later, in retrospect, when his life seemed to parallel it so closely that he became woven into the legend of the era). After you've read the stories, perhaps you'll ask yourself, as I did, "Well, it's absorbing writing, but what's jazzy about it?" The people seem so innocent, somehow, so earnest and well-meaning, that it's hard to detect the abandoned strains of "Charleston" in the background—only the faint strumming of a latter-day "Shine On, Shine On, Harvest Moon," or "By the Sea, By the Sea, By the Beautiful Sea." As one friend whose opinion I asked remarked, "Why, if you didn't know who wrote these stories, you'd guess it was O. Henry!"

If you search closely, you may discover two flappers between these covers: the girl who washes her shoes in gasoline in "The Jelly-Bean," and the one who dances on top of the table at Pulpat's restaurant in "O Russet Witch!" As a matter of fact, the one who dances on top of the table turns out to be a professional dancer, and rightfully belongs less to the flapper family than to the turn-of-the-century soubrettes of Paris. That leaves only Miss Nancy Lamar, the gasoline girl, who's just one step more sophisticated than Mary Pickford in *The New York Hat.*

And another thing which may surprise some youthful readers of this collection is the fact that nobody in it kisses anybody else unless they're related by marriage or parenthood—again with the single exception of the gasoline girl, who rewards Jim with a brush of her irresistible lips for his success at shooting craps. The book is totally devoid of sex as we have come to take it for granted in modern writing. One exasperated wife in "Gretchen's Forty Winks" appears on the verge of going into New York to the theater with another man, but her husband promptly puts a sleeping powder into her coffee and that disposes of the matter summarily. Where, oh where, is this wild and brassy Jazz Age?

I must confess both a special affection for this book of stories and a special prejudice against it. To start with the prejudice, it implies in no uncertain terms that people of my own general age are very old parties indeed. I refer you to the following paragraph in "The Curious Case of Benjamin Button":

"At that time Hildegarde was a woman of thirty-five, with a son, Roscoe, fourteen years old. In the early days of their marriage Benjamin had worshipped her. But, as the years passed, her honey-colored hair became an unexciting brown, the blue enamel of her eyes assumed the aspect of cheap crockery—moreover, and most of all, she had become too settled in her ways, too placid, too content, too anemic in her excitements, and too sober in her taste. As a bride it had been she who had 'dragged' Benjamin to dances and dinners—now conditions were reversed. She went out socially with him, but without enthusiasm, devoured already by that eternal inertia which comes to live with each one of us one day and stays with us to the end."

My husband doesn't mind that part so much—what he takes exception to is another excerpt, this one from "O Russet Witch!":

"At forty, then, Merlin was no different from himself at thirty-five;

a larger paunch, a gray twinkling near his ears, a more certain lack of vivacity in his walk."

I've always wondered why a well-organized group of his readers didn't have my father tarred and feathered for his blatant impertinence. But perhaps this is the one detectible Jazz Age note after all: you had to be young, apparently, during the Jazz Age, or life might as well not have been gone on with at all.

No—those who are looking in the attic for the silver flask and the raccoon coat won't find them here, though they may find many other quaint and delightful things to catch their interest. I have a special fondness for these stories not just because they're fun to read, but because they prove something—that F. Scott Fitzgerald was a good deal more than a wild young man with talent, who came to symbolize a disheveled era to the point where fact and legend were indistinguishable.

Maxwell Perkins, then an editor at Scribners, said it best in a letter to my mother not long after my father died:

"In a way Scott got caught in the public mind in the age that he gave a name to, and there are many things that he wrote that should not belong to any particular time, but to all time . . . he transcended what he called the Jazz Age, and many people did not realize this because of the very success with which he wrote of it."

FRANCES FITZGERALD LANAHAN

December, 1959

CONTENTS

SIX TALES OF THE JAZZ AGE
AND OTHER STORIES

THE JELLY-BEAN

JIM POWELL was a Jelly-bean. Much as I desire to make him an appealing character, I feel that it would be unscrupulous to deceive you on that point. He was a bred-in-the-bone, dyed-in-the-wool, ninety-nine three-quarters per cent Jelly-bean and he grew lazily all during Jelly-bean season, which is every season, down in the land of the Jelly-beans well below the Mason-Dixon line.

Now if you call a Memphis man a Jelly-bean he will quite possibly pull a long sinewy rope from his hip pocket and hang you to a convenient telegraph-pole. If you call a New Orleans man a Jelly-bean he will probably grin and ask you who is taking your girl to the Mardi Gras ball. The particular Jelly-bean patch which produced the protagonist of this history lies somewhere between the two—a little city of forty thousand that has dozed sleepily for forty thousand years in southern Georgia, occasionally stirring in its slumbers and muttering something about a war that took place sometime, somewhere, and that everyone else has forgotten long ago.

Jim was a Jelly-bean. I write that again because it has such a pleasant sound—rather like the beginning of a fairy story—as if Jim were nice. It somehow gives me a picture of him with a round, appetizing face and all sorts of leaves and vegetables growing out of his cap. But Jim was long and thin and bent at the waist from stooping over pool-tables, and he was what might have been known in the indiscriminating North as a corner loafer. "Jelly-bean" is the name throughout the undissolved Confederacy for one who spends his life conjugating the verb to idle in the first person singular—I am idling, I have idled, I will idle.

Jim was born in a white house on a green corner. It had four weather-beaten pillars in front and a great amount of lattice-work in the rear that made a cheerful criss-cross background for a flowery sun-drenched lawn. Originally the dwellers in the white house had owned the ground next door and next door to that and next door to that, but this had been so long ago that even Jim's father scarcely remembered it. He had, in fact, thought it a matter of so little moment that when he was dying from a pistol wound got in a brawl he neglected even to tell little Jim, who was five years old and miserably frightened. The white house became a boarding-house run by a tight-lipped lady from Macon, whom Jim called Aunt Mamie and detested with all his soul.

He became fifteen, went to high school, wore his hair in black snarls, and was afraid of girls. He hated his home where four women and one old man prolonged an interminable chatter from summer to summer about what lots the Powell place had originally included and what sort of flowers would be out next. Sometimes the parents of little girls in town, remembering Jim's mother and fancying a resemblance in the dark eyes and hair, invited him to parties, but parties made him shy and he much preferred sitting on a disconnected axle in Tilly's Garage, rolling the bones or exploring his mouth endlessly with a long straw. For pocket money, he picked up odd jobs, and it was due to this that he stopped going to parties. At his third party little Marjorie Haight had whispered indiscreetly and within hearing distance that he was a boy who brought the groceries sometimes. So instead of the two-step and polka, Jim had learned to throw any number he desired on the dice and had listened to spicy tales of all the shootings that had occurred in the surrounding country during the past fifty years.

He became eighteen. The war broke out and he enlisted as a gob and polished brass in the Charleston Navy-yard for a year. Then, by way of variety, he went North and polished brass in the Brooklyn Navy-yard for a year.

When the war was over he came home. He was twenty-one, his trousers were too short and too tight. His buttoned shoes were long and narrow. His tie was an alarming conspiracy of purple and pink marvellously scrolled, and over it were two blue eyes faded like a piece of very good old cloth long exposed to the sun.

In the twilight of one April evening when a soft gray had drifted down along the cottonfields and over the sultry town, he was a vague figure leaning against a board fence, whistling and gazing at the moon's rim above the lights of Jackson Street. His mind was working persistently on a problem that had held his attention for an hour. The Jelly-bean had been invited to a party.

Back in the days when all the boys had detested all the girls, Clark Darrow and Jim had sat side by side in school. But, while Jim's social aspirations had died in the oily air of the garage, Clark had alternately fallen in and out of love, gone to college, taken to drink, given it up, and, in short, become one of the best beaux of the town. Nevertheless Clark and Jim had retained a friendship that, though casual, was perfectly definite. That afternoon Clark's ancient Ford had slowed up beside Jim, who was on the sidewalk and, out of a clear sky, Clark had invited him to a party at the country club. The impulse that made him do this was no stranger than the impulse which made Jim accept. The latter was probably an unconscious ennui, a half-frightened sense of adventure. And now Jim was soberly thinking it over.

He began to sing, drumming his long foot idly on a stone block in the sidewalk till it wobbled up and down in time to the low throaty tune:

> "One mile from Home in Jelly-bean town,
> Lives Jeanne, the Jelly-bean Queen.
> She loves her dice and treats 'em nice;
> No dice would treat her mean."

He broke off and agitated the sidewalk to a bumpy gallop.

"Daggone!" he muttered, half aloud.

They would all be there—the old crowd, the crowd to which, by right of the white house, sold long since, and the portrait of the officer in gray over the mantel, Jim should have belonged. But that crowd had grown up together into a tight little set as gradually as the girls' dresses had lengthened inch by inch, as definitely as the boys' trousers had dropped suddenly to their ankles. And to that society of first names and dead puppy-loves Jim was an outsider—a running mate of poor whites. Most of the men knew him, condescendingly; he tipped his hat to three or four girls. That was all.

When the dusk had thickened into a blue setting for the moon, he walked through the hot, pleasantly pungent town to Jackson Street. The stores were closing and the last shoppers were drifting homeward, as if borne on the dreamy revolution of a slow merry-go-round. A street-fair farther down made a brilliant alley of vari-colored booths and contributed a blend of music to the night—an oriental dance on a calliope, a melancholy bugle in front of a freak show, a cheerful rendition of "Back Home in Tennessee" on a hand-organ.

The Jelly-bean stopped in a store and bought a collar. Then he sauntered along toward Soda Sam's, where he found the usual three or four cars of a summer evening parked in front and the little darkies running back and forth with sundaes and lemonades.

"Hello, Jim."

It was a voice at his elbow—Joe Ewing sitting in an automobile with Marylyn Wade. Nancy Lamar and a strange man were in the back seat.

The Jelly-bean tipped his hat quickly.

"Hi, Ben—" then, after an almost imperceptible pause—"How y' all?"

Passing, he ambled on toward the garage where he had a room upstairs. His "How y' all" had been said to Nancy Lamar, to whom he had not spoken in fifteen years.

Nancy had a mouth like a remembered kiss and shadowy eyes and blue-black hair inherited from her mother who had been born in Budapest. Jim passed her often in the street, walking small-boy fashion with her hands in her pockets and he knew that with her inseparable Sally Carrol Hopper she had left a trail of broken hearts from Atlanta to New Orleans.

For a few fleeting moments Jim wished he could dance. Then he laughed and as he reached his door began to sing softly to himself:

> "Her Jelly Roll can twist your soul,
> Her eyes are big and brown,
> She's the Queen of the Queens of the Jelly-beans—
> My Jeanne of Jelly-bean Town."

II

At nine-thirty Jim and Clark met in front of Soda Sam's and started for the Country Club in Clark's Ford.

"Jim," asked Clark casually, as they rattled through the jasmine-scented night, "how do you keep alive?"

The Jelly-bean paused, considered.

"Well," he said finally, "I got a room over Tilly's garage. I help him some with the cars in the afternoon an' he gives it to me free. Sometimes I drive one of his taxies and pick up a little thataway. I get fed up doin' that regular though."

"That all?"

"Well, when there's a lot of work I help him by the day—Saturdays usually—and then there's one main source of revenue I don't generally mention. Maybe you don't recollect I'm about the champion crap-shooter of this town. They make me shoot from a cup now because once I get the feel of a pair of dice they just roll for me."

Clark grinned appreciatively.

"I never could learn to set 'em so's they'd do what I wanted. Wish you'd shoot with Nancy Lamar some day and take all her money away from her. She will roll 'em with the boys and she loses more than her daddy can afford to give her. I happen to know she sold a good ring last month to pay a debt."

The Jelly-bean was non-committal.

"The white house on Elm Street still belong to you?"

Jim shook his head.

"Sold. Got a pretty good price, seein' it wasn't in a good part of town no more. Lawyer told me to put it into Liberty bonds. But Aunt Mamie got so she didn't have no sense, so it takes all the interest to keep her up at Great Farms Sanitarium.

"Hm."

"I got an old uncle up-state an' I reckon I kin go up there if ever I get sure enough pore. Nice farm, but not enough niggers around to work it. He's asked me to come up and help him, but I don't guess I'd take much to it. Too doggone lonesome——" He broke off suddenly. "Clark, I want to tell you I'm much obliged to you for askin' me out, but I'd be a lot happier if you'd just stop the car right here an' let me walk back into town."

"Shucks!" Clark grunted. "Do you good to step out. You don't have to dance—just get out there on the floor and shake."

"Hold on," exclaimed Jim uneasily, "Don't you go leadin' me up to any girls and leavin' me there so I'll have to dance with 'em."

Clark laughed.

" 'Cause," continued Jim desperately, "without you swear you won't do that I'm agoin' to get out right here an' my good legs goin' carry me back to Jackson Street."

They agreed after some argument that Jim, unmolested by females, was to view the spectacle from a secluded settee in the corner where Clark would join him whenever he wasn't dancing.

So ten o'clock found the Jelly-bean with his legs crossed and his arms conservatively folded, trying to look casually at home and politely uninterested in the dancers. At heart he was torn between overwhelming self-consciousness and an intense curiosity as to all that went on around him. He saw the girls emerge one by one from the dressing-room, stretching and pluming themselves like bright birds, smiling over their powdered shoulders at the chaperones, casting a quick glance around to take in the room and, simultaneously, the room's reaction to their entrance—and then, again like birds, alighting and nestling in the sober arms of their waiting escorts. Sally Carrol Hopper, blonde and lazy-eyed, appeared clad in her favorite pink and blinking like an awakened rose. Marjorie Haight, Marylyn Wade, Harriet Cary, all the girls he had seen loitering down Jackson Street by noon, now, curled and brilliantined and delicately tinted for the overhead lights, were miraculously strange Dresden figures of pink and blue and red and gold, fresh from the shop and not yet fully dried.

He had been there half an hour, totally uncheered by Clark's jovial visits which were each one accompanied by a "Hello, old boy, how you making out?" and a slap at his knee. A dozen males had spoken to him or stopped for a moment beside him, but he knew that they were each one surprised at finding him there and fancied that one or two were even slightly resentful. But at half past ten his embarrassment suddenly left him and a pull of breathless interest took him completely out of himself—Nancy Lamar had come out of the dressing-room.

She was dressed in yellow organdie, a costume of a hundred cool corners, with three tiers of ruffles and a big bow in back until she shed black and yellow around her in a sort of phosphorescent lustre. The Jelly-bean's eyes opened wide and a lump arose in his throat. For a minute she stood beside the door until her partner hurried up. Jim recognized him as the stranger who had been with her in Joe Ewing's car that afternoon. He saw her set her arms akimbo and say something in a low voice, and laugh. The man laughed too and Jim experienced the quick pang of a weird new kind of pain. Some ray had passed between the pair, a shaft of beauty from that sun that had warmed him a moment since. The Jelly-bean felt suddenly like a weed in a shadow.

A minute later Clark approached him, bright-eyed and glowing.

"Hi, old man," he cried with some lack of originality. "How you making out?"

Jim replied that he was making out as well as could be expected.

"You come along with me," commanded Clark. "I've got something that'll put an edge on the evening."

Jim followed him awkwardly across the floor and up the stairs to the locker-room where Clark produced a flask of nameless yellow liquid.

"Good old corn."

Ginger ale arrived on a tray. Such potent nectar as "good old corn" needed some disguise beyond seltzer.

"Say, boy," exclaimed Clark breathlessly, "doesn't Nancy Lamar look beautiful?"

Jim nodded.

"Mighty beautiful," he agreed.

"She's all dolled up to a fare-you-well to-night," continued Clark. "Notice that fellow she's with?"

"Big fella? White pants?"

"Yeah. Well, that's Ogden Merritt from Savannah. Old man Merritt makes the Merritt safety razors. This fella's crazy about her. Been chasing after her all year.

"She's a wild baby," continued Clark, "but I like her. So does everybody. But she sure does do crazy stunts. She usually gets out alive, but she's got scars all over her reputation from one thing or another she's done."

"That so?" Jim passed over his glass. "That's good corn."

"Not so bad. Oh, she's a wild one. Shoots craps, say, boy! And she do like her high-balls. Promised I'd give her one later on."

"She in love with this—Merritt?"

"Damned if I know. Seems like all the best girls around here marry fellas and go off somewhere."

He poured himself one more drink and carefully corked the bottle.

"Listen, Jim, I got to go dance and I'd be much obliged if you just stick this corn right on your hip as long as you're not dancing. If a man notices I've had a drink he'll come up and ask me and before I know it it's all gone and somebody else is having my good time."

So Nancy Lamar was going to marry. This toast of a town was to become the private property of an individual in white trousers—and all because white trousers' father had made a better razor than his neighbor. As they descended the stairs Jim found the idea inexplicably depressing. For the first time in his life he felt a vague and romantic yearning. A picture of her began to form in his imagination—Nancy walking boylike and debonnaire along the street, taking an orange as tithe from a worshipful fruit-dealer, charging a dope on a mythical account at Soda Sam's, assembling a convoy of beaux and then driving off in triumphal state for an afternoon of splashing and singing.

The Jelly-bean walked out on the porch to a deserted corner, dark between the moon on the lawn and the single lighted door of the ballroom. There he found a chair and, lighting a cigarette, drifted into the thoughtless reverie that was his usual mood. Yet now it was a reverie made sensuous by the night and by the hot smell of damp powder puffs, tucked in the fronts of low dresses and distilling a thousand rich scents to float out through the open door. The music itself, blurred by a loud trombone, became hot and shadowy, a languorous overtone to the scraping of many shoes and slippers.

Suddenly the square of yellow light that fell through the door was obscured by a dark figure. A girl had come out of the dressing-room and was standing on the porch not more than ten feet away. Jim heard a low-breathed "doggone" and then she turned and saw him. It was Nancy Lamar.

Jim rose to his feet.

"Howdy?"

"Hello—" She paused, hesitated and then approached. "Oh, it's —Jim Powell."

He bowed slightly, tried to think of a casual remark.

"Do you suppose," she began quickly, "I mean—do you know anything about gum?"

"What?"

"I've got gum on my shoe. Some utter ass left his or her gum on the floor and of course I stepped in it."

Jim blushed, inappropriately.

"Do you know how to get it off?" she demanded petulantly. "I've tried a knife. I've tried every damn thing in the dressing-room. I've tried soap and water—and even perfume and I've ruined my powder-puff trying to make it stick to that."

Jim considered the question in some agitation.

"Why—I think maybe gasolene——"

The words had scarcely left his lips when she grasped his hand and pulled him at a run off the low veranda, over a flower bed and at a gallop toward a group of cars parked in the moonlight by the first hole of the golf course.

"Turn on the gasolene," she commanded breathlessly.

"What?"

"For the gum of course. I've got to get it off. I can't dance with gum on."

Obediently Jim turned to the cars and began inspecting them with a view to obtaining the desired solvent. Had she demanded a cylinder he would have done his best to wrench one out.

"Here," he said after a moment's search. "Here's one that's easy. Got a handkerchief?"

"It's up-stairs wet. I used it for the soap and water."

Jim laboriously explored his pockets.

"Don't believe I got one either."

"Doggone it! Well, we can turn it on and let it run on the ground."

He turned the spout; a dripping began.

"More!"

He turned it on fuller. The dripping became a flow and formed an oily pool that glistened brightly, reflecting a dozen tremulous moons on its quivering bosom.

"Ah," she sighed contentedly, "let it all out. The only thing to do is to wade in it."

In desperation he turned on the tap full and the pool suddenly widened sending tiny rivers and trickles in all directions.

"That's fine. That's something like."

Raising her skirts she stepped gracefully in.

"I know this'll take it off," she murmured.

Jim smiled.

"There's lots more cars."

She stepped daintily out of the gasolene and began scraping her slippers, side and bottom, on the running-board of the automobile. The Jelly-bean contained himself no longer. He bent double with explosive laughter and after a second she joined in.

"You're here with Clark Darrow, aren't you?" she asked as they walked back toward the veranda.

"Yes."

"You know where he is now?"

"Out dancin', I reckon."

"The deuce. He promised me a highball."

"Well," said Jim, "I guess that'll be all right. I got his bottle right here in my pocket."

She smiled at him radiantly.

"I guess maybe you'll need ginger ale though," he added.

"Not me. Just the bottle."

"Sure enough?"

She laughed scornfully.

"Try me. I can drink anything any man can. Let's sit down."

She perched herself on the side of a table and he dropped into one of the wicker chairs beside her. Taking out the cork she held the flask to her lips and took a long drink. He watched her fascinated.

"Like it?"

She shook her head breathlessly.

"No, but I like the way it makes me feel. I think most people are that way."

Jim agreed.

"My daddy liked it too well. It got him."

"American men," said Nancy gravely, "don't know how to drink."

"What?" Jim was startled.

"In fact," she went on carelessly, "they don't know how to do anything very well. The one thing I regret in my life is that I wasn't born in England."

"In England?"

"Yes. It's the one regret of my life that I wasn't."

"Do you like it over there."

"Yes. Immensely. I've never been there in person, but I've met a lot of Englishmen who were over here in the army, Oxford and Cambridge men—you know, that's like Sewanee and University of Georgia are here—and of course I've read a lot of English novels."

Jim was interested, amazed.

"D' you ever hear of Lady Diana Manners?" she asked earnestly.

No, Jim had not.

"Well, she's what I'd like to be. Dark, you know, like me, and wild as sin. She's the girl who rode her horse up the steps of some cathedral or church or something and all the novelists made their heroines do it afterwards."

Jim nodded politely. He was out of his depths.

"Pass the bottle," suggested Nancy. "I'm going to take another little one. A little drink wouldn't hurt a baby.

"You see," she continued, again breathless after a draught. "People over there have style. Nobody has style here. I mean the boys here aren't really worth dressing up for or doing sensational things for. Don't you know?"

"I suppose so—I mean I suppose not," murmured Jim.

"And I'd like to do 'em an' all. I'm really the only girl in town that has style."

She stretched out her arms and yawned pleasantly.

"Pretty evening."

"Sure is," agreed Jim.

"Like to have boat," she suggested dreamily. "Like to sail out on a silver lake, say the Thames, for instance. Have champagne and caviare sandwiches along. Have about eight people. And one of the men would jump overboard to amuse the party and get drowned like a man did with Lady Diana Manners once."

"Did he do it to please her?"

"Didn't mean drown himself to please her. He just meant to jump overboard and make everybody laugh."

"I reckin they just died laughin' when he drowned."

"Oh, I suppose they laughed a little," she admitted. "I imagine she did, anyway. She's pretty hard, I guess—like I am."

"You hard?"

"Like nails." She yawned again and added, "Give me a little more from that bottle."

Jim hesitated but she held out her hand defiantly.

"Don't treat me like a girl," she warned him. "I'm not like any girl *you* ever saw." She considered. "Still, perhaps you're right. You got—you got old head on young shoulders."

She jumped to her feet and moved toward the door. The Jelly-bean rose also.

"Good-bye," she said politely, "good-bye. Thanks, Jelly-bean."

Then she stepped inside and left him wide-eyed upon the porch.

III

At twelve o'clock a procession of cloaks issued single file from the women's dressing-room and, each one paring with a coated beau like dancers meeting in a cotillion figure, drifted through the door with sleepy happy laughter—through the door into the dark where autos backed and snorted and parties called to one another and gathered around the water-cooler.

Jim, sitting in his corner, rose to look for Clark. They had met at eleven; then Clark had gone in to dance. So, seeking him, Jim wandered into the soft-drink stand that had once been a bar. The room was deserted except for a sleepy negro dozing behind the counter and two boys lazily fingering a pair of dice at one of the tables. Jim was about to leave when he saw Clark coming in. At the same moment Clark looked up.

"Hi, Jim!" he commanded. "C'mon over and help us with this bottle. I guess there's not much left, but there's one all around."

Nancy, the man from Savannah, Marylyn Wade, and Joe Ewing were lolling and laughing in the doorway. Nancy caught Jim's eye and winked at him humorously.

They drifted over to a table and arranging themselves around it waited for the waiter to bring ginger ale. Jim, faintly ill at ease, turned his eyes on Nancy, who had drifted into a nickel crap game with the two boys at the next table.

"Bring them over here," suggested Clark.

Joe looked around.

"We don't want to draw a crowd. It's against club rules."

"Nobody's around," insisted Clark, "except Mr. Taylor. He's walking up and down like a wild-man trying to find out who let all the gasolene out of his car."

There was a general laugh.

"I bet a million Nancy got something on her shoe again. You can't park when she's around."

"O Nancy, Mr. Taylor's looking for you!"

Nancy's cheeks were glowing with excitement over the game. "I haven't seen his silly little flivver in two weeks."

Jim felt a sudden silence. He turned and saw an individual of uncertain age standing in the doorway.

Clark's voice punctuated the embarrassment.

"Won't you join us, Mr. Taylor?"

"Thanks."

Mr. Taylor spread his unwelcome presence over a chair. "Have to, I guess. I'm waiting till they dig me up some gasolene. Somebody got funny with my car."

His eyes narrowed and he looked quickly from one to the other. Jim wondered what he had heard from the doorway—tried to remember what had been said.

"I'm right to-night," Nancy sang out, "and my four bits is in the ring."

"Faded!" snapped Taylor suddenly.

"Why, Mr. Taylor, I didn't know you shot craps!" Nancy was overjoyed to find that he had seated himself and instantly covered her bet. They had openly disliked each other since the night she had definitely discouraged a series of rather pointed advances.

"All right, babies, do it for your mamma. Just one little seven." Nancy was *cooing* to the dice. She rattled them with a brave underhand flourish, and rolled them out on the table.

"Ah-h! I suspected it. And now again with the dollar up."

Five passes to her credit found Taylor a bad loser. She was making it personal, and after each success Jim watched triumph flutter across her face. She was doubling with each throw—such luck could scarcely last.

"Better go easy," he cautioned her timidly.

"Ah, but watch this one," she whispered. It was eight on the dice and she called her number.

"Little Ada, this time we're going South."

Ada from Decatur rolled over the table. Nancy was flushed and half-hysterical, but her luck was holding. She drove the pot up and up, refusing to drag. Taylor was drumming with his fingers on the table, but he was in to stay.

Then Nancy tried for a ten and lost the dice. Taylor seized them avidly. He shot in silence, and in the hush of excitement the clatter of one pass after another on the table was the only sound.

Now Nancy had the dice again, but her luck had broken. An hour passed. Back and forth it went. Taylor had been at it again—and again and again. They were even at last—Nancy lost her ultimate five dollars.

"Will you take my check," she said quickly, "for fifty, and we'll shoot it all?" Her voice was a little unsteady and her hand shook as she reached to the money.

Clark exchanged an uncertain but alarmed glance with Joe Ewing. Taylor shot again. He had Nancy's check.

"How 'bout another?" she said wildly. "Jes' any bank'll do—money everywhere as a matter of fact."

Jim understood—the "good old corn" he had given her—the "good old corn" she had taken since. He wished he dared interfere—a girl of that age and position would hardly have two bank accounts. When the clock struck two he contained himself no longer.

"May I—can't you let me roll 'em for you?" he suggested, his low, lazy voice a little strained.

Suddenly sleepy and listless, Nancy flung the dice down before him.

"All right—old boy! As Lady Diana Manners says, 'Shoot 'em, Jelly-bean'—My luck's gone."

"Mr. Taylor," said Jim, carelessly, "we'll shoot for one of those there checks against the cash."

Half an hour later Nancy swayed forward and clapped him on the back.

"Stole my luck, you did." She was nodding her head sagely.

Jim swept up the last check and putting it with the others tore them into confetti and scattered them on the floor. Someone started singing, and Nancy kicking her chair backward rose to her feet.

"Ladies and gentlemen," she announced. "Ladies—that's you Marylyn. I want to tell the world that Mr. Jim Powell, who is a well-known Jelly-bean of this city, is an exception to a great rule—'lucky in dice—unlucky in love.' He's lucky in dice, and as matter fact I—I *love* him. Ladies and gentlemen, Nancy Lamar, famous dark-haired beauty often featured in the *Herald* as one th' most popular members of younger set as other girls are often featured in this particular case. Wish to announce—wish to announce, anyway, Gentlemen——" She tipped suddenly. Clark caught her and restored her balance.

"My error," she laughed, "she stoops to—stoops to—anyways—— We'll drink to Jelly-bean . . . Mr. Jim Powell, King of the Jelly-beans."

And a few minutes later as Jim waited hat in hand for Clark in the darkness of that same corner of the porch where she had come searching for gasolene, she appeared suddenly beside him.

"Jelly-bean," she said, "are you here, Jelly-bean? I think—" and her slight unsteadiness seemed part of an enchanted dream—"I think you deserve one of my sweetest kisses for that, Jelly-bean."

For an instant her arms were around his neck—her lips were pressed to his.

"I'm a wild part of the world, Jelly-bean, but you did me a good turn."

Then she was gone, down the porch, over the cricket-loud lawn. Jim saw Merritt come out the front door and say something to her angrily—saw her laugh and, turning away, walk with averted eyes to his car. Marylyn and Joe followed, singing a drowsy song about a Jazz baby.

Clark came out and joined Jim on the steps. "All pretty lit, I guess," he yawned. "Merritt's in a mean mood. He's certainly off Nancy."

Over east along the golf course a faint rug of gray spread itself across the feet of the night. The party in the car began to chant a chorus as the engine warmed up.

"Good-night everybody," called Clark.

"Good-night, Clark."

"Good-night."

There was a pause, and then a soft, happy voice added,

"Good-night, Jelly-bean."

The car drove off to a burst of singing. A rooster on a farm across the way took up a solitary mournful crow, and behind them a last negro waiter turned out the porch light. Jim and Clark strolled over toward the Ford, their shoes crunching raucously on the gravel drive.

"Oh boy!" sighed Clark softly, "how you can set those dice!"

It was still too dark for him to see the flush on Jim's thin cheeks —or to know that it was a flush of unfamiliar shame.

IV

Over Tilly's garage a bleak room echoed all day to the rumble and snorting down-stairs and the singing of the negro washers as they turned the hose on the cars outside. It was a cheerless square of a room, punctuated with a bed and a battered table on which lay half a dozen books—Joe Miller's "Slow Train thru Arkansas," "Lucille," in an old edition very much annotated in an old-fashioned hand; "The Eyes of the World," by Harold Bell Wright, and an ancient prayer-book of the Church of England with the name Alice Powell and the date 1831 written on the fly-leaf.

The East, gray when the Jelly-bean entered the garage, became a rich and vivid blue as he turned on his solitary electric light. He snapped it out again, and going to the window rested his elbows on the sill and stared into the deepening morning. With the awakening of his emotions, his first perception was a sense of futility, a dull ache at the utter grayness of his life. A wall had sprung up suddenly around him hedging him in, a wall as definite and tangible as the white wall of his bare room. And with his perception of this wall all that had been the romance of his existence, the casualness, the light-hearted improvidence, the miraculous open-handedness of life faded out. The Jelly-bean strolling up Jackson Street humming a lazy song, known at every shop and street stand, cropful of easy greeting and local wit, sad sometimes for only the sake of sadness and the flight of time—that Jelly-bean was suddenly vanished. The very name was a reproach, a triviality. With a flood of insight he knew that Merritt must despise him, that even Nancy's kiss in the dawn would have awakened not jealousy but only a contempt for Nancy's so lowering herself. And on his part the Jelly-bean had used for her a dingy subterfuge learned from the garage. He had been her moral laundry; the stains were his.

As the gray became blue, brightened and filled the room, he crossed to his bed and threw himself down on it, gripping the edges fiercely.

"I love her," he cried aloud, "God!"

As he said this something gave way within him like a lump melting in his throat. The air cleared and became radiant with dawn, and turning over on his face he began to sob dully into the pillow.

In the sunshine of three o'clock Clark Darrow chugging painfully along Jackson Street was hailed by the Jelly-bean, who stood on the curb with his fingers in his vest pockets.

"Hi!" called Clark, bringing his Ford to an astonishing stop alongside. "Just get up?"

The Jelly-bean shook his head.

"Never did go to bed. Felt sorta restless, so I took a long walk this morning out in the country. Just got into town this minute."

"Should think you *would* feel restless. I been feeling thataway all day——"

"I'm thinkin' of leavin' town," continued the Jelly-bean, absorbed by his own thoughts. "Been thinkin' of goin' up on the farm, and takin' a little that work off Uncle Dun. Reckin I been bummin' too long."

Clark was silent and the Jelly-bean continued:

"I reckin maybe after Aunt Mamie dies I could sink that money of mine in the farm and make somethin' out of it. All my people originally came from that part up there. Had a big place."

Clark looked at him curiously.

"That's funny," he said. "This—this sort of affected me the same way."

The Jelly-bean hesitated.

"I don't know," he began slowly, "somethin' about—about that girl last night talkin' about a lady named Diana Manners—an English lady, sorta got me thinkin'!" He drew himself up and looked oddly at Clark, "I had a family once," he said defiantly.

Clark nodded.

"I know."

"And I'm the last of 'em," continued the Jelly-bean, his voice rising slightly, "and I ain't worth shucks. Name they call me by means jelly—weak and wobbly like. People who weren't nothin' when my folks was a lot turn up their noses when they pass me on the street."

Again Clark was silent.

"So I'm through. I'm goin' to-day. And when I come back to this town it's going to be like a gentleman."

Clark took out his handkerchief and wiped his damp brow.

"Reckon you're not the only one it shook up," he admitted gloomily. "All this thing of girls going round like they do is going to stop right quick. Too bad, too, but everybody'll have to see it that-away."

"Do you mean," demanded Jim in surprise, "that all that's leaked out?"

"Leaked out? How on earth could they keep it secret. It'll be announced in the papers to-night. Doctor Lamar's got to save his name somehow."

Jim put his hands on the sides of the car and tightened his long fingers on the metal.

"Do you mean Taylor investigated those checks?"

It was Clark's turn to be surprised.

"Haven't you heard what happened?"

Jim's startled eyes were answer enough.

"Why," announced Clark dramatically, "those four got another bottle of corn, got tight and decided to shock the town—so Nancy and that fella Merritt were married in Rockville at seven o'clock this morning."

A tiny indentation appeared in the metal under the Jelly-bean's fingers.

"Married?"

"Sure enough. Nancy sobered up and rushed back into town, crying and frightened to death—claimed it'd all been a mistake. First Doctor Lamar went wild and was going to kill Merritt, but finally they got it patched up some way, and Nancy and Merritt went to Savannah on the two-thirty train."

Jim closed his eyes and with an effort overcame a sudden sickness.

"It's too bad," said Clark philosophically. "I don't mean the wedding—reckon that's all right, though I don't guess Nancy cared a darn about him. But it's a crime for a nice girl like that to hurt her family that way."

The Jelly-bean let go the car and turned away. Again something was going on inside him, some inexplicable but almost chemical change.

"Where you going?" asked Clark.

The Jelly-bean turned and looked dully back over his shoulder.

"Got to go," he muttered. "Been up too long; feelin' right sick."

'Oh."

The street was hot at three and hotter still at four, the April dust seeming to enmesh the sun and give it forth again as a world-old joke forever played on an eternity of afternoons. But at half past four a first layer of quiet fell and the shades lengthened under the awnings and heavy foliaged trees. In this heat nothing mattered. All life was weather, a waiting through the hot where events had no significance for the cool that was soft and caressing like a woman's hand on a tired forehead. Down in Georgia there is a feeling—perhaps inarticulate—that this is the greatest wisdom of the South—so after a while the Jelly-bean turned into a pool-hall on Jackson Street where he was sure to find a congenial crowd who would make all the old jokes—the ones he knew.

THE CAMEL'S BACK

THE glazed eye of the tired reader resting for a second on the above title will presume it to be merely metaphorical. Stories about the cup and the lip and the bad penny and the new broom rarely have anything to do with cups or lips or pennies or brooms. This story is the exception. It has to do with a material, visible and large-as-life camel's back.

Starting from the neck we shall work toward the tail. I want you to meet Mr. Perry Parkhurst, twenty-eight, lawyer, native of Toledo. Perry has nice teeth, a Harvard diploma, parts his hair in the middle. You have met him before—in Cleveland, Portland, St. Paul, Indianapolis, Kansas City, and so forth. Baker Brothers, New York, pause on their semi-annual trip through the West to clothe him; Montmorency & Co. dispatch a young man post-haste every three months to see that he has the correct number of little punctures on his shoes. He has a domestic roadster now, will have a French roadster if he lives long enough, and doubtless a Chinese tank if it comes into fashion. He looks like the advertisement of the young man rubbing his sunset-colored chest with liniment and goes East every other year to his class reunion.

I want you to meet his Love. Her name is Betty Medill, and she would take well in the movies. Her father gives her three hundred a month to dress on, and she has tawny eyes and hair and feather fans of five colors. I shall also introduce her father, Cyrus Medill. Though he is to all appearances flesh and blood, he is, strange to say, commonly known in Toledo as the Aluminum Man. But when he sits in his club window with two or three Iron Men, and the White Pine Man, and the Brass Man, they look very much as you and I do, only more so, if you know what I mean.

Now during the Christmas holidays of 1919 there took place in Toledo, counting only the people with the italicized *the,* forty-one dinner parties, sixteen dances, six luncheons, male and female, twelve teas, four stag dinners, two weddings, and thirteen bridge parties. It was the cumulative effect of all this that moved Perry Parkhurst on the twenty-ninth day of December to a decision.

This Medill girl would marry him and she wouldn't marry him.

She was having such a good time that she hated to take such a definite step. Meanwhile, their secret engagement had got so long that it seemed as if any day it might break off of its own weight. A little man named Warburton, who knew it all, persuaded Perry to superman her, to get a marriage license and go up to the Medill house and tell her she'd have to marry him at once or call it off forever. So he presented himself, his heart, his license, and his ultimatum, and within five minutes they were in the midst of a violent quarrel, a burst of sporadic open fighting such as occurs near the end of all long wars and engagements. It brought about one of those ghastly lapses in which two people who are in love pull up sharp, look at each other coolly and think it's all been a mistake. Afterward they usually kiss wholesomely and assure the other person it was all their fault. Say it all was my fault! Say it was! I want to hear you say it!

But while reconciliation was trembling in the air, while each was, in a measure, stalling it off, so that they might the more voluptuously and sentimentally enjoy it when it came, they were permanently interrupted by a twenty-minute phone call for Betty from a garrulous aunt. At the end of eighteen minutes Perry Parkhurst, urged on by pride and suspicion and injured dignity, put on his long fur coat, picked up his light brown soft hat, and stalked out the door.

"It's all over," he muttered brokenly as he tried to jam his car into first. "It's all over—if I have to choke you for an hour, damn you!" This last to the car, which had been standing some time and was quite cold.

He drove downtown—that is, he got into a snow rut that led him downtown. He sat slouched down very low in his seat, much too dispirited to care where he went.

In front of the Clarendon Hotel he was hailed from the sidewalk by a bad man named Baily, who had big teeth and lived at the hotel and had never been in love.

"Perry," said the bad man softly when the roadster drew up beside him at the curb, "I've got six quarts of the doggonedest still champagne you ever tasted. A third of it's yours, Perry, if you'll come up-stairs and help Martin Macy and me drink it."

"Baily," said Perry tensely, "I'll drink your champagne. I'll drink every drop of it. I don't care if it kills me."

"Shut up, you nut!" said the bad man gently. "They don't put wood alcohol in champagne. This is the stuff that proves the world is more than six thousand years old. It's so ancient that the cork is petrified. You have to pull it with a stone drill."

"Take me up-stairs," said Perry moodily. "If that cork sees my heart it'll fall out from pure mortification."

The room up-stairs was full of those innocent hotel pictures of little girls eating apples and sitting in swings and talking to dogs. The other decorations were neckties and a pink man reading a pink paper devoted to ladies in pink tights.

"When you have to go into the highways and byways——" said the pink man, looking reproachfully at Baily and Perry.

"Hello, Martin Macy," said Perry shortly, "where's this stone-age champagne?"

"What's the rush? This isn't an operation, understand. This is a party."

Perry sat down dully and looked disapprovingly at all the neckties.

Baily leisurely opened the door of a wardrobe and brought out six handsome bottles.

"Take off that darn fur coat!" said Martin Macy to Perry. "Or maybe you'd like to have us open all the windows."

"Give me champagne," said Perry.

"Going to the Townsends' circus ball to-night?"

"Am not!"

"'Vited?"

"Uh-huh."

"Why not go?"

"Oh, I'm sick of parties," exclaimed Perry. "I'm sick of 'em. I've been to so many that I'm sick of 'em."

"Maybe you're going to the Howard Tates' party?"

"No, I tell you; I'm sick of 'em."

"Well," said Macy consolingly, "the Tates' is just for college kids anyways."

"I tell you——"

"I thought you'd be going to one of 'em anyways. I see by the papers you haven't missed a one this Christmas."

"Hm," grunted Perry morosely.

He would never go to any more parties. Classical phrases played in his mind—that side of his life was closed, closed. Now when a man says "closed, closed" like that, you can be pretty sure that some woman has double-closed him, so to speak. Perry was also thinking that other classical thought, about how cowardly suicide is. A noble thought that one—warm and inspiring. Think of all the fine men we should lose if suicide were not so cowardly!

An hour later was six o'clock, and Perry had lost all resemblance to the young man in the liniment advertisement. He looked like a rough draft for a riotous cartoon. They were singing—an impromptu song of Baily's improvisation:

"One Lump Perry, the parlor snake,
  Famous through the city for the way he drinks his tea;
Plays with it, toys with it,
Makes no noise with it,
  Balanced on a napkin on his well-trained knee——"

"Trouble is," said Perry, who had just banged his hair with Baily's comb and was tying an orange tie round it to get the effect of Julius Cæsar, "that you fellas can't sing worth a damn. Soon's I leave th' air and start singin' tenor you start singin' tenor too."

"'M a natural tenor," said Macy gravely. "Voice lacks cultivation, tha's all. Gotta natural voice, m'aunt used say. Naturally good singer."

"Singers, singers, all good singers," remarked Baily, who was at the telephone. "No, not the cabaret; I want night egg. I mean some dog-gone clerk 'at's got food—food! I want——"

"Julius Cæsar," announced Perry, turning round from the mirror. "Man of iron will and stern 'termination."

"Shut up!" yelled Baily. "Say, iss Mr. Baily. Sen' up enormous supper. Use y'own judgment. Right away."

He connected the receiver and the hook with some difficulty, and then with his lips closed and an expression of solemn intensity in his eyes went to the lower drawer of his dresser and pulled it open.

"Lookit!" he commanded. In his hands he held a truncated garment of pink gingham.

"Pants," he exclaimed gravely. "Lookit!"

This was a pink blouse, a red tie, and a Buster Brown collar.

"Lookit!" he repeated. "Costume for the Townsends' circus ball. I'm li'l' boy carries water for the elephants."

Perry was impressed in spite of himself.

"I'm going to be Julius Cæsar," he announced after a moment of concentration.

"Thought you weren't going!" said Macy.

"Me? Sure, I'm goin'. Never miss a party. Good for the nerves—like celery."

"Cæsar!" scoffed Baily. "Can't be Cæsar! He is not about a circus. Cæsar's Shakespeare. Go as a clown."

Perry shook his head.

"Nope; Cæsar."

"Cæsar?"

"Sure. Chariot."

Light dawned on Baily.

"That's right. Good idea."

Perry looked round the room searchingly.

"You lend me a bathrobe and this tie," he said finally.

Baily considered.

"No good."

"Sure, tha's all I need. Cæsar was a savage. They can't kick if I come as Cæsar, if he was a savage."

"No," said Baily, shaking his head slowly. "Get a costume over at a costumer's. Over at Nolak's."

"Closed up."

"Find out."

After a puzzling five minutes at the phone a small, weary voice managed to convince Perry that it was Mr. Nolak speaking, and that they would remain open until eight because of the Townsends' ball. Thus assured, Perry ate a great amount of filet mignon and drank his third of the last bottle of champagne. At eight-fifteen the man in the tall hat who stands in front of the Clarendon found him trying to start his roadster.

"Froze up," said Perry wisely. "The cold froze it. The cold air."

"Froze, eh?"

"Yes. Cold air froze it."

"Can't start it?"

"Nope. Let it stand here till summer. One those hot ole August days'll thaw it out awright."

"Goin' let it stand?"

"Sure. Let 'er stand. Take a hot thief to steal it. Gemme taxi."

The man in the tall hat summoned a taxi.

"Where to, mister?"

"Go to Nolak's—costume fella."

II

Mrs. Nolak was short and ineffectual looking, and on the cessation of the world war had belonged for a while to one of the new nationalities. Owing to unsettled European conditions she had never since been quite sure what she was. The shop in which she and her husband performed their daily stint was dim and ghostly, and peopled with suits of armor and Chinese mandarins, and enormous papier-mâché birds suspended from the ceiling. In a vague background many rows of masks glared eyelessly at the visitor, and there were glass cases full of crowns and scepters, and jewels and enormous stomachers, and paints, and crape hair, and wigs of all colors.

When Perry ambled into the shop Mrs. Nolak was folding up the last troubles of a strenuous day, so she thought, in a drawer full of pink silk stockings.

"Something for you?" she queried pessimistically.

"Want costume of Julius Hur, the charioteer."

Mrs. Nolak was sorry, but every stitch of charioteer had been rented long ago. Was it for the Townsends' circus ball?

It was.

"Sorry," she said, "but I don't think there's anything left that's really circus."

This was an obstacle.

"Hm," said Perry. An idea struck him suddenly. "If you've got a piece of canvas I could go's a tent."

"Sorry, but we haven't anything like that. A hardware store is where you'd have to go to. We have some very nice Confederate soldiers."

"No. No soldiers."

"And I have a very handsome king."

He shook his head.

"Several of the gentlemen," she continued hopefully, "are wearing stovepipe hats and swallow-tail coats and going as ringmasters—but we're all out of tall hats. I can let you have some crape hair for a mustache."

"Want somep'n 'stinctive."

"Something—let's see. Well, we have a lion's head, and a goose, and a camel——"

"Camel?" The idea seized Perry's imagination, gripped it fiercely.

"Yes, but it needs two people."

"Camel. That's the idea. Lemme see it."

The camel was produced from his resting place on a top shelf. At first glance he appeared to consist entirely of a very gaunt, cadaverous head and a sizable hump, but on being spread out he was found to possess a dark brown, unwholesome-looking body made of thick, cottony cloth.

"You see it takes two people," explained Mrs. Nolak, holding the camel in frank admiration. "If you have a friend he could be part of it. You see there's sorta pants for two people. One pair is for the fella in front, and the other pair for the fella in back. The fella in front does the lookin' out through these here eyes, an' the fella in back he's just gotta stoop over an' folla the front fella round."

"Put it on," commanded Perry.

Obediently Mrs. Nolak put her tabby-cat face inside the camel's head and turned it from side to side ferociously.

Perry was fascinated.

"What noise does a camel make?"

"What?" asked Mrs. Nolak as her face emerged, somewhat smudgy. "Oh, what noise? Why, he sorta brays."

"Lemme see it in a mirror."

Before a wide mirror Perry tried on the head and turned from side to side appraisingly. In the dim light the effect was distinctly pleasing. The camel's face was a study in pessimism, decorated with numerous abrasions, and it must be admitted that his coat was in that state of general negligence peculiar to camels—in fact, he needed to be cleaned and pressed—but distinctive he certainly was. He was majestic. He would have attracted attention in any gathering, if only by his melancholy cast of feature and the look of hunger lurking round his shadowy eyes.

"You see you have to have two people," said Mrs. Nolak again.

Perry tentatively gathered up the body and legs and wrapped them about him, tying the hind legs as a girdle round his waist. The effect on the whole was bad. It was even irreverent—like one of those mediæval pictures of a monk changed into a beast by the ministrations of Satan. At the very best the ensemble resembled a humpbacked cow sitting on her haunches among blankets.

"Don't look like anything at all," objected Perry gloomily.

"No," said Mrs. Nolak; "you see you got to have two people."

A solution flashed upon Perry.

"You got a date to-night?"

"Oh, I couldn't possibly——"

"Oh, come on," said Perry encouragingly. "Sure you can! Here! Be good sport, and climb into these hind legs."

With difficulty he located them, and extended their yawning depths ingratiatingly. But Mrs. Nolak seemed loath. She backed perversely away.

"Oh, no——"

"C'm on! You can be the front if you want to. Or we'll flip a coin."

"Oh, no——"

"Make it worth your while."

Mrs. Nolak set her lips firmly together.

"Now you just stop!" she said with no coyness implied. "None of the gentlemen ever acted up this way before. My husband——"

"You got a husband?" demanded Perry. "Where is he?"

"He's home."

"Wha's telephone number?"

After considerable parley he obtained the telephone number pertaining to the Nolak penates and got into communication with that small, weary voice he had heard once before that day. But Mr. Nolak, though taken off his guard and somewhat confused by Perry's brilliant flow of logic, stuck staunchly to his point. He refused firmly, but with dignity, to help out Mr. Parkhurst in the capacity of back part of a camel.

Having rung off, or rather having been rung off on, Perry sat down on a three-legged stool to think it over. He named over to himself those friends on whom he might call, and then his mind paused as Betty Medill's name hazily and sorrowfully occurred to him. He had a sentimental thought. He would ask her. Their love affair was over, but she could not refuse this last request. Surely it was not much to ask—to help him keep up his end of social obligation for one short night. And if she insisted, she could be the front part of the camel and he would go as the back. His magnanity pleased him. His mind even turned to rosy-colored dreams of a tender reconciliation inside the camel—there hidden away from all the world. . . .

"Now you'd better decide right off."

The bourgeois voice of Mrs. Nolak broke in upon his mellow fancies and roused him to action. He went to the phone and called up the Medill house. Miss Betty was out; had gone out to dinner.

Then, when all seemed lost, the camel's back wandered curiously into the store. He was a dilapidated individual with a cold in his head and a general trend about him of downwardness. His cap was pulled down low on his head, and his chin was pulled down low on his chest, his coat hung down to his shoes, he looked run-down, down at the heels, and—Salvation Army to the contrary—down and out. He said that he was the taxicab-driver that the gentleman had hired at the Clarendon Hotel. He had been instructed to wait outside, but he had waited some time, and a suspicion had grown upon him that the gentleman had gone out the back way with purpose to defraud him—gentlemen sometimes did—so he had come in. He sank down onto the three-legged stool.

"Wanta go to a party?" demanded Perry sternly.

"I gotta work," answered the taxi-driver lugubriously. "I gotta keep my job."

"It's a very good party."

" 'S a very good job."

"Come on!" urged Perry. "Be a good fella. See—it's pretty!" He held the camel up and the taxi-driver looked at it cynically.

"Huh!"

Perry searched feverishly among the folds of the cloth.

"See!" he cried enthusiastically, holding up a selection of folds. "This is your part. You don't even have to talk. All you have to do is to walk—and sit down occasionally. You do all the sitting down. Think of it. I'm on my feet all the time and *you* can sit down some of the time. The only time *I* can sit down is when we're lying down, and you can sit down when—oh, any time. See?"

"What's 'at thing?" demanded the individual dubiously. "A shroud?"

"Not at all," said Perry indignantly. "It's a camel."

"Huh?"

Then Perry mentioned a sum of money, and the conversation left the land of grunts and assumed a practical tinge. Perry and the taxi-driver tried on the camel in front of the mirror.

"You can't see it," explained Perry, peering anxiously out through the eyeholes, "but honestly, ole man, you look sim'ly great! Honestly!"

A grunt from the hump acknowledged this somewhat dubious compliment.

"Honestly, you look great!" repeated Perry enthusiastically. "Move round a little."

The hind legs moved forward, giving the effect of a huge cat-camel hunching his back preparatory to a spring.

"No; move sideways."

The camel's hips went neatly out of joint; a hula dancer would have writhed in envy.

"Good, isn't it?" demanded Perry, turning to Mrs. Nolak for approval.

"It looks lovely," agreed Mrs. Nolak.

"We'll take it," said Perry.

The bundle was stowed under Perry's arm and they left the shop.

"Go to the party!" he commanded as he took his seat in the back.

"What party?"

"Fanzy-dress party."

"Where'bouts is it?"

This presented a new problem. Perry tried to remember, but the names of all those who had given parties during the holidays danced confusedly before his eyes. He could ask Mrs. Nolak, but on looking out the window he saw that the shop was dark. Mrs. Nolak had already faded out, a little black smudge far down the snowy street.

"Drive uptown," directed Perry with fine confidence. "If you see a party, stop. Otherwise I'll tell you when we get there."

He fell into a hazy daydream and his thoughts wandered again to Betty—he imagined vaguely that they had had a disagreement because she refused to go to the party as the back part of the camel. He was just slipping off into a chilly doze when he was wakened by the taxi-driver opening the door and shaking him by the arm.

"Here we are, maybe."

Perry looked out sleepily. A striped awning led from the curb up to a spreading gray stone house, from which issued the low drummy whine of expensive jazz. He recognized the Howard Tate house.

"Sure," he said emphatically; "'at's it! Tate's party to-night. Sure, everybody's goin'."

"Say," said the individual anxiously after another look at the awning, "you sure these people ain't gonna romp on me for comin' here?"

Perry drew himself up with dignity.

"'F anybody says anything to you, just tell 'em you're part of my costume."

The visualization of himself as a thing rather than a person seemed to reassure the individual.

"All right," he said reluctantly.

Perry stepped out under the shelter of the awning and began unrolling the camel.

"Let's go," he commanded.

Several minutes later a melancholy, hungry-looking camel, emitting clouds of smoke from his mouth and from the tip of his noble hump, might have been seen crossing the threshhold of the Howard Tate residence, passing a startled footman without so much as a snort, and heading directly for the main stairs that led up to the ballroom. The beast walked with a peculiar gait which varied between an uncertain lockstep and a stampede—but can best be described by the word "halting." The camel had a halting gait—and as he walked he alternately elongated and contracted like a gigantic concertina.

III

The Howard Tates are, as every one who lives in Toledo knows, the most formidable people in town. Mrs. Howard Tate was a Chicago Todd before she became a Toledo Tate, and the family generally affect that conscious simplicity which has begun to be the earmark of American aristocracy. The Tates have reached the stage where they talk about pigs and farms and look at you icy-eyed if you are not amused. They have begun to prefer retainers rather than friends as dinner guests, spend a lot of money in a quiet way, and, having lost all sense of competition, are in process of growing quite dull.

The dance this evening was for little Millicent Tate, and though all ages were represented, the dancers were mostly from school and college—the younger married crowd was at the Townsends' circus ball up at the Tallyho Club. Mrs. Tate was standing just inside the ballroom, following Millicent round with her eyes, and beaming whenever she caught her eye. Beside her were two middle-aged sycophants, who were saying what a perfectly exquisite child Millicent was. It was at this moment that Mrs. Tate was grasped firmly by the skirt and her youngest daughter, Emily, aged eleven, hurled herself with an "Oof!" into her mother's arms.

"Why, Emily, what's the trouble?"

"Mamma," said Emily, wild-eyed but voluble, "there's something out on the stairs."

"What?"

"There's a thing out on the stairs, mamma. I think it's a big dog, mamma, but it doesn't look like a dog."

"What do you mean, Emily?"

The sycophants waved their heads sympathetically.

"Mamma, it looks like a—like a camel."

Mrs. Tate laughed.

"You saw a mean old shadow, dear, that's all."

"No, I didn't. No, it was some kind of thing, mamma—big. I was going down-stairs to see if there were any more people, and this dog or something, he was coming up-stairs. Kinda funny, mamma, like he was lame. And then he saw me and gave a sort of growl, and then he slipped at the top of the landing, and I ran."

Mrs. Tate's laugh faded.

"The child must have seen something," she said.

The sycophants agreed that the child must have seen something—and suddenly all three women took an instinctive step away from the door as the sounds of muffled steps were audible just outside.

And then three startled gasps rang out as a dark brown form rounded the corner, and they saw what was apparently a huge beast looking down at them hungrily.

"Oof!" cried Mrs. Tate.

"O-o-oh!" cried the ladies in a chorus.

The camel suddenly humped his back, and the gasps turned to shrieks.

"Oh—look!"

"What is it?"

The dancing stopped, but the dancers hurrying over got quite a different impression of the invader; in fact, the young people immediately suspected that it was a stunt, a hired entertainer come to amuse the party. The boys in long trousers looked at it rather disdainfully, and sauntered over with their hands in their pockets, feeling that their intelligence was being insulted. But the girls uttered little shouts of glee.

"It's a camel!"

"Well, if he isn't the funniest!"

The camel stood there uncertainly, swaying slightly from side to side, and seeming to take in the room in a careful, appraising glance; then as if he had come to an abrupt decision he turned and ambled swiftly out the door.

Mr. Howard Tate had just come out of the library on the lower floor, and was standing chatting with a young man in the hall. Suddenly they heard the noise of shouting up-stairs, and almost immediately a succession of bumping sounds, followed by the precipitous appearance at the foot of the stairway of a large brown beast that seemed to be going somewhere in a great hurry.

"Now what the devil!" said Mr. Tate, starting.

The beast picked itself up not without dignity and, affecting an air of extreme nonchalance, as if he had just remembered an important engagement, started at a mixed gait toward the front door. In fact, his front legs began casually to run.

"See here now," said Mr. Tate sternly. "Here! Grab it, Butterfield! Grab it!"

The young man enveloped the rear of the camel in a pair of compelling arms, and, realizing that further locomotion was impossible, the front end submitted to capture and stood resignedly in a state of some agitation. By this time a flood of young people was pouring down-stairs, and Mr. Tate, suspecting everything from an ingenious burglar to an escaped lunatic, gave crisp directions to the young man:

"Hold him! Lead him in here; we'll soon see."

The camel consented to be led into the library, and Mr. Tate, after locking the door, took a revolver from a table drawer and instructed the young man to take the thing's head off. Then he gasped and returned the revolver to its hiding-place.

"Well, Perry Parkhurst!" he exclaimed in amazement.

"Got the wrong party, Mr. Tate," said Perry sheepishly. "Hope I didn't scare you."

"Well—you gave us a thrill, Perry." Realization dawned on him. "You're bound for the Townsends' circus ball."

"That's the general idea."

"Let me introduce Mr. Butterfield, Mr. Parkhurst." Then turning to Perry: "Butterfield is staying with us for a few days."

"I got a little mixed up," mumbled Perry. "I'm very sorry."

"Perfectly all right; most natural mistake in the world. I've got a clown rig and I'm going down there myself after a while." He turned to Butterfield. "Better change your mind and come down with us."

The young man demurred. He was going to bed.

"Have a drink, Perry?" suggested Mr. Tate.

"Thanks, I will."

"And, say," continued Tate quickly, "I'd forgotten all about your —friend here." He indicated the rear part of the camel. "I didn't mean to seem discourteous. Is it any one I know? Bring him out.

"It's not a friend," explained Perry hurriedly. "I just rented him."

"Does he drink?"

"Do you?" demanded Perry, twisting himself tortuously round.

There was a faint sound of assent.

"Sure he does!" said Mr. Tate heartily. "A really efficient camel ought to be able to drink enough so it'd last him three days."

"Tell you," said Perry anxiously, "he isn't exactly dressed up enough to come out. If you give me the bottle I can hand it back to him and he can take his inside."

From under the cloth was audible the enthusiastic smacking sound inspired by this suggestion. When a butler had appeared with bottles, glasses, and siphon one of the bottles was handed back; thereafter the silent partner could be heard imbibing long potations at frequent intervals.

Thus passed a benign hour. At ten o'clock Mr. Tate decided that they'd better be starting. He donned his clown's costume; Perry replaced the camel's head, and side by side they traversed on foot the single block between the Tate house and the Tallyho Club.

The circus ball was in full swing. A great tent fly had been put up inside the ballroom and round the walls had been built rows of booths representing the various attractions of a circus side show, but these were now vacated and over the floor swarmed a shouting, laughing medley of youth and color—clowns, bearded ladies, acrobats, bareback riders, ringmasters, tattooed men, and charioteers. The Townsends had determined to assure their party of success, so a great quantity of liquor had been surreptitiously brought over from their house and was now flowing freely. A green ribbon ran along the wall completely round the ballroom, with pointing arrows alongside and signs which instructed the uninitiated to "Follow the green line!" The green line led down to the bar, where waited pure punch and wicked punch and plain dark-green bottles.

On the wall above the bar was another arrow, red and very wavy, and under it the slogan: "Now follow this!"

But even amid the luxury of costume and high spirits represented there, the entrance of the camel created something of a stir, and Perry was immediately surrounded by a curious, laughing crowd attempting to penetrate the identity of this beast that stood by the wide doorway eying the dancers with his hungry, melancholy gaze.

And then Perry saw Betty standing in front of a booth, talking to a comic policeman. She was dressed in the costume of an Egyptian snake-charmer: her tawny hair was braided and drawn through brass rings, the effect crowned with a glittering Oriental tiara. Her fair face was stained to a warm olive glow and on her arms and the half moon of her back writhed painted serpents with single eyes of venomous green. Her feet were in sandals and her skirt was slit to the knees, so that when she walked one caught a glimpse of other slim serpents painted just above her bare ankles. Wound about her neck was a glittering cobra. Altogether a charming costume—one that caused the more nervous among the older women to shrink away from her when she passed, and the more troublesome ones to make great talk about "shouldn't be allowed" and "perfectly disgraceful."

But Perry, peering through the uncertain eyes of the camel, saw only her face, radiant, animated, and glowing with excitement, and her arms and shoulders, whose mobile, expressive gestures made her always the outstanding figure in any group. He was fascinated and his fascination exercised a sobering effect on him. With a growing clarity the events of the day came back—rage rose within him, and with a half-formed intention of taking her away from the crowd he started toward her—or rather he elongated slightly, for he had neglected to issue the preparatory command necessary to locomotion.

But at this point fickle Kismet, who for a day had played with him bitterly and sardonically, decided to reward him in full for the amusement he had afforded her. Kismet turned the tawny eyes of the snake-charmer to the camel. Kismet led her to lean toward the man beside her and say, "Who's that? That camel?"

"Darned if I know."

But a little man named Warburton, who knew it all, found it necessary to hazard an opinion:

"It came in with Mr. Tate. I think part of it's probably Warren Butterfield, the architect from New York, who's visiting the Tates."

Something stirred in Betty Medill—that age-old interest of the provincial girl in the visiting man.

"Oh," she said casually after a slight pause.

At the end of the next dance Betty and her partner finished up within a few feet of the camel. With the informal audacity that was the key-note of the evening she reached out and gently rubbed the camel's nose.

"Hello, old camel."

The camel stirred uneasily.

"You 'fraid of me?" said Betty, lifting her eyebrows in reproof.

"Don't be. You see I'm a snake-charmer, but I'm pretty good at camels too."

The camel bowed very low and some one made the obvious remark about beauty and the beast.

Mrs. Townsend approached the group.

"Well, Mr. Butterfield," she said helpfully, "I wouldn't have recognized you."

Perry bowed again and smiled gleefully behind his mask.

"And who is this with you?" she inquired.

"Oh," said Perry, his voice muffled by the thick cloth and quite unrecognizable, "he isn't a fellow, Mrs. Townsend. He's just part of my costume."

Mrs. Townsend laughed and moved away. Perry turned again to Betty.

"So," he thought, "this is how much she cares! On the very day of our final rupture she starts a flirtation with another man—an absolute stranger."

On an impulse he gave her a soft nudge with his shoulder and waved his head suggestively toward the hall, making it clear that he desired her to leave her partner and accompany him.

"By-by, Rus," she called to her partner. "This old camel's got me. Where we going, Prince of Beasts?"

The noble animal made no rejoinder, but stalked gravely along in the direction of a secluded nook on the side stairs.

There she seated herself, and the camel, after some seconds of confusion which included gruff orders and sounds of a heated dispute going on in his interior, placed himself beside her—his hind legs stretching out uncomfortably across two steps.

"Well, old egg," said Betty cheerfully, "how do you like our happy party?"

The old egg indicated that he liked it by rolling his head ecstatically and executing a gleeful kick with his hoofs.

"This is the first time that I ever had a tête-à-tête with a man's valet 'round"—she pointed to the hind legs—"or whatever that is."

"Oh," mumbled Perry, "he's deaf and blind."

"I should think you'd feel rather handicapped—you can't very well toddle, even if you want to."

The camel hung his head lugubriously.

"I wish you'd say something," continued Betty sweetly. "Say you like me, camel. Say you think I'm beautiful. Say you'd like to belong to a pretty snake-charmer."

The camel would.

"Will you dance with me, camel?"

The camel would try.

Betty devoted half an hour to the camel. She devoted at least half an hour to all visiting men. It was usually sufficient. When she approached a new man the current débutantes were accustomed to scatter right and left like a close column deploying before a machine-gun. And so to Perry Parkhurst was awarded the unique privilege of seeing his love as others saw her. He was flirted with violently!

IV

This paradise of frail foundation was broken into by the sounds of a general ingress to the ballroom; the cotillion was beginning. Betty and the camel joined the crowd, her brown hand resting lightly on his shoulder, defiantly symbolizing her complete adoption of him.

When they entered the couples were already seating themselves at tables round the walls, and Mrs. Townsend, resplendent as a super bareback rider with rather too rotund calves, was standing in the centre with the ringmaster in charge of arrangements. At a signal to the band every one rose and began to dance.

"Isn't it just slick!" sighed Betty. "Do you think you can possibly dance?"

Perry nodded enthusiastically. He felt suddenly exuberant. After all, he was here incognito talking to his love—he could wink patronizingly at the world.

So Perry danced the cotillion. I say danced, but that is stretching the word far beyond the wildest dreams of the jazziest terpsichorean. He suffered his partner to put her hands on his helpless shoulders and pull him here and there over the floor while he hung his huge head docilely over her shoulder and made futile dummy motions with his feet. His hind legs danced in a manner all their own, chiefly by hopping first on one foot and then on the other. Never being sure whether dancing was going on or not, the hind legs played safe by going through a series of steps whenever the music started playing. So the spectacle was frequently presented of the front part of the camel standing at ease and the rear keeping up a constant energetic motion calculated to rouse a sympathetic perspiration in any soft-hearted observer.

He was frequently favored. He danced first with a tall lady covered with straw who announced jovially that she was a bale of hay and coyly begged him not to eat her.

"I'd like to; you're so sweet," said the camel gallantly.

Each time the ringmaster shouted his call of "Men up!" he lumbered ferociously for Betty with the cardboard wienerwurst or the photograph of the bearded lady or whatever the favor chanced to be. Sometimes he reached her first, but usually his rushes were unsuccessful and resulted in intense interior arguments.

"For Heaven's sake," Perry would snarl fiercely between his clenched teeth, "get a little pep! I could have gotten her that time if you'd picked your feet up."

"Well, gimme a little warnin'!"

"I did, darn you."

"I can't see a dog-gone thing in here."

"All you have to do is follow me. It's just like dragging a load of sand round to walk with you."

"Maybe you wanta try back here."

"You shut up! If these people found you in this room they'd give you the worst beating you ever had. They'd take your taxi license away from you!"

Perry surprised himself by the ease with which he made this monstrous threat, but it seemed to have a soporific influence on his companion, for he gave out an "aw gwan" and subsided into abashed silence.

The ringmaster mounted to the top of the piano and waved his hand for silence.

"Prizes!" he cried. "Gather round!"

"Yea! Prizes!"

Self-consciously the circle swayed forward. The rather pretty girl who had mustered the nerve to come as a bearded lady trembled with excitement, thinking to be rewarded for an evening's hideousness. The man who had spent the afternoon having tattoo marks painted on him skulked on the edge of the crowd, blushing furiously when any one told him he was sure to get it.

"Lady and gent performers of this circus," announced the ringmaster jovially, "I am sure we will all agree that a good time has been had by all. We will now bestow honor where honor is due by bestowing the prizes. Mrs. Townsend has asked me to bestow the prizes. Now, fellow performers, the first prize is for that lady who has displayed this evening the most striking, becoming"—at this point the bearded lady sighed resignedly—"and original costume." Here the bale of hale pricked up her ears. "Now I am sure that the decision which has been agreed upon will be unanimous with all here present. The first prize goes to Miss Betty Medill, the charming Egyptian snake-charmer."

There was a burst of applause, chiefly masculine, and Miss Betty Medill, blushing beautifully through her olive paint, was passed up to receive her award. With a tender glance the ringmaster handed down to her a huge bouquet of orchids.

"And now," he continued, looking round him, "the other prize is for that man who has the most amusing and original costume. This prize goes without dispute to a guest in our midst, a gentleman who is visiting here but whose stay we all hope will be long and merry—in short, to the noble camel who has entertained us all by his hungry look and his brilliant dancing throughout the evening."

He ceased and there was a violent clapping and yeaing, for it was a popular choice. The prize, a large box of cigars, was put aside for the camel, as he was anatomically unable to accept it in person.

"And now," continued the ringmaster, "we will wind up the cotillion with the marriage of Mirth to Folly!

"Form for the grand wedding march, the beautiful snake-charmer and the nobel camel in front!"

Betty skipped forward cheerily and wound an olive arm round the camel's neck. Behind them formed the procession of little boys, little girls, country jakes, fat ladies, thin men, sword-swallowers, wild men of Borneo, and armless wonders, many of them well in their cups, all of them excited and happy and dazzled by the flow of light and color round them, and by the familiar faces, strangely unfamiliar under bizarre wigs and barbaric paint. The voluptuous chords of the wedding march done in blasphemous syncopation issued in a delirious blend from the trombones and saxophones—and the march began.

"Aren't you glad, camel?" demanded Betty sweetly as they stepped off. "Aren't you glad we're going to be married and you're going to belong to the nice snake-charmer ever afterward?"

The camel's front legs pranced, expressing excessive joy.

"Minister! Minister! Where's the minister?" cried voices out of the revel. "Who's going to be the clergyman?"

The head of Jumbo, obese negro, waiter at the Tallyho Club for many years, appeared rashly through a half-opened pantry door.

"Oh, Jumbo!"

"Get old Jumbo. He's the fella!"

"Come on, Jumbo. How 'bout marrying us a couple?"

"Yea!"

Jumbo was seized by four comedians, stripped of his apron, and escorted to a raised daïs at the head of the ball. There his collar was removed and replaced back side forward with ecclesiastical effect. The parade separated into two lines, leaving an aisle for the bride and groom.

"Lawdy, man," roared Jumbo, "Ah got ole Bible 'n' ev'ythin', sho nuff."

He produced a battered Bible from an interior pocket.

"Yea! Jumbo's got a Bible!"

"Razor, too, I'll bet!"

Together the snake-charmer and the camel ascended the cheering aisle and stopped in front of Jumbo.

"Where's yo license, camel?"

A man near by prodded Perry.

"Give him a piece of paper. Anything'll do."

Perry fumbled confusedly in his pocket, found a folded paper, and pushed it out through the camel's mouth. Holding it upside down Jumbo pretended to scan it earnestly.

"Dis yeah's a special camel's license," he said. "Get you ring ready, camel."

Inside the camel Perry turned round and addressed his worse half.

"Gimme a ring, for Heaven's sake!"

"I ain't got none," protested a weary voice.

"You have. I saw it."

"I ain't goin' to take it offen my hand."

"If you don't I'll kill you."

There was a gasp and Perry felt a huge affair of rhinestone and brass inserted into his hand.

Again he was nudged from the outside.

"Speak up!"

"I do!" cried Perry quickly.

He heard Betty's responses given in a debonair tone, and even in this burlesque the sound thrilled him.

Then he had pushed the rhinestone through a tear in the camel's coat and was slipping it on her finger, muttering ancient and historic words after Jumbo. He didn't want any one to know about this ever. His one idea was to slip away without having to disclose his identity, for Mr. Tate had so far kept his secret well. A dignified young man, Perry—and this might injure his infant law practice.

"Embrace the bride!"

"Unmask, camel, and kiss her!"

Instinctively his heart beat high as Betty turned to him laughingly and began to stroke the card-board muzzle. He felt his self-control giving way, he longed to surround her with his arms and declare his identity and kiss those lips that smiled only a foot away—when suddenly the laughter and applause round them died off and a curious hush fell over the hall. Perry and Betty looked up in surprise. Jumbo had given vent to a huge "Hello!" in such a startled voice that all eyes were bent on him.

"Hello!" he said again. He had turned round the camel's marriage license, which he had been holding upside down, produced specacles, and was studying it agonizingly.

"Why," he exclaimed, and in the pervading silence his words were heard plainly by every one in the room, "this yeah's a sho-nuff marriage permit."

"What?"

"Huh?"

"Say it again, Jumbo!"

"Sure you can read!"

Jumbo waved them to silence and Perry's blood burned to fire in his veins as he realized the break he had made.

"Yassuh!" repeated Jumbo. "This yeah's a sho-nuff license, and the pa'ties concerned one of 'em is dis yeah young lady, Miz Betty Medill, and th' other's Mistah Perry Pa'khurst."

There was a general gasp, and a low rumble broke out as all eyes fell on the camel. Betty shrank away from him quickly, her tawny eyes giving out sparks of fury.

"Is you Mistah Pa'khurst, you camel?"

Perry made no answer. The crowd pressed up closer and stared at him. He stood frozen rigid with embarrassment, his cardboard face still hungry and sardonic as he regarded the ominous Jumbo.

"Y'all bettah speak up!" said Jumbo slowly, "this yeah's a mighty serious mattah. Outside mah duties at this club ah happens to be a sho-nuff minister in the Firs' Baptis' Church. It done look to me as though y'all is gone an' got married."

V

The scene that followed will go down forever in the annals of the Tallyho Club. Stout matrons fainted, one hundred per cent Americans swore, wild-eyed débutantes babbled in lightning groups instantly formed and instantly dissolved, and a great buzz of chatter, virulent yet oddly subdued, hummed through the chaotic ballroom. Feverish youths swore they would kill Perry or Jumbo or themselves or some one, and the Baptis' preacheh was besieged by a tempestuous covey of clamorous amateur lawyers, asking questions, making threats, demanding precedents, ordering the bonds annulled, and especially trying to ferret out any hint of prearrangement in what had occurred.

In the corner Mrs. Townsend was crying softly on the shoulder of Mr. Howard Tate, who was trying vainly to comfort her; they were exchanging "all my fault's" volubly and voluminously. Outside on a snow-covered walk Mr. Cyrus Medill, the Aluminum Man, was being paced slowly up and down between two brawny charioteers, giving vent now to a string of unrepeatables, now to wild pleadings that they'd just let him get at Jumbo. He was facetiously attired for the evening as a wild man of Borneo, and the most exacting stage-manager would have acknowledged any improvement in casting the part to be quite impossible.

Meanwhile the two principals held the real centre of the stage. Betty Medill—or was it Betty Parkhurst?—storming furiously, was surrounded by the plainer girls—the prettier ones were too busy talking about her to pay much attention to her—and over on the other side of the hall stood the camel, still intact except for his head-piece, which dangled pathetically on his chest. Perry was earnestly engaged in making protestations of his innocence to a ring of angry, puzzled men. Every few minutes, just as he had apparently proved his case, some one would mention the marriage certificate, and the inquisition would begin again.

A girl named Marion Cloud, considered the second best belle of Toledo, changed the gist of the situation by a remark she made to Betty.

"Well," she said maliciously, "it'll all blow over, dear. The courts will annul it without question."

Betty's angry tears dried miraculously in her eyes, her lips shut tight together, and she looked stonily at Marion. Then she rose and, scattering her sympathizers right and left, walked directly across the room to Perry, who stared at her in terror. Again silence crept down upon the room.

"Will you have the decency to grant me five minutes' conversation—or wasn't that included in your plans?"

He nodded, his mouth unable to form words.

Indicating coldly that he was to follow her she walked out into the hall with her chin uptilted and headed for the privacy of one of the little card-rooms.

Perry started after her, but was brought to a jerky halt by the failure of his hind legs to function.

"You stay here!" he commanded savagely.

"I can't," whined a voice from the hump, "unless you get out first and let me get out."

Perry hesitated, but unable any longer to tolerate the eyes of the curious crowd he muttered a command and the camel moved carefully from the room on its four legs.

Betty was waiting for him.

"Well," she began furiously, "you see what you've done! You and that crazy license! I told you you shouldn't have gotten it!"

"My dear girl, I——"

"Don't say 'dear girl' to me! Save that for your real wife if you ever get one after this disgraceful performance. And don't try to pretend it wasn't all arranged. You know you gave that colored waiter money! You know you did! Do you mean to say you didn't try to marry me?"

"No—of course——"

"Yes, you'd better admit it! You tried it, and now what are you going to do? Do you know my father's nearly crazy? It'll serve you right if he tries to kill you. He'll take his gun and put some cold steel in you. Even if this wed—this *thing* can be annulled it'll hang over me all the rest of my life!"

Perry could not resist quoting softly: "'Oh, camel, wouldn't you like to belong to the pretty snake-charmer for all your——'"

"Shut up!" cried Betty.

There was a pause.

"Betty," said Perry finally, "there's only one thing to do that will really get us out clear. That's for you to marry me."

"Marry you!"

"Yes. Really it's the only——"

"You shut up! I wouldn't marry you if—if——"

"I know. If I were the last man on earth. But if you care anything about your reputation——"

"Reputation!" she cried. "You're a nice one to think about my reputation *now*. Why didn't you think about my reputation before you hired that horrible Jumbo to—to——"

Perry tossed up his hands hopelessly.

"Very well. I'll do anything you want. Lord knows I renounce all claims!"

"But," said a new voice, "I don't."

Perry and Betty started, and she put her hand to her heart.

"For Heaven's sake, what was that?"

"It's me," said the camel's back.

In a minute Perry had whipped off the camel's' skin, and a lax, limp object, his clothes hanging on him damply, his hand clenched tightly on an almost empty bottle, stood defiantly before them.

"Oh," cried Betty, "you brought that object in her to frighten me! You told me he was deaf—that awful person!"

The camel's back sat down on a chair with a sigh of satisfaction.

"Don't talk 'at way about me, lady. I ain't no person. I'm your husband."

"Husband!"

The cry was wrung simultaneously from Betty and Perry.

"Why, sure. I'm as much your husband as that gink is. The smoke didn't marry you to the camel's front. He married you to the whole camel. Why, that's my ring you got on your finger!"

With a little yelp she snatched the ring from her finger and flung it passionately at the floor.

"What's all this?" demanded Perry dazedly.

"Jes' that you better fix me an' fix me right. If you don't I'm a-gonna have the same claim you got to bein' married to her!"

"That's bigamy," said Perry, turning gravely to Betty.

Then came the supreme moment of Perry's evening, the ultimate chance on which he risked his fortunes. He rose and looked first at

Betty, where she sat weakly, aghast at this new complication, and then at the individual who swayed from side to side on his chair, uncertainly, menacingly.

"Very well," said Perry slowly to the individual, "you can have her. Betty, I'm going to prove to you that as far as I'm concerned our marriage was entirely accidental. I'm going to renounce utterly my rights to have you as my wife, and give you to—to the man whose ring you wear—your lawful husband."

There was a pause and four horror-stricken eyes were turned on him.

"Good-by, Betty," he said brokenly. "Don't forget me in your new-found happiness. I'm going to leave for the Far West on the morning train. Think of me kindly, Betty."

With a last glance at them he turned and his head rested on his chest as his hand touched the door-knob.

"Good-by," he repeated. He turned the door-knob.

But at this sound the snakes and silk and tawny hair precipitated themselves violently toward him.

"Oh, Perry, don't leave me! Perry, Perry, take me with you!"

Her tears flowed damply on his neck. Calmly he folded his arms about her.

"I don't care," she cried. "I love you and if you can wake up a minister at this hour and have it done over again I'll go West with you."

Over her shoulder the front part of the camel looked at the back part of the camel—and they exchanged a particularly subtle, esoteric sort of wink that only true camels can understand.

THE CURIOUS CASE OF BENJAMIN BUTTON

As LONG ago as 1860 it was the proper thing to be born at home. At present, so I am told, the high gods of medicine have decreed that the first cries of the young shall be uttered upon the anesthetic air of a hospital, preferably a fashionable one. So young Mr. and Mrs. Roger Button were fifty years ahead of style when they decided, one day in the summer of 1860, that their first baby should be born in a hospital. Whether this anachronism had any bearing upon the astonishing history I am about to set down will never be known.

I shall tell you what occurred, and let you judge for yourself.

The Roger Buttons held an enviable position, both social and financial, in ante-bellum Baltimore. They were related to the This Family and the That Family, which, as every Southerner knew, entitled them to membership in that enormous peerage which largely populated the Confederacy. This was their first experience with the charming old custom of having babies—Mr. Button was naturally nervous. He hoped it would be a boy so that he could be sent to Yale College in Connecticut, at which institution Mr. Button himself had been known for four years by the somewhat obvious nickname of "Cuff."

On the September morning consecrated to the enormous event he arose nervously at six o'clock, dressed himself, adjusted an impeccable stock, and hurried forth through the streets of Baltimore to the hospital, to determine whether the darkness of the night had borne in new life upon its bosom.

When he was approximately a hundred yards from the Maryland Private Hospital for Ladies and Gentlemen he saw Doctor Keene, the family physician, descending the front steps, rubbing his hands together with a washing movement—as all doctors are required to do by the unwritten ethics of their profession.

Mr. Roger Button, the president of Roger Button & Co., Wholesale Hardware, began to run toward Doctor Keene with much less dignity than was expected from a Southern gentleman of that picturesque period. "Doctor Keene!" he called. "Oh, Doctor Keene!"

The doctor heard him, faced around, and stood waiting, a curious expression settling on his harsh, medicinal face as Mr. Button drew near.

"What happened?" demanded Mr. Button, as he came up in a gasping rush. "What was it? How is she? A boy? Who is it? What——"

"Talk sense!" said Doctor Keene sharply. He appeared somewhat irritated.

"Is the child born?" begged Mr. Button.

Doctor Keene frowned. "Why, yes, I suppose so—after a fashion." Again he threw a curious glance at Mr. Button.

"Is my wife all right?"

"Yes."

"Is it a boy or a girl?"

"Here now!" cried Doctor Keene in a perfect passion of irritation, "I'll ask you to go and see for yourself. Outrageous!" He snapped the last word out in almost one syllable, then he turned away muttering: "Do you imagine a case like this will help my professional reputation? One more would ruin me—ruin anybody."

"What's the matter?" demanded Mr. Button, appalled. "Triplets?"

"No, not triplets!" answered the doctor cuttingly. "What's more, you can go and see for yourself. And get another doctor. I brought you into the world, young man, and I've been physician to your family for forty years, but I'm through with you! I don't want to see you or any of your relatives ever again! Good-by!"

Then he turned sharply, and without another word climbed into his phaeton, which was waiting at the curbstone, and drove severely away.

Mr. Button stood there upon the sidewalk, stupefied and trembling from head to foot. What horrible mishap had occurred? He had suddenly lost all desire to go into the Maryland Private Hospital for Ladies and Gentlemen—it was with the greatest difficulty that, a moment later, he forced himself to mount the steps and enter the front door.

A nurse was sitting behind a desk in the opaque gloom of the hall. Swallowing his shame, Mr. Button approached her.

"Good-morning," she remarked, looking up at him pleasantly.

"Good-morning. I—I am Mr. Button."

At this a look of utter terror spread itself over the girl's face. She rose to her feet and seemed about to fly from the hall, restraining herself only with the most apparent difficulty.

"I want to see my child," said Mr. Button.

The nurse gave a little scream. "Oh—of course!" she cried hysterically. "Up-stairs. Right up-stairs. Go—*up!*"

She pointed the direction, and Mr. Button, bathed in a cool perspiration, turned falteringly, and began to mount to the second floor. In the upper hall he addressed another nurse who approached him, basin in hand. "I'm Mr. Button," he managed to articulate. "I want to see my——"

Clank! The basin clattered to the floor and rolled in the direction of the stairs. Clank! Clank! It began a methodical descent as if sharing in the general terror which this gentleman provoked.

"I want to see my child!" Mr. Button almost shrieked. He was on the verge of collapse.

Clank! The basin had reached the first floor. The nurse regained control of herself, and threw Mr. Button a look of hearty contempt.

All *right,* Mr. Button," she agreed in a hushed voice. "Very *well!* But if you *knew* what state it's put us all in this morning! It's perfectly outrageous! The hospital will never have the ghost of a reputation after——"

"Hurry!" he cried hoarsely. "I can't stand this!"

"Come this way, then, Mr. Button."

He dragged himself after her. At the end of a long hall they reached a room from which proceeded a variety of howls—indeed, a room which, in later parlance, would have been known as the "crying-room." They entered. Ranged around the walls were half a dozen white-enameled rolling cribs, each with a tag tied at the head.

"Well," gasped Mr. Button, "which is mine?"

"There!" said the nurse.

Mr. Button's eyes followed her pointing finger, and this is what he saw. Wrapped in a voluminous white blanket, and partially crammed into one of the cribs, there sat an old man apparently about seventy years of age. His sparse hair was almost white, and from his chin dripped a long smoke-colored beard, which waved absurdly back and forth, fanned by the breeze coming in at the window. He looked up at Mr. Button with dim, faded eyes in which lurked a puzzled question.

"Am I mad?" thundered Mr. Button, his terror resolving into rage. "Is this some ghastly hospital joke?"

"It doesn't seem like a joke to us," replied the nurse severely. "And I don't know whether you're mad or not—but that is most certainly your child."

The cool perspiration redoubled on Mr. Button's forehead. He closed his eyes, and then, opening them, looked again. There was no mistake—he was gazing at a man of threescore and ten—a *baby* of threescore and ten, a baby whose feet hung over the sides of the crib in which it was reposing.

The old man looked placidly from one to the other for a moment, and then suddenly spoke in a cracked and ancient voice. "Are you my father?" he demanded.

Mr. Button and the nurse started violently.

"Because if you are," went on the old man querulously, "I wish you'd get me out of this place—or, at least, get them to put a comfortable rocker in here."

"Where in God's name did you come from? Who are you?" burst out Mr. Button frantically.

"I can't tell you *exactly* who I am," replied the querulous whine, "because I've only been born a few hours—but my last name is certainly Button."

"You lie! You're an imposter!"

The old man turned wearily to the nurse. "Nice way to welcome a new-born child," he complained in a weak voice. "Tell him he's wrong, why don't you?"

"You're wrong, Mr. Button," said the nurse severely. "This is your child, and you'll have to make the best of it. We're going to ask you to take him home with you as soon as possible—some time to-day."

"Home?" repeated Mr. Button incredulously.

"Yes, we can't have him here. We really can't, you know?"

"I'm right glad of it," whined the old man. "This is a fine place to keep a youngster of quiet tastes. With all this yelling and howling, I haven't been able to get a wink of sleep. I asked for something to eat"—here his voice rose to a shrill note of protest—"and they brought me a bottle of milk!"

Mr. Button sank down upon a chair near his son and concealed his face in his hands. "My heavens!" he murmured, in an ecstasy of horror. "What will people say? What must I do?"

"You'll have to take him home," insisted the nurse—"immediately!"

A grotesque picture formed itself with dreadful clarity before the eyes of the tortured man—a picture of himself walking through the crowded streets of the city with this appalling apparition stalking by his side. "I can't. I can't," he moaned.

People would stop to speak to him, and what was he going to say?

He would have to introduce this—this septuagenarian: "This is my son, born early this morning." And then the old man would gather his blanket around him and they would plod on, past the bustling stores, the slave market—for a dark instant Mr. Button wished passionately that his son was black—past the luxurious houses of the residential district, past the home for the aged. . . .

"Come! Pull yourself together," commanded the nurse.

"See here," the old man announced suddenly, "if you think I'm going to walk home in this blanket, you're entirely mistaken."

"Babies always have blankets."

With a malicious crackle the old man held up a small white swaddling garment. "Look!" he quavered. "*This* is what they had ready for me."

"Babies always wear those," said the nurse primly.

"Well," said the old man, "this baby's not going to wear anything in about two minutes. This blanket itches. They might at least have given me a sheet."

"Keep it on! Keep it on!" said Mr. Button hurriedly. He turned to the nurse. "What'll I do?"

"Go down and buy your son some clothes."

Mr. Button's son's voice followed him down into the hall: "And a cane, father. I want to have a cane."

Mr. Button banged the outer door savagely. . . .

II

"Good-morning," Mr. Button said, nervously, to the clerk in the Chesapeake Dry Goods Company. "I want to buy some clothes for my child."

"How old is your child, sir?"

"About six hours," answered Mr. Button, without due consideration.

"Babies' supply department in the rear."

"Why, I don't think—I'm not sure that's what I want. It's—he's an unusually large-size child. Exceptionally—ah—large."

"They have the largest child's sizes."

"Where is the boys' department?" inquired Mr. Button, shifting his ground desperately. He felt that the clerk must surely scent his shameful secret.

"Right here."

"Well—" He hesitated. The notion of dressing his son in men's clothes was repugnant to him. If, say, he could only find a *very* large boy's suit, he might cut off that long and awful beard, dye the white hair brown, and thus manage to conceal the worst, and to retain something of his own self-respect—not to mention his position in Baltimore society.

But a frantic inspection of the boys' department revealed no suits to fit the new-born Button. He blamed the store, of course—in such cases it is the thing to blame the store.

"How old did you say that boy of yours was?" demanded the clerk curiously.

"He's—sixteen."

"Oh, I beg your pardon. I thought you said six *hours*. You'll find the youths' department in the next aisle."

Mr. Button turned miserably away. Then he stopped, brightened, and pointed his finger toward a dressed dummy in the window display. "There!" he exclaimed. "I'll take that suit, out there on the dummy."

The clerk stared. "Why," he protested, "that's not a child's suit. At least it *is*, but it's for fancy dress. You could wear it yourself!"

"Wrap it up," insisted his customer nervously. "That's what I want."

The astonished clerk obeyed.

Back at the hospital Mr. Button entered the nursery and almost threw the package at his son. "Here's your clothes," he snapped out.

The old man untied the package and viewed the contents with a quizzical eye.

"They look sort of funny to me," he complained. "I don't want to be made a monkey of——"

"You've made a monkey of me!" retorted Mr. Button fiercely. "Never you mind how funny you look. Put them on—or I'll—or I'll *spank* you." He swallowed uneasily at the penultimate word, feeling nevertheless that it was the proper thing to say.

"All right, father"—this with a grotesque simulation of filial respect—"you've lived longer; you know best. Just as you say."

As before, the sound of the word "father" caused Mr. Button to start violently.

"And hurry."

"I'm hurrying, father."

When his son was dressed Mr. Button regarded him with depression. The costume consisted of dotted socks, pink pants, and a belted blouse with a wide white collar. Over the latter waved the long whitish beard, drooping almost to the waist. The effect was not good.

"Wait!"

Mr. Button seized a hospital shears and with three quick snaps amputated a large section of the beard. But even with this improvement the ensemble fell far short of perfection. The remaining brush of scraggly hair, the watery eyes, the ancient teeth, seemed oddly out of tone with the gayety of the costume. Mr. Button, however, was obdurate—he held out his hand. "Come along!" he said sternly.

His son took the hand trustingly. "What are you going to call me, dad?" he quavered as they walked from the nursery—"just 'baby' for a while? till you think of a better name?"

Mr. Button grunted. "I don't know," he answered harshly. "I think we'll call you Methuselah."

III

Even after the new addition to the Button family had had his hair cut short and then dyed to a sparse unnatural black, had had his face shaved so close that it glistened, and had been attired in small-boy clothes made to order by a flabbergasted tailor, it was impossible for Mr. Button to ignore the fact that his son was a poor excuse for a first family baby. Despite his aged stoop, Benjamin Button—for it was by this name they called him instead of by the appropriate but invidious Methuselah—was five feet eight inches tall. His clothes did not conceal this, nor did the clipping and dyeing of his eyebrows disguise the fact that the eyes underneath were faded and watery and tired. In fact, the baby-nurse who had been engaged in advance left the house after one look, in a state of considerable indignation.

But Mr. Button persisted in his unwavering purpose. Benjamin was a baby, and a baby he should remain. At first he declared that if Benjamin didn't like warm milk he could go without food altogether, but he was finally prevailed upon to allow his son bread and butter, and even oatmeal by way of a compromise. One day he brought home a rattle and, giving it to Benjamin, insisted in no uncertain terms that he should "play with it," whereupon the old man took it with a weary expression and could be heard jingling it obediently at intervals throughout the day.

There can be no doubt, though, that the rattle bored him, and that he found other and more soothing amusements when he was left alone. For instance, Mr. Button discovered one day that during the preceding week he had smoked more cigars than ever before—a phenomenon which was explained a few days later when, entering the nursery unexpectedly, he found the room full of faint blue haze and Benjamin, with a guilty expression on his face, trying to conceal the butt of a dark Havana. This, of course, called for a severe spanking, but Mr. Button found that he could not bring himself to administer it. He merely warned his son that he would "stunt his growth."

Nevertheless he persisted in his attitude. He brought home lead soldiers, he brought toy trains, he brought large pleasant animals made of cotton, and, to perfect the illusion which he was creating—for himself at least—he passionately demanded of the clerk in the toy-store whether "the paint would come off the pink duck if the baby put it in his mouth." But, despite all his father's efforts, Benjamin refused to be interested. He would steal down the back stairs and return to the nursery with a volume of the "Encyclopaedia Britannica," over which he would pore through an afternoon, while his cotton cows and his Noah's ark were left neglected on the floor. Against such a stubbornness Mr. Button's efforts were of little avail.

The sensation created in Baltimore was, at first, prodigious. What the mishap would have cost the Buttons and their kinsfolk socially cannot be determined, for the outbreak of the Civil War drew the city's attention to other things. A few people who were unfailingly polite racked their brains for compliments to give to the parents—and finally hit upon the ingenious device of declaring that the baby resembled his grandfather, a fact which, due to the standard state of decay common to all men of seventy, could not be denied. Mr. and Mrs. Roger Button were not pleased, and Benjamin's grandfather was furiously insulted.

Benjamin, once he left the hospital, took life as he found it. Several small boys were brought to see him, and he spent a stiff-jointed afternoon trying to work up an interest in tops and marbles—he even managed, quite accidentally, to break a kitchen window with a stone from a sling shot, a feat which secretly delighted his father.

Thereafter Benjamin contrived to break something every day, but he did these things only because they were expected of him, and because he was by nature obliging.

When his grandfather's initial antagonism wore off, Benjamin and that gentleman took enormous pleasure in one another's company. They would sit for hours, these two so far apart in age and experience, and, like old cronies, discuss with tireless monotony the slow events of the day. Benjamin felt more at ease in his grandfather's presence than in his parents'—they seemed always somewhat in awe of him and, despite the dictatorial authority they exercised over him, frequently addressed him as "Mr."

He was as puzzled as any one else at the apparently advanced age of his mind and body at birth. He read up on it in the medical journal, but found that no such case had been previously recorded. At his father's urging he made an honest attempt to play with other boys, and frequently he joined in the milder games—football shook him up too much, and he feared that in case of a fracture his ancient bones would refuse to knit.

When he was five he was sent to kindergarten, where he was initiated into the art of pasting green paper on orange paper, of weaving colored maps and manufacturing eternal cardboard necklaces. He was inclined to drowse off to sleep in the middle of these tasks, a habit which both irritated and frightened his young teacher. To his relief she complained to his parents, and he was removed from the school. The Roger Buttons told their friends that they felt he was too young.

By the time he was twelve years old his parents had grown used to him. Indeed, so strong is the force of custom that they no longer felt that he was different from any other child—except when some curious anomaly reminded them of the fact. But one day a few weeks after his twelfth birthday, while looking in the mirror, Benjamin made, or thought he made, an astonishing discovery. Did his eyes deceive him, or had his hair turned in the dozen years of his life from white to iron-gray under its concealing dye? Was the network of wrinkles on his face becoming less pronounced? Was his skin healthier and firmer, with even a touch of ruddy winter color? He could not tell. He knew that he no longer stooped and that his physical condition had improved since the early days of his life.

"Can it be——?" he thought to himself, or, rather, scarcely dared to think.

He went to his father. "I am grown," he announced determinedly. "I want to put on long trousers."

His father hesitated. "Well," he said finally, "I don't know. Fourteen is the age for putting on long trousers—and you are only twelve."

"But you'll have to admit," protested Benjamin, "that I'm big for my age."

His father looked at him with illusory speculation. "Oh, I'm not so sure of that," he said. "I was as big as you when I was twelve."

This was not true—it was all part of Roger Button's silent agreement with himself to believe in his son's normality.

Finally a compromise was reached. Benjamin was to continue to dye his hair. He was to make a better attempt to play with boys of his own age. He was not to wear his spectacles or carry a cane in the street. In return for these concessions he was allowed his first suit of long trousers. . . .

IV

Of the life of Benjamin Button between his twelfth and twenty-first year I intend to say little. Suffice to record that they were years of normal ungrowth. When Benjamin was eighteen he was erect as a man of fifty; he had more hair and it was of a dark gray; his step was firm, his voice had lost its cracked quaver and descended to a healthy baritone. So his father sent him up to Connecticut to take examinations for entrance to Yale College. Benjamin passed his examination and became a member of the freshman class.

On the third day following his matriculation he received a notification from Mr. Hart, the college registrar, to call at his office and arrange his schedule. Benjamin, glancing in the mirror, decided that his hair needed a new application of its brown dye, but an anxious inspection of his bureau drawer disclosed that the dye bottle was not there. Then he remembered—he had emptied it the day before and thrown it away.

He was in a dilemma. He was due at the registrar's in five minutes. There seemed to be no help for it—he must go as he was. He did.

"Good-morning," said the registrar politely. "You've come to inquire about your son."

"Why, as a matter of fact, my name's Button—" began Benjamin, but Mr. Hart cut him off.

"I'm very glad to meet you, Mr. Button. I'm expecting your son here any minute."

"That's me!" burst out Benjamin. "I'm a freshman."

"What!"

"I'm a freshman."

"Surely you're joking."

"Not at all."

The registrar frowned and glanced at a card before him. "Why, I have Mr. Benjamin Button's age down here as eighteen."

"That's my age," asserted Benjamin, flushing slightly.

The registrar eyed him wearily. "Now surely, Mr. Button, you don't expect me to believe that."

Benjamin smiled wearily. "I am eighteen," he repeated.

The registrar pointed sternly to the door. "Get out," he said. "Get out of college and get out of town. You are a dangerous lunatic."

"I am eighteen."

Mr. Hart opened the door. "The idea!" he shouted. "A man of your age trying to enter here as a freshman. Eighteen years old, are you? Well, I'll give you eighteen minutes to get out of town."

Benjamin Button walked with dignity from the room, and half a dozen undergraduates, who were waiting in the hall, followed him curiously with their eyes. When he had gone a little way he turned around, faced the infuriated registrar, who was still standing in the doorway, and repeated in a firm voice: "I am eighteen years old."

To a chorus of titters which went up from the group of undergraduates, Benjamin walked away.

But he was not fated to escape so easily. On his melancholy walk to the railroad station he found that he was being followed by a group, then by a swarm, and finally by a dense mass of undergraduates. The word had gone around that a lunatic had passed the entrance examinations for Yale and attempted to palm himself off as a youth of eighteen. A fever of excitement permeated the college. Men ran hatless out of classes, the football team abandoned its practice and joined the mob, professors' wives with bonnets awry and bustles out of position, ran shouting after the procession, from which proceeded a continual succession of remarks aimed at the tender sensibilities of Benjamin Button.

"He must be the Wandering Jew!"

"He ought to go to prep school at his age!"

"Look at the infant prodigy!"

"He thought this was the old men's home!"

"Go up to Harvard!"

Benjamin increased his gait, and soon he was running. He would show them! He *would* go to Harvard, and then they would regret these ill-considered taunts!

Safely on board the train for Baltimore, he put his head from the window. "You'll regret this!" he shouted.

"Ha-ha!" the undergraduates laughed. "Ha-ha-ha!" It was the biggest mistake that Yale College had ever made. . . .

V

In 1880 Benjamin Button was twenty years old, and he signalized his birthday by going to work for his father in Roger Button & Co., Wholesale Hardware. It was in that same year that he began "going out socially"—that is, his father insisted on taking him to several fashionable dances. Roger Button was now fifty, and he and his son were more and more companionable—in fact, since Benjamin had ceased to dye his hair (which was still grayish) they appeared about the same age, and could have passed for brothers.

One night in August they got into the phaeton attired in their full-dress suits and drove out to a dance at the Shevlins' country house, situated just outside of Baltimore. It was a gorgeous evening. A full moon drenched the road to the lustreless color of platinum, and late-blooming harvest flowers breathed into the motionless air aromas that were like low, half-heard laughter. The open country, carpeted for rods around with bright wheat, was translucent as in the day. It was almost impossible not to be affected by the sheer beauty of the sky—almost.

"There's a great future in the dry-goods business," Roger Button was saying. He was not a spiritual man—his esthetic sense was rudimentary.

"Old fellows like me can't learn new tricks," he observed profoundly. "It's you youngsters with energy and vitality that have the great future before you."

Far up the road the lights of the Shevlins' country house drifted into view, and presently there was a sighing sound that crept persistently toward them—it might have been the fine plaint of violins or the rustle of the silver wheat under the moon.

They pulled up behind a handsome brougham whose passengers were disembarking at the door. A lady got out, then an elderly gentleman, then another young lady, beautiful as sin. Benjamin started; an almost chemical change seemed to dissolve and recompose the very elements of his body. A rigor passed over him, blood rose into his cheeks, his forehead, and there was a steady thumping in his ears. It was first love.

The girl was slender and frail, with hair that was ashen under the moon and honey-colored under the sputtering gas-lamps of the porch. Over her shoulders was thrown a Spanish mantilla of softest yellow, butterflied in black; her feet were glittering buttons at the hem of her bustled dress.

Roger Button leaned over to his son. "That," he said, "is young Hildegarde Moncrief, the daughter of General Moncrief."

Benjamin nodded coldly. "Pretty little thing," he said indifferently. But when the negro boy had led the buggy away, he added: "Dad, you might introduce me to her."

They approached a group of which Miss Moncrief was the centre. Reared in the old tradition, she courtesied low before Benjamin. Yes, he might have a dance. He thanked her and walked away—staggered away.

The interval until the time for his turn should arrive dragged itself out interminably. He stood close to the wall, silent, inscrutable, watching with murderous eyes the young bloods of Baltimore as they eddied around Hildegarde Moncrief, passionate admiration in their faces. How obnoxious they seemed to Benjamin; how intolerably rosy! Their curling brown whiskers aroused in him a feeling equivalent to indigestion.

But when his own time came, and he drifted with her out upon the changing floor to the music of the latest waltz from Paris, his jealousies and anxieties melted from him like a mantle of snow. Blind with enchantment, he felt that life was just beginning.

"You and your brother got here just as we did, didn't you?" asked Hildegarde, looking up at him with eyes that were like bright blue enamel.

Benjamin hesitated. If she took him for his father's brother, would it be best to enlighten her? He remembered his experience at Yale, so he decided against it. It would be rude to contradict a lady; it would be criminal to mar this exquisite occasion with the grotesque story of his origin. Later, perhaps. So he nodded, smiled, listened, was happy.

"I like men of your age," Hildegarde told him. "Young boys are so idiotic. They tell me how much champagne they drink at college, and how much money they lose playing cards. Men of your age know how to appreciate women."

Benjamin felt himself on the verge of a proposal—with an effort he choked back the impulse.

"You're just the romantic age," she continued—"fifty. Twenty-five is too worldly-wise; thirty is apt to be pale from overwork; forty is the age of long stories that take a whole cigar to tell; sixty is—oh, sixty is too near seventy; but fifty is the mellow age. I love fifty."

Fifty seemed to Benjamin a glorious age. He longed passionately to be fifty.

"I've always said," went on Hildegarde, "that I'd rather marry a man of fifty and be taken care of than marry a man of thirty and take care of *him*."

For Benjamin the rest of the evening was bathed in a honey-colored mist. Hildegarde gave him two more dances, and they discovered that they were marvellously in accord on all the questions of the day. She was to go driving with him on the following Sunday, and then they would discuss all these questions further.

Going home in the phaeton just before the crack of dawn, when the first bees were humming and the fading moon glimmered in the cool dew, Benjamin knew vaguely that his father was discussing wholesale hardware.

". . . . And what do you think should merit our biggest attention after hammers and nails?" the elder Button was saying.

"Love," replied Benjamin absent-mindedly.

"Lugs?" exclaimed Roger Button. "Why, I've just covered the question of lugs."

Benjamin regarded him with dazed eyes just as the eastern sky was suddenly cracked with light, and an oriole yawned piercingly in the quickening trees. . . .

VI

When, six months later, the engagement of Miss Hildegarde Moncrief to Mr. Benjamin Button was made known (I say "made known," for General Moncrief declared he would rather fall upon his sword than announce it), the excitement in Baltimore society reached a feverish pitch. The almost forgotten story of Benjamin's birth was remembered and sent out upon the winds of scandal in picaresque and incredible forms. It was said that Benjamin was really the father of Roger Button, that he was his brother who had been in prison for forty years, that he was John Wilkes Booth in disguise—and, finally, that he had two small conical horns sprouting from his head.

The Sunday supplements of the New York papers played up the case with fascinating sketches which showed the head of Benjamin Button attached to a fish, to a snake, and, finally, to a body of solid brass. He became known, journalistically, as the Mystery Man of Maryland. But the true story, as is usually the case, had a very small circulation.

However, every one agreed with General Moncrief that it was "criminal" for a lovely girl who could have married any beau in Baltimore to throw herself into the arms of a man who was assuredly fifty. In vain Mr. Roger Button published his son's birth certificate in large type in the Baltimore *Blaze*. No one believed it. You had only to look at Benjamin and see.

On the part of the two people most concerned there was no wavering. So many of the stories about her fiancé were false that Hildegarde refused stubbornly to believe even the true one. In vain General Moncrief pointed out to her the high mortality among men of fifty—or, at least, among men who looked fifty; in vain he told her of the instability of the wholesale hardware business. Hildegarde had chosen to marry for mellowness—and marry she did. . . .

VII

In one particular, at least, the friends of Hildegarde Moncrief were mistaken. The wholesale hardware business prospered amazingly. In the fifteen years between Benjamin Button's marriage in 1880 and his father's retirement in 1895, the family fortune was doubled—and this was due largely to the younger member of the firm.

Needless to say, Baltimore eventually received the couple to its bosom. Even old General Moncrief became reconciled to his son-in-law when Benjamin gave him the money to bring out his "History of the Civil War" in twenty volumes, which had been refused by nine prominent publishers.

In Benjamin himself fifteen years had wrought many changes. It seemed to him that the blood flowed with new vigor through his veins. It began to be a pleasure to rise in the morning, to walk with an active step along the busy, sunny street, to work untiringly with his shipments of hammers and his cargoes of nails. It was in 1890 that he executed his famous business coup: he brought up the suggestion that *all nails used in nailing up the boxes in which nails are shipped are the property of the shippee,* a proposal which became a statute, was approved by Chief Justice Fossile, and saved Roger Button and Company, Wholesale Hardware, more than *six hundred nails every year.*

In addition, Benjamin discovered that he was becoming more and more attracted by the gay side of life. It was typical of his growing enthusiasm for pleasure that he was the first man in the city of Baltimore to own and run an automobile. Meeting him on the street, his contemporaries would stare enviously at the picture he made of health and vitality.

"He seems to grow younger every year," they would remark. And if old Roger Button, now sixty-five years old, had failed at first to give a proper welcome to his son he atoned at last by bestowing on him what amounted to adulation.

And here we come to an unpleasant subject which it will be well to pass over as quickly as possible. There was only one thing that worried Benjamin Button: his wife had ceased to attract him.

At that time Hildegarde was a woman of thirty-five, with a son, Roscoe, fourteen years old. In the early days of their marriage Benjamin had worshipped her. But, as the years passed, her honey-colored hair became an unexciting brown, the blue enamel of her eyes assumed the aspect of cheap crockery—moreover, and most of all, she had become too settled in her ways, too placid, too content, too anemic in her excitements, and too sober in her taste. As a bride it had been she who had "dragged" Benjamin to dances and dinners—now conditions were reversed. She went out socially with him, but without enthusiasm, *devoured already by that eternal inertia which comes to live with each of us one day and stays with us to the end.*

Benjamin's discontent waxed stronger. At the outbreak of the Spanish-American War in 1898 his home had for him so little charm that he decided to join the army. With his business influence he obtained a commission as captain, and proved so adaptable to the work that he was made a major, and finally a lieutenant-colonel just in time to participate in the celebrated charge up San Juan Hill. He was slightly wounded, and received a medal.

Benjamin had become so attached to the activity and excitement of army life that he regretted to give it up, but his business required attention, so he resigned his commission and came home. He was met at the station by a brass band and escorted to his house.

VIII

Hildegarde, waving a large silk flag, greeted him on the porch, and even as he kissed her he felt with a sinking of the heart that these three years had taken their toll. She was a woman of forty now, with a faint skirmish line of gray hairs in her head. The sight depressed him.

Up in his room he saw his reflection in the familiar mirror—he went closer and examined his own face with anxiety, comparing it after a moment with a photograph of himself in uniform taken just before the war.

"Good Lord!" he said aloud. The process was continuing. There was no doubt of it—he looked now like a man of thirty. Instead of being delighted, he was uneasy—he was growing younger. He had hitherto hoped that once he reached a bodily age equivalent to his age in years, the grotesque phenomenon which had marked his birth would cease to function. He shuddered. His destiny seemed to him awful, incredible.

When he came down-stairs Hildegarde was waiting for him. She appeared annoyed, and he wondered if she had at last discovered that there was something amiss. It was with an effort to relieve the tension between them that he broached the matter at dinner in what he considered a delicate way.

"Well," he remarked lightly, "everybody says I look younger than ever."

Hildegarde regarded him with scorn. She sniffed. "Do you think it's anything to boast about?"

"I'm not boasting," he asserted uncomfortably.

She sniffed again. "The idea," she said, and after a moment: "I should think you'd have enough pride to stop it."

"How can I?" he demanded.

"I'm not going to argue with you," she retorted. "But there's a right way of doing things and a wrong way. If you've made up your mind to be different from everybody else, I don't suppose I can stop you, but I really don't think it's very considerate."

"But, Hildegarde, I can't help it."

"You can too. You're simply stubborn. You think you don't want to be like any one else. You always have been that way, and you always will be. But just think how it would be if every one else looked at things as you do—what would the world be like?"

As this was an inane and unanswerable argument Benjamin made no reply, and from that time on a chasm began to widen between them. He wondered what possible fascination she had ever exercised over him.

To add to the breach, he found, as the new century gathered headway, that his thirst for gayety grew stronger. Never a party of any kind in the city of Baltimore but he was there, dancing with the prettiest of the young married women, chatting with the most popular of the débutantes, and finding their company charming, while his wife, a dowager of evil omen, sat among the chaperons, now in haughty disapproval, and now following him with solemn, puzzled, and reproachful eyes.

"Look!" people would remark. "What a pity! A young fellow that age tied to a woman of forty-five. He must be twenty years younger than his wife." They had forgotten—as people inevitably forget—that back in 1880 their mammas and papas had also remarked about this same ill-matched pair.

Benjamin's growing unhappiness at home was compensated for by his many new interests. He took up golf and made a great success of it. He went in for dancing: in 1906 he was an expert at "The Boston," and in 1908 he was considered proficient at the "Maxixe," while in 1909 his "Castle Walk" was the envy of every young man in town.

His social activities, of course, interfered to some extent with his business, but then he had worked hard at wholesale hardware for twenty-five years and felt that he could soon hand it on to his son, Roscoe, who had recently graduated from Harvard.

He and his son were, in fact, often mistaken for each other. This pleased Benjamin—he soon forgot the insidious fear which had come over him on his return from the Spanish-American War, and grew to take a naïve pleasure in his appearance. There was only one fly in the delicious ointment—he hated to appear in public with his wife. Hildegarde was almost fifty, and the sight of her made him feel absurd. . . .

IX

One September day in 1910—a few years after Roger Button & Co., Wholesale Hardware, had been handed over to young Roscoe Button—a man, apparently about twenty years old, entered himself as a freshman at Harvard University in Cambridge. He did not make the mistake of announcing that he would never see fifty again nor did he mention the fact that his son had been graduated from the same institution ten years before.

He was admitted, and almost immediately attained a prominent position in the class, partly because he seemed a little older than the other freshmen, whose average age was about eighteen.

But his success was largely due to the fact that in the football game with Yale he played so brilliantly, with so much dash and with such a cold, remorseless anger that he scored seven touchdowns and fourteen field goals for Harvard, and caused one entire eleven of Yale men to be carried singly from the field, unconscious. He was the most celebrated man in college.

Strange to say, in his third or junior year he was scarcely able to "make" the team. The coaches said that he had lost weight, and it seemed to the more observant among them that he was not quite as tall as before. He made no touchdowns—indeed, he was retained on the team chiefly in hope that his enormous reputation would bring terror and disorganization to the Yale team.

In his senior year he did not make the team at all. He had grown so slight and frail that one day he was taken by some sophomores for a freshman, an incident which humiliated him terribly. He became known as something of a prodigy—a senior who was surely no more than sixteen—and he was often shocked at the worldliness of some of his classmates. His studies seemed harder to him—he felt that they were too advanced. He had heard his classmates speak of St. Midas', the famous preparatory school, at which so many of them had prepared for college, and he determined after his graduation to enter himself at St. Midas', where the sheltered life among boys his own size would be more congenial to him

Upon his graduation in 1914 he went home to Baltimore with his Harvard diploma in his pocket. Hildegarde was now residing in Italy, so Benjamin went to live with his son, Roscoe. But though he was welcomed in a general way, there was obviously no heartiness in Roscoe's feeling toward him—there was even perceptible a tendency on his son's part to think that Benjamin, as he moped about the house in adolescent mooniness, was somewhat in the way. Roscie was married now and prominent in Baltimore life, and he wanted no scandal to creep out in connection with his family.

Benjamin, no longer persona grata with the débutantes and younger college set, found himself left much alone, except for the companionship of three or four fifteen-year-old boys in the neighborhood. His idea of going to St. Midas' school recurred to him.

"Say," he said to Roscoe one day, "I've told you over and over that I want to go to prep school."

"Well, go, then," replied Roscoe shortly. The matter was distasteful to him, and he wished to avoid a discussion.

"I can't go alone," said Benjamin helplessly. "You'll have to enter me and take me up there."

"I haven't got time," declared Roscoe abruptly. His eyes narrowed and he looked uneasily at his father. "As a matter of fact," he added, "you'd better not go on with this business much longer. You better pull up short. You better—you better"—he paused and his face crimsoned as he sought for words—"you better turn right around and start back the other way. This has gone too far to be a joke. It isn't funny any longer. You—you behave yourself!"

Benjamin looked at him, on the verge of tears.

"And another thing," continued Roscoe, "when visitors are in the house I want you to call me 'Uncle'—not 'Roscoe,' but 'Uncle,' do you understand? It looks absurd for a boy of fifteen to call me by my first name. Perhaps you'd better call me 'Uncle' *all* the time, so you'll get used to it."

With a harsh look at his father, Roscoe turned away. . . .

X

At the termination of this interview, Benjamin wandered dismally up-stairs and stared at himself in the mirror. He had not shaved for three months, but he could find nothing on his face but a faint white down with which it seemed unnecessary to meddle. When he had first come home from Harvard, Roscoe had approached him with the proposition that he should wear eye-glasses and imitation whiskers glued to his cheeks, and it had seemed for a moment that the farce of his early years was to be repeated. But whiskers had itched and made him ashamed. He wept and Roscoe had reluctantly relented.

Benjamin opened a book of boys' stories, "The Boy Scouts in Bimini Bay," and began to read. But he found himself thinking persistently about the war. America had joined the Allied cause during the preceding month, and Benjamin wanted to enlist, but, alas, sixteen was the minimum age, and he did not look that old. His true age, which was fifty-seven, would have disqualified him, anyway.

There was a knock at his door, and the butler appeared with a letter bearing a large official legend in the corner and addressed to Mr. Benjamin Button. Benjamin tore it open eagerly, and read the enclosure with delight. It informed him that many reserve officers who had served in the Spanish-American War were being called back into service with a higher rank, and it enclosed his commission as brigadier-general in the United States army with orders to report immediately.

Benjamin jumped to his feet fairly quivering with enthusiasm. This was what he had wanted. He seized his cap and ten minutes later he had entered a large tailoring establishment on Charles Street, and asked in his uncertain treble to be measured for a uniform.

"Want to play soldier, sonny?" demanded a clerk, casually.

Benjamin flushed. "Say! Never mind what I want!" he retorted angrily. "My name's Button and I live on Mt. Vernon Place, so you know I'm good for it."

"Well," admitted the clerk, hesitantly, "if you're not, I guess your daddy is, all right."

Benjamin was measured, and a week later his uniform was completed. He had difficulty in obtaining the proper general's insignia because the dealer kept insisting to Benjamin that a nice Y. W. C. A. badge would look just as well and be much more fun to play with.

Saying nothing to Roscoe, he left the house one night and proceeded by train to Camp Mosby, in South Carolina, where he was to command an infantry brigade. On a sultry April day he approached the entrance to the camp, paid off the taxicab which had brought him from the station, and turned to the sentry on guard.

"Get some one to handle my luggage!" he said briskly.

The sentry eyed him reproachfully. "Say," he remarked, "where you goin' with the general's duds, sonny?"

Benjamin, veteran of the Spanish-American War, whirled upon him with fire in his eye, but with, alas, a changing treble voice.

"Come to attention!" he tried to thunder; he paused for breath—then suddenly he saw the sentry snap his heels together and bring his rifle to the present. Benjamin concealed a smile of gratification, but when he glanced around his smile faded. It was not he who had inspired obedience, but an imposing artillery colonel who was approaching on horseback.

"Colonel!" called Benjamin shrilly.

The colonel came up, drew rein, and looked coolly down at him with a twinkle in his eyes. "Whose little boy are you?" he demanded kindly.

"I'll soon darn well show you whose little boy I am!" retorted Benjamin in a ferocious voice. "Get down off that horse!"

The colonel roared with laughter.

"You want him, eh, general?"

"Here!" cried Benjamin desperately. "Read this." And he thrust his commission toward the colonel.

The colonel read it, his eyes popping from their sockets.

"Where'd you get this?" he demanded, slipping the document into his own pocket.

"I got it from the Government, as you'll soon find out!"

"You come along with me," said the colonel with a peculiar look. "We'll go up to headquarters and talk this over. Come along."

The colonel turned and began walking his horse in the direction of headquarters. There was nothing for Benjamin to do but follow with as much dignity as possible—meanwhile promising himself a stern revenge.

But this revenge did not materialize. Two days later, however, his son Roscoe materialized from Baltimore, hot and cross from a hasty trip, and escorted the weeping general, *sans* uniform, back to his home.

XI

In 1920 Roscoe Button's first child was born. During the attendant festivities, however, no one thought it "the thing" to mention that the little grubby boy, apparently about ten years of age who played around the house with lead soldiers and a miniature circus, was the new baby's own grandfather.

No one disliked the little boy whose fresh, cheerful face was crossed with just a hint of sadness, but to Roscoe Button his presence was a source of torment. In the idiom of his generation Roscoe did not consider the matter "efficient." It seemed to him that his father, in refusing to look sixty, had not behaved like a "red-blooded he-man"—this was Roscoe's favorite expression—but in a curious and perverse manner. Indeed, to think about the matter for as much as a half an hour drove him to the edge of insanity. Roscoe believed that "live wires" should keep young, but carrying it out on such a scale was—was—was inefficient. And there Roscoe rested.

Five years later Roscoe's little boy had grown old enough to play childish games with little Benjamin under the supervision of the same nurse. Roscoe took them both to kindergarten on the same day and Benjamin found that playing with little strips of colored paper, making mats and chains and curious and beautiful designs, was the most fascinating game in the world. Once he was bad and had to stand in the corner—then he cried—but for the most part there were gay hours in the cheerful room, with the sunlight coming in the windows and Miss Bailey's kind hand resting for a moment now and then in his tousled hair.

Roscoe's son moved up into the first grade after a year, but Benjamin stayed on in the kindergarten. He was very happy. Sometimes when other tots talked about what they would do when they grew up a shadow would cross his little face as if in a dim, childish way he realized that those were things in which he was never to share.

The days flowed on in monotonous content. He went back a third year to the kindergarten, but he was too little now to understand what the bright shining strips of paper were for. He cried because the other boys were bigger than he and he was afraid of them. The teacher talked to him, but though he tried to understand he could not understand at all.

He was taken from the kindergarten. His nurse, Nana, in her starched gingham dress, became the centre of his tiny world. On bright days they walked in the park; Nana would point at a great gray monster and say "elephant," and Benjamin would say it after her, and when he was being undressed for bed that night he would say it over and over aloud to her: "Elyphant, elyphant, elyphant." Sometimes Nana let him jump on the bed, which was fun, because if you sat down exactly right it would bounce you up on your feet again, and if you said "Ah" for a long time while you jumped you got a very pleasing broken vocal effect.

He loved to take a big cane from the hatrack and go around hitting chairs and tables with it and saying: "Fight, fight, fight." When there were people there the old ladies would cluck at him, which interested him, and the young ladies would try to kiss him, which he submitted to with mild boredom. And when the long day was done at five o'clock he would go up-stairs with Nana and be fed oatmeal and nice soft mushy foods with a spoon.

There were no troublesome memories in his childish sleep; no token came to him of his brave days at college, of the glittering years when he flustered the hearts of many girls. There were only the white, safe walls of his crib and Nana and a man who came to see him sometimes, and a great big orange ball that Nana pointed at just before his twilight bed hour and called "sun." When the sun went his eyes were sleepy—there were no dreams, no dreams to haunt him.

The past—the wild charge at the head of his men up San Juan Hill; the first years of his marriage when he worked late into the summer dusk down in the busy city for young Hildegarde whom he loved; the days before that when he sat smoking far into the night in the gloomy old Button house on Monroe Street with his grandfather—all these had faded like unsubstantial dreams from his mind as though they had never been.

He did not remember. He did not remember clearly whether the milk was warm or cool at his last feeding or how the days passed—there was only his crib and Nana's familiar presence. And then he remembered nothing. When he was hungry he cried—that was all. Through the noons and nights he breathed and over him there were soft mumblings and murmurings that he scarcely heard, and faintly differentiated smells, and light and darkness.

Then it was all dark, and his white crib and the dim faces that moved above him, and the warm sweet aroma of the milk, faded out altogether from his mind.

TARQUIN OF CHEAPSIDE

Running footsteps—light, soft-soled shoes made of curious leathery cloth brought from Ceylon setting the pace; thick flowing boots, two pairs, dark blue and gilt, reflecting the moonlight in blunt gleams and splotches, following a stone's throw behind.

Soft Shoes flashes through a patch of moonlight, then darts into a blind labyrinth of alleys and becomes only an intermittent scuffle ahead somewhere in the enfolding darkness. In go Flowing Boots, with short swords lurching and long plumes awry, finding a breath to curse God and the black lanes of London.

Soft Shoes leaps a shadowy gate and crackles through a hedgerow. Flowing Boots leap the gate and crackles through the hedgerow—and there, startlingly, is the watch ahead—two murderous pikemen of ferocious cast of mouth acquired in Holland and the Spanish marches.

But there is no cry for help. The pursued does not fall panting at the feet of the watch, clutching a purse; neither do the pursuers raise a hue and cry. Soft Shoes goes by in a rush of swift air. The watch curse and hesitate, glance after the fugitive, and then spread their pikes firmly across the road and wait for Flowing Boots. Darkness, like a great hand, cuts off the even flow of the moon.

The hand moves off the moon whose pale caress finds again the eaves and lintels, and the watch, wounded and tumbled in the dust. Up the street one of Flowing Boots leaves a black trail of spots until he binds himself, clumsily as he runs, with fine lace caught from his throat.

It was no affair for the watch: Satan was at large tonight and Satan seemed to be he who appeared dimly in front, heel over gate, knee over fence. Moreover, the adversary was obviously travelling near home or at least in that section of London consecrated to his coarser whims, for the street narrowed like a road in a picture and the houses bent over further and further, cooping in natural ambushes suitable for murder and its histrionic sister, sudden death.

Down long and sinuous lanes twisted the hunted and the harriers, always in and out of the moon in a perpetual queen's move over a checker-board of glints and patches. Ahead, the quarry, minus his leather jerkin now and half blinded by drips of sweat, had taken to scanning his ground desperately on both sides. As a result he suddenly slowed short, and retracing his steps a bit scooted up an alley so dark that it seemed that here sun and moon had been in eclipse since the last glacier slipped roaring over the earth. Two hundred yards down he stopped and crammed himself into a niche in the wall where he huddled and panted silently, a grotesque god without bulk or outline in the gloom.

Flowing Boots, two pairs, drew near, came up, went by, halted twenty yards beyond him, and spoke in deep-lunged, scanty whispers:

"I was attune to that scuffle; it stopped."

"Within twenty paces."

"He's hid."

"Stay together now and we'll cut him up."

The voice faded into a low crunch of a boot, nor did Soft Shoes wait to hear more—he sprang in three leaps across the alley, where he bounded up, flapped for a moment on the top of the wall like a huge bird, and disappeared, gulped down by the hungry night at a mouthful.

II

"He read at wine, he read in bed,
He read aloud, had he the breath,
His every thought was with the dead,
And so he read himself to death."

Any visitor to the old James the First graveyard near Peat's Hill may spell out this bit of doggerel, undoubtedly one of the worst recorded of an Elizabethan, on the tomb of Wessel Caxter.

This death of his, says the antiquary, occurred when he was thirty-seven, but as this story is concerned with the night of a certain chase through darkness, we find him still alive, still reading. His eyes were somewhat dim, his stomach somewhat obvious—he was a misbuilt man and indolent—oh, Heavens! But an era is an era, and in the reign of Elizabeth, by the grace of Luther, Queen of England, no man could help but catch the spirit of enthusiasm. Every loft in

Cheapside published its *Magnum Folium* (or magazine) of the new blank verse; the Cheapside Players would produce anything on sight as long as it "got away from those reactionary miracle plays," and the English Bible had run through seven "very large" printings in as many months.

So Wessel Caxter (who in his youth had gone to sea) was now a reader of all on which he could lay his hands—he read manuscripts in holy friendship; he dined rotten poets; he loitered about the shops where the *Magna Folia* were printed, and he listened tolerantly while the young playwrights wrangled and bickered among themselves, and behind each other's backs made bitter and malicious charges of plagiarism or anything else they could think of.

To-night he had a book, a piece of work which, though inordinately versed, contained, he thought, some rather excellent political satire. "The Faerie Queene" by Edmund Spenser lay before him under the tremulous candle-light. He had ploughed through a canto; he was beginning another:

THE LEGEND OF BRITOMARTIS OR OF CHASTITY

It falls me here to write of Chastity.
The fayrest vertue, far above the rest. . . .

A sudden rush of feet on the stairs, a rusty swing-open of the thin door, and a man thrust himself into the room, a man without a jerkin, panting, sobbing, on the verge of collapse.

"Wessel," words choked him, "stick me away somewhere, love of Our Lady!"

Caxter rose, carefully closing his book, and bolted the door in some concern.

"I'm pursued," cried out Soft Shoes. "I vow there's two short-witted blades trying to make me into mincemeat and near succeeding. They saw me hop the back wall!"

"It would need," said Wessel, looking at him curiously, "several battalions armed with blunderbusses, and two or three Armadas, to keep you reasonably secure from the revenges of the world."

Soft Shoes smiled with satisfaction. His sobbing gasps were giving way to quick, precise breathing; his hunted air had faded to a faintly perturbed irony.

"I feel little surprise," continued Wessel.

"They were two such dreary apes.

"Making a total of three."

"Only two unless you stick me away. Man, man, come alive; they'll be on the stairs in a spark's age."

Wessel took a dismantled pike-staff from the corner, and raising it to the high ceiling, dislodged a rough trap-door opening into a garret above.

"There's no ladder."

He moved a bench under the trap, upon which Soft Shoes mounted, crouched, hesitated, crouched again, and then leaped amazingly upward. He caught at the edge of the aperture and swung back and forth for a moment, shifting his hold; finally doubled up and disappeared into the darkness above. There was a scurry, a migration of rats, as the trap-door was replaced; . . . silence.

Wessel returned to his reading-table, opened to the Legend of Britomartis or of Chastity—and waited. Almost a minute later there was a scramble on the stairs and an intolerable hammering at the door. Wessel sighed and, picking up his candle, rose.

"Who's there?"

"Open the door!"

"Who's there?"

An aching blow frightened the frail wood, splintered it around the edge. Wessel opened it a scarce three inches, and held the candle high. His was to play the timorous, the super-respectable citizen, disgracefully disturbed.

"One small hour of the night for rest. Is that too much to ask from every brawler and——"

"Quiet, gossip! Have you seen a perspiring fellow?"

The shadows of two gallants fell in immense wavering outlines over the narrow stairs; by the light Wessel scrutinized them closely. Gentlemen, they were, hastily but richly dressed—one of them wounded severely in the hand, both radiating a sort of furious horror. Waving aside Wessel's ready miscomprehension, they pushed by him into the room and with their swords went through the business of poking carefully into all suspected dark spots in the room, further extending their search to Wessel's bedchamber.

"Is he hid here?" demanded the wounded man fiercely.

"Is who here?"

"Any man but you."

"Only two others that I know of."

For a second Wessel feared that he had been too damned funny, for the gallants made as though to prick him through.

"I heard a man on the stairs," he said hastily, "full five minutes ago, it was. He most certainly failed to come up."

He went on to explain his absorption in "The Faerie Queene" but, for the moment at least, his visitors, like the great saints, were anæsthetic to culture.

"What's been done?" inquired Wessel.

"Violence!" said the man with the wounded hand. Wessel noticed that his eyes were quite wild. "My own sister. Oh, Christ in heaven, give us this man!"

Wessel winced.

"Who is the man?"

"God's word! We know not even that. What's that trap up there?" he added suddenly.

"It's nailed down. It's not been used for years." He thought of the pole in the corner and quailed in his belly, but the utter despair of the two men dulled their astuteness.

"It would take a ladder for any one not a tumbler," said the wounded man listlessly.

His companion broke into hysterical laughter.

"A tumbler. Oh, a tumbler. Oh——"

Wessel stared at them in wonder.

"That appeals to my most tragic humor," cried the man, "that no one—oh, no one—could get up there but a tumbler."

The gallant with the wounded hand snapped his good fingers impatiently.

"We must go next door—and then on——"

Helplessly they went as two walking under a dark and storm-swept sky.

Wessel closed and bolted the door and stood a moment by it, frowning in pity.

A low-breathed "Ha!" made him look up. Soft Shoes had already raised the trap and was looking down into the room, his rather elfish face squeezed into a grimace, half of distaste, half of sardonic amusement.

"They take off their heads with their helmets," he remarked in a whisper, "but as for you and me, Wessel, we are two cunning men."

"Now you be cursed," cried Wessel vehemently. "I knew you for a dog, but when I hear even the half of a tale like this, I know you for such a dirty cur that I am minded to club your skull."

Soft Shoes stared at him, blinking.

"At all events," he replied finally, "I find dignity impossible in this position."

With this he let his body through the trap, hung for an instant, and dropped the seven feet to the floor.

"There was a rat considered my ear with the air of a gourmet," he continued, dusting his hands on his breeches. "I told him in the rat's peculiar idiom that I was deadly poison, so he took himself off."

"Let's hear of this night's lechery!" insisted Wessel angrily.

Soft Shoes touched his thumb to his nose and wiggled the fingers derisively at Wessel.

"Street gamin!" muttered Wessel.

"Have you any paper?" demanded Soft Shoes irrelevantly, and then rudely added, "or can you write?"

"Why should I give you paper?"

"You wanted to hear of the night's entertainment. So you shall, an you give me pen, ink, a sheaf of paper, and a room to myself."

Wessel hesitated.

"Get out!" he said finally.

"As you will. Yet you have missed a most intriguing story."

Wessel wavered—he was soft as taffy, that man—gave in. Soft Shoes went into the adjoining room with the begrudged writing materials and precisely closed the door. Wessel grunted and returned to "The Faerie Queene"; so silence came once more upon the house.

III

Three o'clock went into four. The room paled, the dark outside was shot through with damp and chill, and Wessel, cupping his brain in his hands, bent low over his table, tracing through the pattern of knights and fairies and the harrowing distresses of many girls. There were dragons chortling along the narrow street outside; when the sleepy armorer's boy began his work at half-past five the heavy clink and chank of plate and linked mail swelled to the echo of a marching cavalcade.

A fog shut down at the first flare of dawn, and the room was grayish yellow at six when Wessel tiptoed to his cupboard bed-chamber and pulled open the door. His guest turned on him a face pale as parchment in which two distraught eyes burned like great red letters. He had drawn a chair close to Wessel's *prie-dieu* which he was using as a desk; and on it was an amazing stack of closely written pages. With a long sigh Wessel withdrew and returned to his siren, calling himself fool for not claiming his bed here at dawn.

The clump of boots outside, the croaking of old beldames from attic to attic, the dull murmur of morning, unnerved him, and, dozing, he slumped in his chair, his brain, overladen with sound and color, working intolerably over the imagery that stacked it. In this restless dream of his he was one of a thousand groaning bodies crushed near the sun, a helpless bridge for the strong-eyed Apollo. The dream tore at him, scraped along his mind like a ragged knife. When a hot hand touched his shoulder, he awoke with what was nearly a scream to find the fog thick in the room and his guest, a gray ghost of misty stuff, beside him with a pile of paper in his hand.

"It should be a most intriguing tale, I believe, though it requires some going over. May I ask you to lock it away, and in God's name let me sleep?"

He waited for no answer, but thrust the pile at Wessel, and literally poured himself like stuff from a suddenly inverted bottle upon a couch in the corner; slept, with his breathing regular, but his brow wrinkled in a curious and somewhat uncanny manner.

Wessel yawned sleepily and, glancing at the scrawled, uncertain first page, he began reading aloud very softly:

The Rape of Lucrece

"From the besieged Ardea all in post,
Borne by the trustless wings of false desire,
Lust-breathing Tarquin leaves the Roman host——"

"O RUSSET WITCH"

MERLIN GRAINGER was employed by the Moonlight Quill Bookshop, which you may have visited, just around the corner from the Ritz-Carlton on Forty-seventh Street. The Moonlight Quill is, or rather was, a very romantic little store, considered radical and admitted dark. It was spotted interiorly with red and orange posters of breathless exotic intent, and lit no less by the shiny reflecting bindings of special editions than by the great squat lamp of crimson satin that, lighted through all the day, swung overhead. It was truly a mellow bookshop. The words "Moonlight Quill" were worked over the door in a sort of serpentine embroidery. The windows seemed always full of something that had passed the literary censors with little to spare; volumes with covers of deep orange which offer their titles on little white paper squares. And over all there was the smell of the musk, which the clever, inscrutable Mr. Moonlight Quill ordered to be sprinkled about—the smell half of a curiosity shop in Dickens' London and half of a coffee-house on the warm shores of the Bosphorus.

From nine until five-thirty Merlin Grainger asked bored old ladies in black and young men with dark circles under their eyes if they "cared for this fellow" or were interested in first editions. Did they buy novels with Arabs on the cover, or books which gave Shakespeare's newest sonnets as dictated psychically to Miss Sutton of South Dakota? he sniffed. As a matter of fact, his own taste ran to these latter, but as an employee at the Moonlight Quill he assumed for the working day the attitude of a disillusioned connoisseur.

After he had crawled over the window display to pull down the front shade at five-thirty every afternoon, and said good-bye to the mysterious Mr. Moonlight Quill and the lady clerk, Miss McCracken, and the lady stenographer, Miss Masters, he went home to the girl, Caroline. He did not eat supper with Caroline. It is unbelievable that Caroline would have considered eating off his bureau with the collar buttons dangerously near the cottage cheese, and the ends of Merlin's necktie just missing his glass of milk—he had never asked her to eat with him. He ate alone. He went into Braegdort's delicatessen on Sixth Avenue and bought a box of crackers, a tube of anchovy paste, and some oranges, or else a little jar of sausages and some potato salad and a bottled soft drink, and with these in a brown package he went to his room at Fifty-something West Fifty-eighth Street and ate his supper and saw Caroline.

Caroline was a very young and gay person who lived with some older lady and was possibly nineteen. She was like a ghost in that she never existed until evening. She sprang into life when the lights went on in her apartment at about six, and she disappeared, at the latest, about midnight. Her apartment was a nice one, in a nice building with a white stone front, opposite the south side of Central Park. The back of her apartment faced the single window of the single room occupied by the single Mr. Grainger.

He called her Caroline because there was a picture that looked like her on the jacket of a book of that name down at the Moonlight Quill.

Now, Merlin Grainger was a thin young man of twenty-five, with dark hair and no mustache or beard or anything like that, but Caroline was dazzling and light, with a shimmering morass of russet waves to take the place of hair, and the sort of features that remind you of kisses—the sort of features you thought belonged to your first love, but know, when you come across an old picture, didn't. She dressed in pink or blue usually, but of late she had sometimes put on a slender black gown that was evidently her especial pride, for whenever she wore it she would stand regarding a certain place on the wall, which Merlin thought must be a mirror. She sat usually in the profile chair near the window, but sometimes honored the *chaise longue* by the lamp, and often she leaned 'way back and smoked a cigarette with posturings of her arms and hands that Merlin considered very graceful.

At another time she had come to the window and stood in it magnificently, and looked out because the moon had lost its way and was dripping the strangest and most transforming brilliance into the areaway between, turning the motif of ash-cans and clothes-lines intc a vivid impressionism of silver casks and gigantic gossamer cobwebs. Merlin was sitting in plain sight, eating cottage cheese with sugar and milk on it; and so quickly did he reach out for the window cord that he tipped the cottage cheese into his lap with his free hand—and the milk was cold and the sugar made spots on his trousers, and he was sure that she had seen him after all.

Sometimes there were callers—men in dinner coats, who stood

and bowed, hat in hand and coat on arm, as they talked to Caroline; then bowed some more and followed her out of the light, obviously bound for a play or for a dance. Other young men came and sat and smoked cigarettes, and seemed trying to tell Caroline something—she sitting either in the profile chair and watching them with eager intentness or else in the *chaise longue* by the lamp, looking very lovely and youthfully inscrutable indeed.

Merlin enjoyed these calls. Of some of the men he approved. Others won only his grudging toleration, one or two he loathed—especially the most frequent caller, a man with black hair and a black goatee and a pitch-dark soul, who seemed to Merlin vaguely familiar, but whom he was never quite able to recognize.

Now, Merlin's whole life was not "bound up with this romance he had constructed"; it was not "the happiest hour of his day." He never arrived in time to rescue Caroline from "clutches"; nor did he even marry her. A much stranger thing happened than any of these, and it is this strange thing that will presently be set down here. It began one October afternoon when she walked briskly into the mellow interior of the Moonlight Quill.

It was a dark afternoon, threatening rain and the end of the world, and done in that particularly gloomy gray in which only New York afternoons indulge. A breeze was crying down the streets, whisking along battered newspapers and pieces of things, and little lights were pricking out all the windows—it was so desolate that one was sorry for the tops of sky-scrapers lost up there in the dark green and gray heaven, and felt that now surely the farce was to close, and presently all the buildings would collapse like card houses, and pile up in a dusty, sardonic heap upon all the millions who presumed to wind in and out of them.

At least these were the sort of musings that lay heavily upon the soul of Merlin Grainger, as he stood by the window putting a dozen books back in a row, after a cyclonic visit by a lady with ermine trimmings. He looked out of the window full of the most distressing thoughts—of the early novels of H. G. Wells, of the book of Genesis, of how Thomas Edison had said that in thirty years there would be no dwelling-houses upon the island, but only a vast and turbulent bazaar; and then he set the last book right side up, turned—and Caroline walked coolly into the shop.

She was dressed in a jaunty but conventional walking costume—he remembered this when he thought about it later. Her skirt was plaid, pleated like a concertina; her jacket was a soft but brisk tan; her shoes and spats were brown and her hat, small and trim, completed her like the top of a very expensive and beautifully filled candy box.

Merlin, breathless and startled, advanced nervously toward her.

"Good-afternoon—" he said, and then stopped—why, he did not know, except that it came to him that something very portentous in his life was about to occur, and that it would need no furbishing but silence, and the proper amount of expectant attention. And in that minute before the thing began to happen he had the sense of a breathless second hanging suspended in time: he saw through the glass partition that bounded off the little office the malevolent conical head of his employer, Mr. Moonlight Quill, bent over his correspondence. He saw Miss McCracken and Miss Masters as two patches of hair drooping over piles of paper; he saw the crimson lamp overhead, and noticed with a touch of pleasure how really pleasant and romantic it made the book-store seem.

Then the thing happened, or rather it began to happen. Caroline picked up a volume of poems lying loose upon a pile, fingered it absently with her slender white hand, and suddenly, with an easy gesture, tossed it upward toward the ceiling, where it disappeared in the crimson lamp and lodged there, seen through the illuminated silk as a dark, bulging rectangle. This pleased her—she broke into young, contagious laughter, in which Merlin found himself presently joining.

"It stayed up!" she cried merrily. "It stayed up, didn't it?" To both of them this seemed the height of brilliant absurdity. Their laughter mingled, filled the bookshop, and Merlin was glad to find that her voice was rich and full of sorcery.

"Try another," he found himself suggesting—"try a red one."

At this her laughter increased, and she had to rest her hands upon the stack to steady herself.

"Try another," she managed to articulate between spasms of mirth. "Oh, golly, try another!"

"Try two."

"Yes, try two. Oh, I'll choke if I don't stop laughing. Here it goes."

Suiting her action to the word, she picked up a red book and sent it in a gentle hyperbola toward the ceiling, where it sank into the lamp beside the first. It was a few minutes before either of them could do more than rock back and forth in helpless glee; but then by mutual agreement they took up the sport anew, this time in unison. Merlin seized a large, specially bound French classic and whirled it upward. Applauding his own accuracy, he took a best-seller in one hand and a book on barnacles in the other, and waited breathlessly while she made her shot. Then the business waxed fast and furious —sometimes they alternated, and, watching, he found how supple she was in every movement; sometimes one of them made shot after shot, picking up the nearest book, sending it off, merely taking time to follow it with a glance before reaching for another. Within three minutes they had cleared a little place on the table, and the lamp of crimson satin was so bulging with books that it was near breaking.

"Silly game, basket-ball," she cried scornfully as a book left her hand. "High-school girls play it in hideous bloomers."

"Idiotic," he agreed.

She paused in the act of tossing a book, and replaced it suddenly in its position on the table.

"I think we've got room to sit down now," she said gravely.

They had; they had cleared an ample space for two. With a faint touch of nervousness Merlin glanced toward Mr. Moonlight Quill's glass partition, but the three heads were still bent earnestly over their work, and it was evident that they had not seen what had gone on in the shop. So when Caroline put her hands on the table and hoisted herself up Merlin calmly imitated her, and they sat side by side looking very earnestly at each other.

"I had to see you," she began, with a rather pathetic expression in her brown eyes.

"I know."

"It was that last time," she continued, her voice trembling a little, though she tried to keep it steady. "I was frightened. I don't like you to eat off the dresser. I'm so afraid you'll—you'll swallow a collar button."

"I did once—almost," he confessed reluctantly, "but it's not so easy, you know. I mean you can swallow the flat part easy enough or else the other part—that is, separately—but for a whole collar button you'd have to have a specially made throat." He was astonishing himself by the debonnaire appropriateness of his remarks. Words seemed for the first time in his life to run at him shrieking to be used, gathering themselves into carefully arranged squads and platoons, and being presented to him by punctilious adjutants of paragraphs.

"That's what scared me," she said. "I knew you had to have a specially made throat—and I knew, at least I felt sure, that you didn't have one."

He nodded frankly.

"I haven't. It costs money to have one—more money unfortunately than I possess."

He felt no shame in saying this—rather a delight in making the admission—he knew that nothing he could say or do would be beyond her comprehension; least of all his poverty, and the practical impossibility of ever extricating himself from it.

Caroline looked down at her wrist watch, and with a little cry slid from the table to her feet.

"It's after five," she cried. "I didn't realize. I have to be at the Ritz at five-thirty. Let's hurry and get this done. I've got a bet on it."

With one accord they set to work. Caroline began the matter by seizing a book on insects and sending it whizzing, and finally crashing through the glass partition that housed Mr. Moonlight Quill. The proprietor glanced up with a wild look, brushed a few pieces of glass from his desk, and went on with his letters. Miss McCracken gave no sign of having heard—only Miss Masters started and gave a little frightened scream before she bent to her task again.

But to Merlin and Caroline it didn't matter. In a perfect orgy of energy they were hurling book after book in all directions, until sometimes three or four were in the air at once, smashing against shelves, cracking the glass of pictures on the walls, falling in bruised and torn heaps upon the floor. It was fortunate that no customers happened to come in, for it is certain they would never have come in again—the noise was too tremendous, a noise of smashing and ripping and tearing, mixed now and then with the tinkling of glass, the quick breathing of the two throwers, and the intermittent outbursts of laughter to which both of them periodically surrendered.

At five-thirty Caroline tossed a last book at the lamp, and so gave the final impetus to the load it carried. The weakened silk tore and dropped its cargo in one vast splattering of white and color to the already littered floor. Then with a sigh of relief she turned to Merlin and held out her hand.

"Good-by," she said simply.

"Are you going?" He knew she was. His question was simply a lingering wile to detain her and extract for another moment that dazzling essence of light he drew from her presence, to continue his enormous satisfaction in her features, which were like kisses and, he thought, like the features of a girl he had known back in 1910. For a minute he pressed the softness of her hand—then she smiled and withdrew it and, before he could spring to open the door, she had done it herself and was gone out into the turbid and ominous twilight that brooded narrowly over Forty-seventh Street.

I would like to tell you how Merlin, having seen how beauty regards the wisdom of the years, walked into the little partition of Mr. Moonlight Quill and gave up his job then and there; thence issuing out into the street a much finer and nobler and increasingly ironic man. But the truth is much more commonplace. Merlin Grainger stood up and surveyed the wreck of the bookshop, the ruined volumes, the torn silk remnants of the once beautiful crimson lamp, the crystalline sprinkling of broken glass which lay in iridescent dust over the whole interior—and then he went to a corner where a broom was kept and began cleaning up and rearranging and, as far as he was able, restoring the shop to its former condition. He found that, though some few of the books were uninjured, most of them had suffered in varying extents. The backs were off some, the pages were torn from others, still others were just slightly cracked in the front, which, as all careless book returners know, makes a book unsalable, and therefore second-hand.

Nevertheless by six o'clock he had done much to repair the damage. He had returned the books to their original places, swept the floor, and put new lights in the sockets overhead. The red shade itself was ruined beyond redemption, and Merlin thought in some trepidation that the money to replace it might have to come out of his salary. At six, therefore, having done the best he could, he crawled over the front window display to pull down the blind. As he was treading delicately back, he saw Mr. Moonlight Quill rise from his desk, put on his overcoat and hat, and emerge into the shop. He nodded mysteriously at Merlin and went toward the door. With his hand on the knob he paused, turned around, and in a voice curiously compounded of ferocity and uncertainty, he said:

"If that girl comes in here again, you tell her to behave."

With that he opened the door, drowning Merlin's meek "Yessir" in its creak, and went out.

Merlin stood there for a moment, deciding wisely not to worry about what was for the present only a possible futurity, and then he went into the back of the shop and invited Miss Masters to have supper with him at Pulpat's French Restaurant, where one could still obtain red wine at dinner, despite the Great Federal Government. Miss Masters accepted.

"Wine makes me feel all tingly," she said.

Merlin laughed inwardly as he compared her to Caroline, or rather as he didn't compare her. There was no comparison.

II

Mr. Moonlight Quill, mysterious, exotic, and oriental in temperament was, nevertheless, a man of decision. And it was with decision that he approached the problem of his wrecked shop. Unless he should make an outlay equal to the original cost of his entire stock —a step which for certain private reasons he did not wish to take— it would be impossible for him to continue in business with the Moonlight Quill as before. There was but one thing to do. He promptly turned his establishment from an up-to-the-minute bookstore into a second-hand bookshop. The damaged books were marked down from twenty-five to fifty per cent, the name over the door whose serpentine embroidery had once shone so insolently bright, was allowed to grow dim and take on the indescribably vague color of old paint, and, having a strong penchant for ceremonial, the proprietor even went so far as to buy two skull-caps of shoddy red felt, one for himself and one for his clerk, Merlin Grainger. Moreover, he let his goatee grow until it resembled the tail-feathers of an ancient sparrow and substituted for a once dapper business suit a reverence-inspiring affair of shiny alpaca.

In fact, within a year after Caroline's catastrophic visit to the bookshop the only thing in it that preserved any semblance of being up to date was Miss Masters. Miss McCracken had followed in the footsteps of Mr. Moonlight Quill and become an intolerable dowd.

For Merlin too, from a feeling compounded of loyalty and listlessness, had let his exterior take on the semblance of a deserted garden. He accepted the red felt skull-cap as a symbol of his decay. Always a young man known as a "pusher," he had been, since the day of his graduation from the manual training department of a New York High School, an inveterate brusher of clothes, hair, teeth, and even eyebrows, and had learned the value of laying all his clean socks toe upon toe and hell upon heel in a certain drawer of his bureau, which would be known as the sock drawer.

These things, he felt, had won him his place in the greatest splendor of the Moonlight Quill. It was due to them that he was not still making "chests useful for keeping things," as he was taught with breathless practicality in High School, and selling them to whoever had use of such chests—possibly undertakers. Nevertheless when the progressive Moonlight Quill became the retrogressive Moonlight Quill he preferred to sink with it, and so took to letting his suits gather undisturbed the wispy burdens of the air and to throwing his socks indiscriminately into the shirt drawer, the underwear drawer, and even into no drawer at all. It was not uncommon in his new carelessness to let many of his clean clothes go directly back to the laundry without having ever been worn, a common eccentricity of impoverished bachelors. And this in the face of his favorite magazines, which at that time were fairly staggering with articles by successful authors against the frightful impudence of the condemned poor, such as the buying of wearable shirts and nice cuts of meat, and the fact that they preferred good investments in personal jewelry to respectable ones in four per cent saving-banks.

It was indeed a strange state of affairs and a sorry one for many worthy and God-fearing men. For the first time in the history of the Republic almost any negro north of Georgia could change a one-dollar bill. But as at that time the cent was rapidly approaching the purchasing power of the Chinese ubu and was only a thing you got back occasionally after paying for a soft drink, and could use merely in getting your correct weight, this was perhaps not so strange a phenomenon as it at first seems. It was too curious a state of things, however, for Merlin Grainger to take the step that he did take—the hazardous, almost involuntary step of proposing to Miss Masters. Stranger still that she accepted him.

It was at Pulpat's on Saturday night and over a $1.75 bottle of water diluted with *vin ordinaire* that the proposal occurred.

"Wine makes me feel all tingly, doesn't it you?" chattered Miss Masters gaily.

"Yes, answered Merlin absently; and then, after a long and pregnant pause: "Miss Masters—Olive—I want to say something to you if you'll listen to me."

The tingliness of Miss Masters (who knew what was coming) increased until it seemed that she would shortly be electrocuted by her own nervous reactions. But her "Yes, Merlin," came without a sign or flicker of interior disturbance. Merlin swallowed a stray bit of air that he found in his mouth.

"I have no fortune," he said with the manner of making an announcement. "I have no fortune at all."

Their eyes met, locked, became wistful, and dreamy and beautiful.

"Olive," he told her, "I love you."

"I love you too, Merlin," she answered simply. "Shall we have another bottle of wine?"

"Yes," he cried, his heart beating at a great rate. "Do you mean——"

"To drink to our engagement," she interrupted bravely. "May it be a short one!"

"No!" he almost shouted, bringing his fist fiercely down upon the table. "May it last forever!"

"What?"

"I mean—oh, I see what you mean. You're right. May it be a short one." He laughed and added, "My error."

After the wine arrived they discussed the matter thoroughly.

"We'll have to take a small apartment at first," he said, "and I believe, yes, by golly, I know there's a small one in the house where I live, a big room and a sort of a dressing-room-kitchenette and the use of a bath on the same floor."

She clapped her hands happily, and he thought how pretty she was really, that is, the upper part of her face—from the bridge of the nose down she was somewhat out of true. She continued enthusiastically:

"And as soon as we can afford it we'll take a real swell apartment, with an elevator and a telephone girl."

"And after that a place in the country—and a car."

"I can't imagine nothing more fun. Can you?"

Merlin fell silent a moment. He was thinking that he would have to give up his room, the fourth floor rear. Yet it mattered very little now. During the past year and a half—in fact, from the very date of Caroline's visit to the Moonlight Quill—he had never seen her. For a week after that visit her lights had failed to go on—darkness brooded out into the areaway, seemed to grope blindly in at his expectant, uncurtained window. Then the lights had appeared at last, and instead of Caroline and her callers they showed a stodgy family —a little man with a bristly mustache and a full-bosomed woman who spent her evenings patting her hips and rearranging bric-a-brac. After two days of them Merlin had callously pulled down his shade.

No, Merlin could think of nothing more fun than rising in the world with Olive. There would be a cottage in a suburb, a cottage painted blue, just one class below the sort of cottages that are of white stucco with a green roof. In the grass around the cottage would be rusty trowels and a broken green bench and a baby-carriage with a wicker body that sagged to the left. And around the grass and the baby-carriage and the cottage itself, around his whole world there would be the arms of Olive, a little stouter, the arms of her neo-Olivian period, when, as she walked, her cheeks would tremble up and down ever so slightly from too much face-massaging. He could hear her voice now, two spoons' length away:

"I knew you were going to say this to-night, Merlin. I could see——"

She could see. Ah—suddenly he wondered how much she could see. Could she see that the girl who had come in with a party of three men and sat down at the next table was Caroline? Ah, could she see that? Could she see that the men brought with them liquor far more potent than Pulpat's red ink condensed threefold . . . ?

Merlin stared breathlessly, half-hearing through an auditory ether Olive's low, soft monologue, as like a persistent honey-bee she sucked sweetness from her memorable hour. Merlin was listening to the clinking of ice and the fine laughter of all four at some pleasantry—and that laughter of Caroline's that he knew so well stirred him, lifted him, called his heart imperiously over to her table, whither it obediently went. He could see her quite plainly, and he fancied that in the last year and a half she had changed, if ever so slightly. Was it the light or were her cheeks a little thinner and her eyes less fresh, if more liquid, than of old? Yet the shadows were still purple in her russet hair; her mouth hinted yet of kisses, as did the profile that came sometimes between his eyes and a row of books, when it was twilight in the bookshop where the crimson lamp presided no more.

And she had been drinking. The threefold flush in her cheeks was compounded of youth and wine and fine cosmetic—that he could tell. She was making great amusement for the young man on her left and the portly person on her right, and even for the old fellow opposite her, for the latter from time to time uttered the shocked and mildly reproachful cackles of another generation. Merlin caught the words of a song she was intermittently singing——

> "Just snap your fingers at care,
> Don't cross the bridge 'til you're there——"

The portly person filled her glass with chill amber. A waiter after several trips about the table, and many helpless glances at Caroline, who was maintaining a cheerful, futile questionnaire as to the succulence of this dish or that, managed to obtain the semblance of an order and hurried away. . . .

Olive was speaking to Merlin——

"When, then?" she asked, her voice faintly shaded with disappointment. He realized that he had just answered no to some question she had asked him.

"Oh, sometime."

"Don't you—care?"

A rather pathetic poignancy in her question brought his eyes back to her.

"As soon as possible, dear," he replied with surprising tenderness. "In two months—in June."

"So soon?" Her delightful excitement quite took her breath away.

"Oh, yes, I think we'd better say June. No use waiting."

Olive began to pretend that two months was really too short a time for her to make preparations. Wasn't he a bad boy! Wasn't he impatient, though! Well, she'd show him he mustn't be too quick with *her*. Indeed he was so sudden she didn't exactly know whether she ought to marry him at all.

"June," he repeated sternly.

Olive sighed and smiled and drank her coffee, her little finger lifted high above the others in true refined fashion. A stray thought came to Merlin that he would like to buy five rings and throw at it.

"By gosh!" he exclaimed aloud. Soon he *would* be putting rings on one of her fingers.

His eyes swung sharply to the right. The party of four had become so riotous that the head-waiter had approached and spoken to them. Caroline was arguing with this head-waiter in a raised voice, a voice so clear and young that it seemed as though the whole restaurant would listen—the whole restaurant except Olive Masters, self-absorbed in her new secret.

"How do you do?" Caroline was saying. "Probably the handsomeest head-waiter in captivity. Too much noise? Very unfortunate. Something'll have to be done about it. Gerald"—she addressed the man on her right—"the head-waiter says there's too much noise. Appeals to us to have it stopped. What'll I say?"

"Sh!" remonstrated Gerald, with laughter. "Sh!" and Merlin heard him add in an undertone: "All the bourgeoisie will be aroused. This is where the floorwalkers learn French."

Caroline sat up straight in sudden alertness.

"Where's a floorwalker?" she cried. "Show me a floorwalker." This seemed to amuse the party, for they all, including Caroline, burst into renewed laughter. The head-waiter, after a last conscientious but despairing admonition, became Gallic with his shoulders and retired into the background.

Pulpat's, as every one knows, has the unvarying respectability of the table d'hôte. It is not a gay place in the conventional sense. One comes, drinks the red wine, talks perhaps a little more and a little louder than usual under the low, smoky ceilings, and then goes home. It closes up at nine-thirty, tight as a drum; the policeman is paid off and given an extra bottle of wine for the missis, the coat-room girl hands her tips to the collector, and then darkness crushes the little round tables out of sight and life. But excitement was prepared for Pulpat's this evening—excitement of no mean variety. A girl with russet, purple-shadowed hair mounted to her table-top and began to dance thereon.

"*Sacré nom de Dieu!* Come down off there!" cried the head-waiter. "Stop that music!"

But the musicians were already playing so loud that they could pretend not to hear his order; having once been young, they played louder and gayer than ever, and Caroline danced with grace and vivacity, her pink, filmy dress swirling about her, her agile arms playing in supple, tenuous gestures along the smoky air.

A group of Frenchmen at a table near by broke into cries of applause, in which other parties joined—in a moment the room was full of clapping and shouting; half the diners were on their feet, crowding up, and on the outskirts the hastily summoned proprietor was giving indistinct vocal evidences of his desire to put an end to this thing as quickly as possible.

"... Merlin!" cried Olive, awake, aroused at last; "she's such a wicked girl! Let's get out—now!"

The fascinated Merlin protested feebly that the check was not paid.

"It's all right. Lay five dollars on the table. I despise that girl. I can't *bear* to look at her." She was on her feet now, tugging at Merlin's arm.

Helplessly, listlessly, and then with what amounted to downright unwillingness, Merlin rose, followed Olive dumbly as she picked her way through the delirious clamor, now approaching its height and threatening to become a wild and memorable riot. Submissively he took his coat and stumbled up half a dozen steps into the moist April air outside, his ears still ringing with the sound of light feet on the table and of laughter all about and over the little world of the café. In silence they walked along toward Fifth Avenue and a bus.

It was not until next day that she told him about the wedding—how she had moved the date forward: it was much better that they should be married on the first of May.

III

And married they were, in a somewhat stuffy manner, under the chandelier of the flat where Olive lived with her mother. After marriage came elation, and then, gradually, the growth of weariness. Responsibility descended upon Merlin, the responsibility of making his thirty dollars a week and her twenty suffice to keep them respectably fat and to hide with decent garments the evidence that they were.

It was decided after several weeks of disastrous and well-nigh humiliating experiments with restaurants that they would join the great army of the delicatessen-fed, so he took up his old way of life again, in that he stopped every evening at Braegdort's delicatessen and bought potatoes in salad, ham in slices, and sometimes even stuffed tomatoes in bursts of extravagance.

Then he would trudge homeward, enter the dark hallway, and climb three rickety flights of stairs covered by an ancient carpet of long obliterated design. The hall had an ancient smell—of the vegetables of 1880, of the furniture polish in vogue when "Adam-and-Eve" Bryan ran against William McKinley, of portieres an ounce heavier with dust, from worn-out shoes and lint from dresses turned long since into patch-work quilts. This smell would pursue him up the stairs, revivified and made poignant at each landing by the aura of contemporary cooking, then, as he began the next flight, diminishing into the odor of the dead routine of dead generations.

Eventually would occur the door of his room, which slipped open with indecent willingness and closed with almost a sniff upon his "Hello, dear! Got a treat for you to-night."

Olive, who always rode home on the bus to "get a morsel of air," would be making the bed and hanging up things. At his call she would come up to him and give him a quick kiss with wide-open eyes, while he held her upright like a ladder, his hands on her two arms, as though she were a thing without equilibrium, and would, once he relinquished hold, fall stiffly backward to the floor. This is the kiss that comes in with the second year of marriage, succeeding the bridegroom kiss (which is rather stagey at best, say those who know about such things, and apt to be copied from passionate movies).

Then came supper, and after that they went out for a walk, up two blocks and through Central Park, or sometimes to a moving picture, which taught them patiently that they were the sort of people for whom life was ordered, and that something very grand and brave and beautiful would soon happen to them if they were docile and obedient to their rightful superiors and kept away from pleasure.

Such was their day for three years. Then change came into their lives: Olive had a baby, and as a result Merlin had a new influx of material resources. In the third week of Olive's confinement, after an hour of nervous rehearsing, he went into the office of Mr. Moonlight Quill and demanded an enormous increase in salary.

"I've been here ten years," he said; "since I was nineteen. I've always tried to do my best in the interests of the business."

Mr. Moonlight Quill said that he would think it over. Next morning he announced, to Merlin's great delight, that he was going to put into effect a project long premeditated—he was going to retire from active work in the bookshop, confining himself to periodic visits and leaving Merlin as manager with a salary of fifty dollars a week and a one-tenth interest in the business. When the old man finished, Merlin's cheeks were glowing and his eyes full of tears. He seized his employer's hand and shook it violently, saying over and over again:

"It's very nice of you, sir. It's very white of you. It's very, very nice of you."

So after ten years of faithful work in the store he had won out at last. Looking back, he saw his own progress toward this hill of elation no longer as a sometimes sordid and always gray decade of worry and failing enthusiasm and failing dreams, years when the moonlight had grown duller in the areaway and the youth had faded out of Olive's face, but as a glorious and triumphant climb over obstacles which he had determinedly surmounted by unconquerable will-power. The optimistic self-delusion that had kept him from misery was seen now in the golden garments of stern resolution. Half a dozen times he had taken steps to leave the Moonlight Quill and soar upward, but through sheer faint-heartedness he had stayed on. Strangely enough he now thought that those were times when he had exerted tremendous persistence and had "determined" to fight it out where he was.

At any rate, let us not for this moment begrudge Merlin his new and magnificent view of himself. He had arrived. At thirty he had reached a post of importance. He left the shop that evening fairly radiant, invested every penny in his pocket in the most tremendous feast that Braegdort's delicatessen offered, and staggered homeward with the great news and four gigantic paper bags. The fact that Olive was too sick to eat, that he made himself faintly but unmistakably ill by a struggle with four stuffed tomatoes, and that most of the food deteriorated rapidly in an iceless ice-box all next day did not mar the occasion. For the first time since the week of his marriage Merlin Grainger lived under a sky of unclouded tranquillity.

The baby boy was christened Arthur, and life became dignified, significant, and, at length, centered. Merlin and Olive resigned themselves to a somewhat secondary place in their own cosmos; but what they lost in personality they regained in a sort of primordial pride. The country house did not come, but a month in an Asbury Park boarding-house each summer filled the gap; and during Merlin's two weeks' holiday this excursion assumed the air of a really merry jaunt—especially when, with the baby asleep in a wide room opening technically on the sea, Merlin strolled with Olive along the thronged board-walk puffing at his cigar and trying to look like twenty thousand a year.

With some alarm at the slowing up of the days and the accelerating of the years, Merlin became thirty-one, thirty-two—then almost with a rush arrived at that age which, with all its washing and panning, can only muster a bare handful of the precious stuff of youth: he became thirty-five. And one day on Fifth Avenue he saw Caroline.

It was Sunday, a radiant, flowerful Easter morning and the avenue was a pageant of lilies and cutaways and happy April-colored bonnets. Twelve o'clock: the great churches were letting out their people—St. Simon's, St. Hilda's, the Church of the Epistles, opened their doors like wide mouths until the people pouring forth surely resembled happy laughter as they met and strolled and chattered, or else waved white bouquets at waiting chauffeurs.

In front of the Church of the Epistles stood its twelve vestrymen, carrying out the time-honored custom of giving away Easter eggs full of face-powder to the church-going débutantes of the year. Around them delightedly danced the two thousand miraculously groomed children of the very rich, correctly cute and curled, shining like sparkling little jewels upon their mothers' fingers. Speaks the sentimentalist for the children of the poor? Ah, but the children of the rich, laundered, sweet-smelling, complexioned of the country, and, above all, with soft, in-door voices.

Little Arthur was five, child of the middle class. Undistinguished, unnoticed, with a nose that forever marred what Grecian yearnings his features might have had, he held tightly to his mother's warm, sticky hand, and, with Merlin on his other side, moved upon the home-coming throng. At Fifty-third Street, where there were two churches, the congestion was at its thickest, its richest. Their progress was of necessity retarded to such an extent that even little Arthur had not the slightest difficulty in keeping up. Then it was that Merlin perceived an open landaulet of deepest crimson, with handsome nickel trimmings, glide slowly up to the curb and come to a stop. In it sat Caroline.

She was dressed in black, a tight-fitting gown trimmed with lavender, flowered at the waist with a corsage of orchids. Merlin started and then gazed at her fearfully. For the first time in the eight years since his marriage he was encountering the girl again. But a girl no longer. Her figure was slim as ever—or perhaps not quite, for a certain boyish swagger, a sort of insolent adolescence, had gone the way of the first blooming of her cheeks. But she was beautiful; dignity was there now, and the charming lines of a fortuitous nine-and-twenty; and she sat in the car with such perfect appropriateness and self-possession that it made him breathless to watch her.

Suddenly she smiled—the smile of old, bright as that very Easter and its flowers, mellower than ever—yet somehow with not quite the radiance and infinite promise of that first smile back there in the bookshop nine years before. It was a steelier smile, disillusioned and sad.

But it was soft enough and smile enough to make a pair of young men in cutaway coats hurry over, to pull their high hats off their wetted, iridescent hair; to bring them, flustered and bowing, to the edge of her landaulet, where her lavender gloves gently touched their gray ones. And these two were presently joined by another, and then two more, until there was a rapidly swelling crowd around the landaulet. Merlin would hear a young man beside him say to his perhaps well-favored companion:

"If you'll just pardon me a moment, there's some one I *have* to speak to. Walk right ahead. I'll catch up."

Within three minutes every inch of the landaulet, front, back, and side, was occupied by a man—a man trying to construct a sentence clever enough to find its way to Caroline through the stream of conversation. Luckily for Merlin a portion of little Arthur's clothing had chosen the opportunity to threaten a collapse, and Olive had hurriedly rushed him over against a building for some extemporaneous repair work, so Merlin was able to watch, unhindered, the salon in the street.

The crowd swelled. A row formed in back of the first, two more behind that. In the midst, an orchid rising from a black bouquet, sat Caroline enthroned in her obliterated car, nodding and crying salutations and smiling with such true happiness that, of a sudden, a new relay of gentlemen had left their wives and consorts and were striding toward her.

The crowd, now phalanx deep, began to be augmented by the merely curious; men of all ages who could not possibly have known Caroline jostled over and melted into the circle of ever-increasing diameter, until the lady in lavender was the centre of a vast impromptu auditorium.

All about her were faces—clean-shaven, bewhiskered, old, young, ageless, and now, here and there, a woman. The mass was rapidly spreading to the opposite curb, and, as St. Anthony's around the corner let out its box-holders, it overflowed to the sidewalk and crushed up against the iron picket-fence of a millionaire across the street. The motors speeding along the avenue were compelled to stop, and in a jiffy were piled three, five, and six deep at the edge of the crowd;

auto-busses, top-heavy turtles of traffic, plunged into the jam, their passengers crowding to the edges of the roofs in wild excitement and peering down into the centre of the mass, which presently could hardly be seen from the mass's edge.

The crush had become terrific. No fashionable audience at a Yale-Princeton football game, no damp mob at a world's series, could be compared with the panoply that talked, stared, laughed, and honked about the lady in black and lavender. It was stupendous; it was terrible. A quarter mile down the block a half-frantic policeman called his precinct; on the same corner a frightened civilian crashed in the glass of a fire-alarm and sent in a wild paean for all the fire-engines of the city; up in an apartment high in one of the tall buildings a hysterical old maid telephoned in turn for the prohibition enforcement agent, the special deputies on Bolshevism, and the maternity ward of Bellevue Hospital.

The noise increased. The first fire-engine arrived, filling the Sunday air with smoke, clanging and crying a brazen, metallic message down the high, resounding walls. In the notion that some terrible calamity had overtaken the city, two excited deacons ordered special services immediately and set tolling the great bells of St. Hilda's and St. Anthony's, presently joined by the jealous gongs of St. Simon's and the Church of the Epistles. Even far off in the Hudson and the East River the sounds of the commotion were heard, and the ferry-boats and tugs and ocean liners set up sirens and whistles that sailed in melancholy cadence, now varied, now reiterated, across the whole diagonal width of the city from Riverside Drive to the gray water-fronts of the lower East Side. . . .

In the centre of her landaulet sat the lady in black and lavender, chatting pleasantly first with one, then with another of that fortunate few in cutaways who had found their way to speaking distance in the first rush. After a while she glanced around her and beside her with a look of growing annoyance.

She yawned and asked the man nearest her if he couldn't run in somewhere and get her a glass of water. The man apologized in some embarrassment. He could not have moved hand or foot. He could not have scratched his own ear. . . .

As the first blast of the river sirens keened along the air, Olive fastened the last safety-pin in little Arthur's rompers and looked up. Merlin saw her start, stiffen slowly like hardening stucco, and then give a little gasp of surprise and disapproval.

"That woman," she cried suddenly. "Oh!"

She flashed a glance at Merlin that mingled reproach and pain, and without another word gathered up little Arthur with one hand, grasped her husband by the other, and darted amazingly in a winding, bumping canter through the crowd. Somehow people gave way before her; somehow she managed to retain her grasp on her son and husband; somehow she managed to emerge two blocks up, battered and dishevelled, into an open space, and, without slowing up her pace, darted down a side-street. Then at last, when uproar had died away into a dim and distant clamor, did she come to a walk and set little Arthur upon his feet.

"And on Sunday, too! Hasn't she disgraced herself enough?" This was her only comment. She said it to Arthur, as she seemed to address her remarks to Arthur throughout the remainder of the day. For some curious and esoteric reason she had never once looked at her husband during the entire retreat.

IV

The years between thirty-five and sixty-five revolve before the passive mind as one unexplained, confusing merry-go-round. True, they are a merry-go-round of ill-gaited and wind-broken horses, painted first in pastel colors, then in dull grays and browns, but perplexing and intolerably dizzy the thing is, as never were the merry-go-rounds of childhood or adolescence, as never, surely, were the certain-coursed, dynamic roller-coasters of youth. For most men and women these thirty years are taken up with a gradual withdrawal from life, a retreat first from a front with many shelters, those myriad amusements and curiosities of youth, to a line with less, when we peel down our ambitions to one ambition, our recreations to one recreation, our friends to a few to whom we are anaesthetic; ending up at last in a solitary, desolate strong point that is not strong, where the shells now whistle abominably, now are but half-heard as, by turns frightened and tired, we sit waiting for death.

At forty, then, Merlin was no different from himself at thirty-five; a larger paunch, a gray twinkling near his ears, a more certain lack of vivacity in his walk. His forty-five differed from his forty by a like margin, unless one mention a slight deafness in his left ear. But at fifty-five the process had become a chemical change of immense rapidity. Yearly he was more and more an "old man" to his family—senile almost, so far as his wife was concerned. He was by this time complete owner of the bookshop. The mysterious Mr. Moonlight Quill, dead some five years and not survived by his wife, had deeded the whole stock and store to him, and there he still spent his days, conversant now by name with almost all that man has recorded for three thousand years, a human catalogue, an authority upon tooling and binding, upon folios and first editions, an accurate inventory of a thousand authors whom he could never have understood and had certainly never read.

At sixty-five he distinctly doddered. He had assumed the melancholy habits of the aged so often portrayed by the second old man in standard Victorian comedies. He consumed vast warehouses of time searching for mislaid spectacles. He "nagged" his wife and was nagged in turn. He told the same jokes three or four times a year at the family table, and gave his son weird, impossible directions as to his conduct in life. Mentally and materially he was so entirely different from the Merlin Grainger of twenty-five that it seemed incongruous that he should bear the same name.

He worked still in the bookshop with the assistance of a youth, whom, of course, he considered very idle, indeed, and a new young woman, Miss Gaffney. Miss McCracken, ancient and unvenerable as himself, still kept the accounts. Young Arthur was gone into Wall Street to sell bonds, as all the young men seemed to be doing in that day. This, of course, was as it should be. Let old Merlin get what magic he could from his books—the place of young King Arthur was in the countinghouse.

One afternoon at four when he had slipped noiselessly up to the front of the store on his soft-soled slippers, led by a newly formed habit, of which, to be fair, he was rather ashamed, of spying upon the young man clerk, he looked casually out of the front window, straining his faded eyesight to reach the street. A limousine, large, portentous, impressive, had drawn to the curb, and the chauffeur, after dismounting and holding some sort of conversation with persons in the interior of the car, turned about and advanced in a bewildered fashion toward the entrance of the Moonlight Quill. He opened the door, shuffled in, and, glancing uncertainly at the old man in the skull-cap, addressed him in a thick, murky voice, as though his words came through a fog.

"Do you—do you sell additions?"

Merlin nodded.

"The arithmetic books are in the back of the store."

The chauffeur took off his cap and scratched a close-cropped, fuzzy head.

"Oh, naw. This I want's a detecatif story." He jerked a thumb back toward the limousine. "She seen it in the paper. Firs' addition."

Merlin's interest quickened. Here was possibly a big sale.

"Oh, editions. Yes, we've advertised some firsts, but—detective stories, I—don't—believe—What was the title?"

"I forget. About a crime."

"About a crime. I have—well, I have 'The Crimes of the Borgias'—full morocco, London 1769, beautifully——"

"Naw," interrupted the chauffeur, "this was one fella did this crime. She seen you had it for sale in the paper." He rejected several possible titles with the air of connoisseur.

" 'Silver Bones,' " he announced suddenly out of a slight pause.

"What?" demanded Merlin, suspecting that the stiffness of his sinews were being commented on.

"Silver Bones. That was the guy that done the crime."

"Silver Bones?"

"Silver Bones. Indian, maybe."

Merlin stroked his grizzly cheeks.

"Gees, Mister," went on the prospective purchaser, "if you wanna save me an awful bawlin' out jes' try an' think. The old lady goes wile if everything don't run smooth."

But Merlin's musings on the subject of Silver Bones were as futile as his obliging search through the shelves, and five minutes later a very dejected charioteer wound his way back to his mistress. Through the glass Merlin could see the visible symbols of a tremendous uproar going on in the interior of the limousine. The chauffeur made wild, appealing gestures of his innocence, evidently to no avail, for when he turned around and climbed back into the driver's seat his expression was not a little dejected.

Then the door of the limousine opened and gave forth a pale and slender young man of about twenty, dressed in the attenuation of fashion and carrying a wisp of a cane. He entered the shop, walked past Merlin, and proceeded to take out a cigarette and light it. Merlin approached him.

"Anything I can do for you, sir?"

"Old boy," said the youth coolly, "there are seveereal things. You can first let me smoke my ciggy in here out of sight of that old lady in the limousine, who happens to be my grandmother. Her knowledge as to whether I smoke it or not before my majority happens to be a matter of five thousand dollars to me. The second thing is that you should look up your first edition of the 'Crime of Sylvester Bonnard' that you advertised in last Sunday's *Times*. My grandmother there happens to want to take if off your hands."

Detecatif story! Crime of somebody! Silver Bones! All was explained. With a faint deprecatory chuckle, as if to say that he would have enjoyed this had life put him in the habit of enjoying anything, Merlin doddered away to the back of his shop where his treasures were kept, to get this latest investment which he had picked up rather cheaply at the sale of a big collection.

When he returned with it the young man was drawing on his cigarette and blowing out quantities of smoke with immense satisfaction.

"My God!" he said. "She keeps me so close to her the entire day running idiotic errands that this happens to be my first puff in six hours. What's the world coming to, I ask you, when a feeble old lady in the milk-toast era can dictate to a man as to his personal vices? I happen to be unwilling to be so dictated to. Let's see the book."

Merlin passed it to him tenderly and the young man, after opening it with a carelessness that gave a momentary jump to the bookdealer's heart, ran through the pages with his thumb.

"No illustrations, eh?" he commented. "Well, old boy, what's it worth? Speak up! We're willing to give you a fair price, though why I don't know."

"One hundred dollars," said Merlin with a frown.

The young man gave a startled whistle.

"Whew! Come on. You're not dealing with somebody from the cornbelt. I happen to be a city-bred man and my grandmother happens to be a city-bred woman, though I'll admit it'd take a special tax appropriation to keep her in repair. We'll give you twenty-five dollars, and let me tell you that's liberal. We've got books in our attic, up in our attic with my old playthings, that were written before the old boy that wrote this was born."

Merlin stiffened, expressing a rigid and meticulous horror.

"Did your grandmother give you twenty-five dollars to buy this with?"

"She did not. She gave me fifty, but she expects change. I know that old lady."

"You tell her," said Merlin with dignity, "that she has missed a very great bargain."

"Give you forty," urged the young man. "Come on now—be reasonable and don't try to hold us up——"

Merlin had wheeled around with the precious volume under his arm and was about to return it to its special drawer in his office when there was a sudden interruption. With unheard-of magnificence the front door burst rather than swung open, and admitted into the dark interior a regal apparition in black silk and fur which bore rapidly down upon him. The cigarette leaped from the fingers of the urban young man and he gave breath to an inadvertent "Damn!"—but it was upon Merlin that the entrance seemed to have the most remarkable and incongruous effect—so strong an effect that the greatest treasure of his shop slipped from his hand and joined the cigarette on the floor. Before him stood Caroline.

She was an old woman, an old woman remarkably preserved, unusually handsome, unusually erect, but still an old woman. Her hair was a soft, beautiful white, elaborately dressed and jewelled; her face, faintly rouged à la grande dame, showed webs of wrinkles at the edges of her eyes and two deeper lines in the form of stanchions connected her nose with the corners of her mouth. Her eyes were dim, ill natured, and querulous.

But it was Caroline without a doubt: Caroline's features though in decay; Caroline's figure, if brittle and stiff in movement; Caroline's manner, unmistakably compounded of a delightful insolence and an enviable self assurance; and, most of all, Caroline's voice, broken and shaky, yet with a ring in it that still could and did make chauffeurs want to drive laundry wagons and cause cigarettes to fall from the fingers of urban grandsons.

She stood and sniffed. Her eyes found the cigarette upon the floor.

"What's that?" she cried. The words were not a question—they were an entire litany of suspicion, accusation, confirmation, and decision. She tarried over them scarcely an instant. "Stand up!" she said to her grandson, "stand up and blow that nicotine out of your lungs!"

The young man looked at her in trepidation.

"Blow!" she commanded.

He pursed his lips feebly and blew into the air.

"Blow!" she repeated, more peremptorily than before.

He blew again, helplessly, ridiculously.

"Do you realize," she went on briskly, "that you've forfeited five thousand dollars in five minutes?"

Merlin momentarily expected the young man to fall pleading upon his knees, but such is the nobility of human nature that he remained standing—even blew again into the air, partly from nervousness, partly, no doubt, with some vague hope of reingratiating himself.

"Young ass!" cried Caroline. "Once more, just once more and you leave college and go to work."

This threat had such an overwhelming effect upon the young man that he took on an even paler pallor than was natural to him. But Caroline was not through.

"Do you think I don't know what you and your brothers, yes, and your asinine father too, think of me? Well, I do. You think I'm senile. You think I'm soft. I'm not!" She struck herself with her fist as though to prove that she was a mass of muscle and sinew. "And I'll have more brains left when you've got me laid out in the drawing-room some sunny day than you and the rest of them were born with."

"But Grandmother——"

"Be quiet. You, a thin little stick of a boy, who if it weren't for my money might have risen to be a journeyman barber out in the Bronx—Let me see your hands. Ugh! The hands of a barber—*you* presume to be smart with *me*, who once had three counts and a bona-fide duke, not to mention half a dozen papal titles pursue me from the city of Rome to the city of New York." She paused, took breath. "Stand up! Blow!"

The young man obediently blew. Simultaneously the door opened and an excited gentleman of middle age who wore a coat and hat trimmed with fur, and seemed, moreover, to be trimmed with the same sort of fur himself on upper lip and chin, rushed into the store and up to Caroline.

"Found you at last," he cried. "Been looking for you all over town. Tried your house on the 'phone and your secretary told me he thought you'd gone to a bookshop called the Moonlight——"

Caroline turned to him irritably.

"Do I employ you for your reminiscenses?" she snapped. "Are you my tutor or my broker?"

"Your broker," confessed the fur-trimmed man, taken somewhat aback. "I beg your pardon. I came about that phonograph stock. I can sell for a hundred and five."

"Then do it."

"Very well. I thought I'd better——"

"Go sell it. I'm talking to my grandson."

"Very well. I——"

"Good-by."

"Good-by, Madame." The fur-trimmed man made a slight bow and hurried in some confusion from the shop.

"As for you," said Caroline, turning to her grandson, "you stay just where you are and be quiet."

She turned to Merlin and included his entire length in a not unfriendly survey. Then she smiled and he found himself smiling too. In an instant they had both broken into a cracked but none the less spontaneous chuckle. She seized his arm and hurried him to the other side of the store. There they stopped, faced each other, and gave vent to another long fit of senile glee.

"It's the only way," she gasped in a sort of triumphant malignity. "The only thing that keeps old folks like me happy is the sense that they can make other people step around. To be old and rich and have poor descendants is almost as much fun as to be young and beautiful and have ugly sisters."

"Oh, yes," chuckled Merlin. "I know. I envy you."

She nodded, blinking.

"The last time I was in here, forty years ago," she said, "you were a young man very anxious to kick up your heels."

"I was," he confessed.

"My visit must have meant a good deal to you."

"You have all along," he exclaimed. "I thought—I used to think at first that you were a real person—human, I mean."

She laughed.

"Many men have thought me inhuman."

"But now," continued Merlin excitedly, "I understand. Understanding is allowed to us old people—after nothing much matters. I see now that on a certain night when you danced upon a table-top you were nothing but my romantic yearning for a beautiful and perverse woman."

Her old eyes were far away, her voice no more than the echo of a forgotten dream.

"How I danced that night! I remember."

"You were making an attempt at me. Olive's arms were closing about me and you warned me to be free and keep my measure of youth and irresponsibility. But it seemed like an effect gotten up at the last moment. It came too late."

"You are very old," she said inscrutably. "I did not realize."

"Also I have not forgotten what you did to me when I was thirty-five. You shook me with that traffic tie-up. It was a magnificent effort. The beauty and power you radiated! You became personified even to my wife, and she feared you. For weeks I wanted to slip out of the house at dark and forget the stuffiness of life with music and cocktails and a girl to make me young. But then—I no longer knew how."

"And now you are so very old."

With a sort of awe she moved back and away from him.

"Yes, leave me!" he cried. "You are old also; the spirit withers with the skin. Have you come here only to tell me something I had best forget: that to be old and poor is perhaps more wretched than to be old and rich; to remind me that *my* son hurls my gray failure in my face?"

"Give me my book," she commanded harshly. "Be quick, old man!"

Merlin looked at her once more and then patiently obeyed. He picked up the book and handed it to her, shaking his head when she offered him a bill.

"Why go through the farce of paying me? Once you made me wreck these very premises."

"I did," she said in anger, "and I'm glad. Perhaps there had been enough done to ruin *me*."

She gave him a glance, half disdain, half ill-concealed uneasiness, and with a brisk word to her urban grandson moved toward the door.

Then she was gone—out of his shop—out of his life. The door clicked. With a sigh he turned and walked brokenly back toward the glass partition that enclosed the yellowed accounts of many years as well as the mellowed, wrinkled Miss McCracken.

Merlin regarded her parched, cobwebbed face with an odd sort of pity. She, at any rate, had had less from life than he. No rebellious, romantic spirit cropping out unbidden had, in its memorable moments, given her life a zest and a glory.

Then Miss McCracken looked up and spoke to him:

"Still a spunky old piece, isn't she?"

Merlin started.

"Who?"

"Old Alicia Dare. Mrs. Thomas Allerdyce she is now, of course; has been these thirty years."

"What? I don't understand you." Merlin sat down suddenly in his swivel chair; his eyes were wide.

"Why, surely, Mr. Grainger, you can't tell me that you've forgotten her, when for ten years she was the most notorious character in New York. Why, one time when she was the correspondent in the Throckmorton divorce case she attracted so much attention on Fifth Avenue that there was a traffic tie-up. Didn't you read about it in the papers."

"I never used to read the papers." His ancient brain was whirring.

"Well, you can't have forgotten the time she came in here and ruined the business. Let me tell you I came near asking Mr. Moonlight Quill for my salary, and clearing out."

"Do you mean that—that you *saw* her?"

"Saw her! How could I help it with the racket that went on. Heaven knows Mr. Moonlight Quill didn't like it either, but of course *he* didn't say anything. He was daffy about her and she could twist him around her little finger. The second he opposed one of her whims she'd threaten to tell his wife on him. Served him right. The idea of that man falling for a pretty adventuress! Of course he was never rich enough for *her*, even though the shop paid well in those days."

"But when I saw her," stammered Merlin, "that is, when I *thought* I saw her, she lived with her mother."

"Mother, trash!" said Miss McCracken indignantly. "She had a woman there she called 'Aunty' who was no more related to her than I am. Oh, she was a bad one—but clever. Right after the Throckmorton divorce case she married Thomas Allerdyce, and made herself secure for life."

"Who was she?" cried Merlin. "For God's sake what was she—a witch?"

"Why, she was Alicia Dare, the dancer, of course. In those days you couldn't pick up a paper without finding her picture."

Merlin sat very quiet, his brain suddenly fatigued and stilled. He was an old man now indeed, so old that it was impossible for him to dream of ever having been young, so old that the glamour was gone out of the world, passing not into the faces of children and into the persistent comforts of warmth and life, but passing out of the range of sight and feeling. He was never to smile again or to sit in a long reverie when spring evenings wafted the cries of children in at his window until gradually they became the friends of his boyhood out there, urging him to come and play before the last dark came down. He was too old now even for memories.

That night he sat at supper with his wife and son, who had used him for their blind purposes. Olive said:

"Don't sit there like a death's-head. Say something."

"Let him sit quiet," growled Arthur. "If you encourage him he'll tell us a story we've heard a hundred times before."

Merlin went up-stairs very quietly at nine o'clock. When he was in his room and had closed the door tight he stood by it for a moment, his thin limbs trembling. He knew now that he had always been a fool.

"O Russet Witch!"

But it was too late. He had angered Providence by resisting too many temptations. There was nothing left but heaven, where he would meet only those who, like him, had wasted earth.

THE LEES OF HAPPINESS

If you should look through the files of old magazines for the first years of the present century you would find, sandwiched in between the stories of Richard Harding Davis and Frank Norris and others long since dead, the work of one Jeffrey Curtain: a novel or two, and perhaps three or four dozen short stories. You could, if you were interested, follow them along until, say, 1908, when they suddenly disappeared.

When you had read them all you would have been quite sure that here were no masterpieces—here were passably amusing stories, a bit out of date now, but doubtless the sort that would then have whiled away a dreary half hour in a dental office. The man who did them was of good intelligence, talented, glib, probably young. In the samples of his work you found there would have been nothing to stir you to more than a faint interest in the whims of life—no deep interior laughs, no sense of futility or hint of tragedy.

After reading them you would yawn and put the number back in the files, and perhaps, if you were in some library reading-room, you would decide that by way of variety you would look at a newspaper of the period and see whether the Japs had taken Port Arthur. But if by any chance the newspaper you had chosen was the right one and had crackled open at the theatrical page, your eyes would have been arrested and held, and for at least a minute you would have forgotten Port Arthur as quickly as you forgot Chateau Thierry. For you would, by this fortunate chance, be looking at the portrait of an exquisite woman.

Those were the days of "Florodora" and of sextets, of pinched-in waists and blown-out sleeves, of almost bustles and absolute ballet skirts, but here, without doubt, disguised as she might be by the unaccustomed stiffness and old fashion of her costume, was a butterfly of butterflies. Here was the gayety of the period—the soft wine of eyes, the songs that flurried hearts, the toasts and the bouquets, the dances and the dinners. Here was a Venus of the hansom cab, the Gibson girl in her glorious prime. Here was . . .

. . . here was, you find by looking at the name beneath, one Roxanne Milbank, who had been chorus girl and understudy in

"The Daisy Chain," but who, by reason of an excellent performance when the star was indisposed, had gained a leading part.

You would look again—and wonder. Why you had never heard of her. Why did her name not linger in popular songs and vaudeville jokes and cigar bands, and the memory of that gay old uncle of yours along with Lillian Runssell and Stella Mayhew and Anna Held? Roxanne Milbank—whither had she gone? What dark trap-door had opened suddenly and swallowed her up? Her name was certainly not in last Sunday's supplement on that list of actresses married to English noblemen. No doubt she was dead—poor beautiful young lady—and quite forgotten.

I am hoping too much. I am having you stumble on Jeffrey Curtain's stories and Roxanne Milbank's picture. It would be incredible that you should find a newspaper item six months later, a single item two inches by four, which informed the public of the marriage, very quietly, of Miss Roxanne Milbank, who had been on tour with "The Daisy Chain," to Mr. Jeffrey Curtain, the popular author. "Mrs. Curtain," it added dispassionately, "will retire from the stage."

It was a marriage of love. He was sufficiently spoiled to be charming; she was ingenuous enough to be irresistible. Like two floating logs they met in a head-on rush, caught, and sped along together. Yet had Jeffrey Curtain kept at scrivening for twoscore years he could not have put a quirk into one of his stories weirder than the quirk that came into his own life. Had Roxanne Milbank played three dozen parts and filled five thousand houses she could never have had a rôle with more happiness and more despair than were in the fate prepared for Roxanne Curtain.

For a year they lived in hotels, travelled to California, to Alaska, to Florida, to Mexico, loved and quarreled gently, and gloried in the golden triflings of his wit with her beauty—they were young and gravely passionate; they demanded everything and then yielded everything again in ecstasies of unselfishness and pride. She loved the swift tones of his voice and his frantic, unfounded jealousy. He loved her dark radiance, the white irises of her eyes, the warm, lustrous enthusiasm of her smile.

"Don't you like her?" he would demand rather excitedly and shyly. "Isn't she wonderful? Did you ever see——"

"Yes," they would answer, grinning. "She's a wonder You're lucky."

The year passed. They tired of hotels. They bought an old house and twenty acres near the town of Marlowe, half an hour from Chicago; bought a little car, and moved out riotously with a pioneering hallucination that would have confounded Balboa.

"Your room will be here!" they cried in turn.

—And then:

"And my room here!"

"And the nursery here when we have children."

"And we'll build a sleeping porch—oh, next year."

They moved out in April. In July Jeffrey's closest friend, Harry Cromwell, came to spend a week—they met him at the end of the long lawn and hurried him proudly to the house.

Harry was married also. His wife had had a baby some six months before and was still recuperating at her mother's in New York. Roxanne had gathered from Jeffrey that Harry's wife was not as attractive as Harry—Jeffrey had met her once and considered her—"shallow." But Harry had been married nearly two years and was apparently happy, so Jeffrey guessed that she was probably all right . . .

"I'm making biscuits," chattered Roxanne gravely. "Can your wife make biscuits? The cook is showing me how. I think every woman should know how to make biscuits. It sounds so utterly disarming. A woman who can make biscuits can surely do no——"

"You'll have to come out here and live," said Jeffrey. "Get a place out in the country like us, for you and Kitty."

"You don't know Kitty. She hates the country. She's got to have her theatres and vaudevilles."

"Bring her out," repeated Jeffrey. "We'll have a colony. There's an awfully nice crowd here already. Bring her out!"

They were at the porch steps now and Roxanne made a brisk gesture toward a dilapidated structure on the right.

"The garage," she announced. "It will also be Jeffrey's writing-room within the month. Meanwhile dinner is at seven. Meanwhile to that I will mix a cocktail."

The two men ascended to the second floor—that is, they ascended half-way, for at the first landing Jeffrey dropped his guest's suitcase and in a cross between a query and a cry exclaimed:

"For God's sake, Harry, how do you like her?"

"We will go up-stairs," answered his guest, "and we will shut the door."

Half an hour later as they were sitting together in the library Roxanne reissued from the kitchen, bearing before her a pan of biscuits. Jeffrey and Harry rose.

"They're beautiful, dear," said the husband, intensely.

"Exquisite," murmured Harry.

Roxanne beamed.

"Taste one. I couldn't bear to touch them before you'd seen them all and I can't bear to take them back until I find what they taste like."

"Like manna, darling."

Simultaneously the two men raised the biscuits to their lips, nibbled tentatively. Simultaneously they tried to change the subject. But Roxanne, undeceived, set down the pan and seized a biscuit. After a second her comment rang out with lugubrious finality:

"Absolutely bum!"

"Really——"

"Why, I didn't notice——"

Roxanne roared.

"Oh, I'm useless," she cried laughing. "Turn me out, Jeffrey—I'm a parasite; I'm no good——"

Jeffrey put his arm around her.

"Darling, I'll eat your biscuits."

"They're beautiful, anyway," insisted Roxanne.

"They're—they're decorative," suggested Harry.

Jeffrey took him up wildly.

"That's the word. They're decorative; they're masterpieces. We'll use them."

He rushed to the kitchen and returned with a hammer and a handful of nails.

"We'll use them, by golly, Roxanne! We'll make a frieze out of them."

"Don't!" wailed Roxanne. "Our beautiful house."

"Never mind. We're going to have the library re-papered in October. Don't you remember?"

"Well——"

Bang! The first biscuit was impaled to the wall, where it quivered for a moment like a live thing.

Bang! . . .

When Roxanne returned with a second round of cocktails the

biscuits were in a perpendicular row, twelve of them, like a collection of primitive spear-heads.

"Roxanne," exclaimed Jeffrey, "you're an artist! Cook?—nonsense! You shall illustrate my books!"

During dinner the twilight faltered into dusk, and later it was a starry dark outside, filled and permeated with the frail gorgeousness of Roxanne's white dress and her tremulous, low laugh.

—Such a little girl she is, thought Harry. Not as old as Kitty.

He compared the two. Kitty—nervous without being sensitive, temperamental without temperament, a woman who seemed to flit and never light—and Roxanne, who was as young as spring night, and summed up in her own adolescent laughter.

—A good match for Jeffrey, he thought again. Two very young people, the sort who'll stay very young until they suddenly find themselves old.

Harry thought these things between his constant thoughts about Kitty. He was depressed about Kitty. It seemed to him that she was well enough to come back to Chicago and bring his little son. He was thinking vaguely of Kitty when he said good-night to his friend's wife and his friend at the foot of the stairs.

"You're our first real house guest," called Roxanne after him. "Aren't you thrilled and proud?"

When he was out of sight around the stair corner she turned to Jeffrey, who was standing beside her resting his hand on the end of the banister.

"Are you tired, my dearest?"

Jeffrey rubbed the centre of his forehead with his fingers.

"A little. How did you know?"

"Oh, how could I help knowing about you?"

"It's a headache," he said moodily. "Splitting. I'll take some aspirin."

She reached over and snapped out the light, and with his arm tight about her waist they walked up the stairs together.

II

Harry's week passed. They drove about the dreaming lanes or idled in cheerful inanity upon lake or lawn. In the evening Roxanne, sitting inside, played to them while the ashes whitened on the glowing ends of their cigars. Then came a telegram from Kitty saying that she wanted Harry to come East and get her, so Roxanne and Jeffrey were left alone in that privacy of which they never seemed to tire.

"Alone" thrilled them again. They wandered about the house, each feeling intimately the presence of the other; they sat on the same side of the table like honeymooners; they were intensely absorbed, intensely happy.

The town of Marlowe, though a comparatively old settlement, had only recently acquired a "society." Five or six years before, alarmed at the smoky swelling of Chicago, two or three young married couples, "bungalow people," had moved out; their friends had followed. The Jeffrey Curtains found an already formed "set" prepared to welcome them; a country club, ballroom, and golf links yawned for them, and there were bridge parties, and poker parties, and parties where they drank beer, and parties where they drank nothing at all.

It was at a poker party that they found themselves a week after Harry's departure. There were two tables, and a good proportion of the young wives were smoking and shouting their bets, and being very daringly mannish for those days.

Roxanne had left the game early and taken to perambulation; she wandered into the pantry and found herself some grape juice—beer gave her a headache—and then passed from table to table, looking over shoulders at the hands, keeping an eye on Jeffrey and being pleasantly unexcited and content. Jeffrey, with intense concentration, was raising a pile of chips of all colors, and Roxanne knew by the deepened wrinkle between his eyes that he was interested. She liked to see him interested in small things.

She crossed over quietly and sat down on the arm of his chair.

She sat there five minutes, listening to the sharp intermittent comments of the men and the chatter of the women, which rose from the table like soft smoke—and yet scarcely hearing either. Then quite innocently she reached out her hand, intending to place it on Jeffrey's shoulder—as it touched him he started of a sudden, gave a short grunt, and, sweeping back his arm furiously, caught her a glancing blow on her elbow.

There was a general gasp. Roxanne regained her balance, gave a little cry, and rose quickly to her feet. It had been the greatest shock of her life. This, from Jeffrey, the heart of kindness, of consideration —this instinctively brutal gesture.

The gasp became a silence. A dozen eyes were turned on Jeffrey, who looked up as though seeing Roxanne for the first time. An expression of bewilderment settled on his face.

"Why—Roxanne——" he said haltingly.

Into a dozen minds entered a quick suspicion, a rumor of scandal. Could it be that behind the scenes with this couple, apparently so in love, lurked some curious antipathy? Why else this streak of fire across such a cloudless heaven?

"Jeffrey!"—Roxanne's voice was pleading—startled and horrified, she yet knew that it was a mistake. Not once did it occur to her to blame him or to resent it. Her word was a trembling supplication—"Tell me, Jeffrey," it said, "tell Roxanne, your own Roxanne."

"Why, Roxanne—" began Jeffrey again. The bewildered look changed to pain. He was clearly as startled as she. "I didn't intend that," he went on; "you startled me. You—I felt as if some one were attacking me. I—how—why, how idiotic!"

"Jeffrey!" Again the word was a prayer, incense offered up to a high God through this new and unfathomable darkness.

They were both on their feet, they were saying good-by, faltering, apologizing, explaining. There was no attempt to pass it off easily. That way lay sacrilege. Jeffrey had not been feeling well, they said. He had become nervous. Back of both their minds was the unexplained horror of that blow—the marvel that there had been for an instant something between them—his anger and her fear—and now to both a sorrow, momentary, no doubt, but to be bridged at once, at once, while there was yet time. Was that swift water lashing under their feet—the fierce glint of some uncharted chasm?

Out in their car under the harvest moon he talked brokenly. It was just—incomprehensible to him, he said. He had been thinking of the poker game—absorbed—and the touch on his shoulder had seemed like an attack. An attack! He clung to that word, flung it up as a shield. He had hated what touched him. With the impact of his hand it had gone, that—nervousness. That was all he knew.

Both their eyes filled with tears and they whispered love there under the broad night as the serene streets of Marlowe sped by. Later, when they went to bed, they were quite calm. Jeffrey was to take a week off all work—was simply to loll, and sleep, and go on long walks until this nervousness left him. When they had decided this safety settled down upon Roxanne. The pillows underhead became soft and friendly; the bed on which they lay seemed wide, and white, and sturdy beneath the radiance that streamed in at the window.

Five days later, in the first cool of late afternoon, Jeffrey picked up an oak chair and sent it crashing through his own front window. Then he lay down on the couch like a child, weeping piteously and begging to die. A blood clot the size of a marble had broken in his brain.

III

There is a sort of waking nightmare that sets in sometimes when one has missed a sleep or two, a feeling that comes with extreme fatigue and a new sun, that the quality of the life around has changed. It is a fully articulate conviction that somehow the existence one is then leading is a branch shoot of life and is related to life only as a moving picture or a mirror—that the people, and streets, and houses are only projections from a very dim and chaotic past. It was in such a state that Roxanne found herself during the first months of Jeffrey's illness. She slept only when she was utterly exhausted; she awoke under a cloud. The long, sober-voiced consultations, the faint aura of medicine in the halls, the sudden tiptoeing in a house that had echoed to many cheerful footsteps, and, most of all, Jeffrey's white face amid the pillows of the bed they had shared—these things subdued her and made her indelibly older. The doctors held out hope, but that was all. A long rest, they said, and quiet. So responsibility came to Roxanne. It was she who paid the bills, pored over his bankbook, corresponded with his publishers. She was in the kitchen constantly. She learned from the nurse how to prepare his meals and after the first month took complete charge of the sick-room. She had had to let the nurse go for reasons of economy. One of the two colored girls left at the same time. Roxanne was realizing that they had been living from short story to short story.

The most frequent visitor was Harry Cromwell. He had been shocked and depressed by the news, and though his wife was now living with him in Chicago he found time to come out several times a month. Roxanne found his sympathy welcome—there was some quality of suffering in the man, some inherent pitifulness that made her comfortable when he was near. Roxanne's nature had suddenly deepened. She felt sometimes that with Jeffrey she was losing her children also, those children that now most of all she needed and should have had.

It was six months after Jeffrey's collapse and when the nightmare had faded, leaving not the old world but a new one, grayer and colder, that she went to see Harry's wife. Finding herself in Chicago with an extra hour before train time, she decided out of courtesy to call.

As she stepped inside the door she had an immediate impression that the apartment was very like some place she had seen before—and almost instantly she remembered a round-the-corner bakery of her childhood, a bakery full of rows and rows of pink frosted cakes—a stuffy pink, pink as a food, pink triumphant, vulgar, and odious.

And this apartment was like that. It was pink. It smelled pink!

Mrs. Cromwell, attired in a wrapper of pink and black, opened the door. Her hair was yellow, heightened, Roxanne imagined, by a dash of peroxide in the rinsing water every week. Her eyes were a thin waxen blue—she was pretty and too consciously graceful. Her cordiality was strident and intimate, hostility melted so quickly to hospitality that it seemed they were both merely in the face and voice—never touching nor touched by the deep core of egotism beneath.

But to Roxanne these things were secondary; her eyes were caught and held in uncanny fascination by the wrapper. It was vilely unclean. From its lowest hem up four inches it was sheerly dirty with the blue dust of the floor; for the next three inches it was gray—then it shaded off into its natural color, which was—pink. It was dirty at the sleeves, too, and at the collar—and when the woman turned to lead the way into the parlor, Roxanne was sure that her neck was dirty.

A one-sided rattle of conversation began. Mrs. Cromwell became explicit about her likes and dislikes, her head, her stomach, her teeth, her apartment—avoiding with a sort of insolent meticulousness any inclusion of Roxanne with life, as if presuming that Roxanne, having been dealt a blow, wished life to be carefully skirted.

Roxanne smiled. That kimono! That neck!

After five minutes a little boy toddled into the parlor—a dirty little boy clad in dirty pink rompers. His face was smudgy—Roxanne wanted to take him into her lap and wipe his nose; other parts in the vicinity of his head needed attention, his tiny shoes were kicked out at the toes. Unspeakable!

"What a darling little boy!" exclaimed Roxanne, smiling radiantly. "Come here to me."

Mrs. Cromwell looked coldly at her son.

"He *will* get dirty. Look at that face!" She held her head on one side and regarded it critically.

"Isn't he a *darling?*" repeated Roxanne.

"Look at his rompers," frowned Mrs. Cromwell.

"He needs a change, don't you, George?"

George stared at her curiously. To his mind the word rompers connotated a garment extraneously smeared, as this one.

"I tried to make him look respectable this morning," complained Mrs. Cromwell as one whose patience had been sorely tried, "and I found he didn't have any more rompers—so rather than have him go round without any I put him back in those—and his face——"

"How many pairs has he?" Roxanne's voice was pleasantly curious. "How many feather fans have you?" she might have asked.

"Oh,——" Mrs. Cromwell considered, wrinkling her pretty brow. "Five, I think. Plenty, I know."

"You can get them for fifty cents a pair."

Mrs. Cromwell's eyes showed surprise—and the faintest superiority. The price of rompers!

"Can you really? I had no idea. He ought to have plenty, but I haven't had a minute all week to send the laundry out." Then, dismissing the subject as irrelevant—"I must show you some things——"

They rose and Roxanne followed her past an open bathroom door whose garment-littered floor showed indeed that the laundry hadn't been sent out for some time, into another room that was, so to speak, the quintessence of pinkness. This was Mrs. Cromwell's room.

Here the hostess opened a closet door and displayed before Roxanne's eyes an amazing collection of lingerie. There were dozens of filmy marvels of lace and silk, all clean, unruffled, seemingly not yet touched. On hangers beside them were three new evening dresses.

"I have some beautiful things," said Mrs. Cromwell, "but not much of a chance to wear them. Harry doesn't care about going out." Spite crept into her voice. "He's perfectly content to let me play nursemaid and housekeeper all day and loving wife in the evening."

Roxanne smiled again.

"You've got some beautiful clothes here."

"Yes, I have. Let me show you——"

"Beautiful," repeated Roxanne, interrupting, "but I'll have to run if I'm going to catch my train."

She felt that her hands were trembling. She wanted to put them on this woman and shake her—shake her. She wanted her locked up somewhere and set to scrubbing floors.

"Beautiful," she repeated, "and I just came in for a moment."

"Well, I'm sorry Harry isn't here."

They moved toward the door.

"—and, oh," said Roxanne with an effort—yet her voice was still gentle and her lips were smiling—"I think it's Argile's where you can get those rompers. Good-by."

It was not until she had reached the station and bought her ticket to Marlowe that Roxanne realized it was the first five minutes in six months that her mind had been off Jeffrey.

IV

A week later Harry appeared at Marlowe, arrived unexpectedly at five o'clock, and coming up the walk sank into a porch chair in a state of exhaustion. Roxanne herself had had a busy day and was worn out. The doctors were coming at five-thirty, bringing a celebrated nerve specialist from New York. She was excited and thoroughly depressed, but Harry's eyes made her sit down beside him.

"What's the matter?"

"Nothing, Roxanne," he denied. "I came to see how Jeff was doing. Don't you bother about me."

"Harry," insisted Roxanne, "there's something the matter."

"Nothing," he repeated. "How's Jeff?"

Anxiety darkened her face.

"He's a little worse, Harry. Doctor Jewett has come on from New York. They thought he could tell me something definite. He's going to try and find whether this paralysis has anything to do with the original blood clot."

Harry rose.

"Oh, I'm sorry," he said jerkily. "I didn't know you expected a consultation. I wouldn't have come. I thought I'd just rock on your porch for an hour——"

"Sit down," she commanded.

Harry hesitated.

"Sit down, Harry, dear boy." Her kindness flooded out now—enveloped him. "I know there's something the matter. You're white as a sheet. I'm going to get you a cool bottle of beer."

All at once he collapsed into his chair and covered his face with his hands.

"I can't make her happy," he said slowly. "I've tried and I've tried. This morning we had some words about breakfast—I'd been getting my breakfast down town—and—well, just after I went to the office she left the house, went East to her mother's with George and a suitcase full of lace underwear."

"Harry!"

"And I don't know—"

There was a crunch on the gravel, a car turning into the drive. Roxanne uttered a little cry.

"It's Doctor Jewett."

"Oh, I'll——"

"You'll wait, won't you?" she interrupted abstractedly. He saw that his problem had already died on the troubled surface of her mind.

There was an embarrassing minute of vague, elided introductions and then Harry followed the party inside and watched them disappear up the stairs. He went into the library and sat down on the big sofa.

For an hour he watched the sun creep up the patterned folds of the chintz curtains. In the deep quiet a trapped wasp buzzing on the inside of the window pane assumed the proportions of a clamor. From time to time another buzzing drifted down from up-stairs, resembling several more larger wasps caught on larger window-panes. He heard low footfalls, the clink of bottles, the clamor of pouring water.

What had he and Roxanne done that life should deal these crashing blows to them? Up-stairs there was taking place a living inquest on the soul of his friend; he was sitting here in a quiet room listening to the plaint of a wasp, just as when he was a boy he had been compelled by a strict aunt to sit hour-long on a chair and atone for some misbehavior. But who had put him here? What ferocious aunt had leaned out of the sky to make him atone for—what?

About Kitty he felt a great hopelessness. She was too expensive—that was the irremediable difficulty. Suddenly he hated her. He wanted to throw her down and kick at her—to tell her she was a cheat and a leech—that she was dirty. Moreover, she must give him his boy.

He rose and began pacing up and down the room. Simultaneously he heard some one begin walking along the hallway up-stairs in exact time with him. He found himself wondering if they would walk in time until the person reached the end of the hall.

Kitty had gone to her mother. God help her, what a mother to go to! He tried to imagine the meeting: the abused wife collapsing upon the mother's breast. He could not. That Kitty was capable of any deep grief was unbelievable. He had gradually grown to think of her as something unapproachable and callous. She would get a divorce, of course, and eventually she would marry again. He began to consider this. Whom would she marry? He laughed bitterly, stopped; a picture flashed before him—of Kitty's arms around some man whose face he could not see, of Kitty's lips pressed close to other lips in what was surely passion.

"God!" he cried aloud. "God! God! God!"

Then the pictures came thick and fast. The Kitty of this morning faded; the soiled kimono rolled up and disappeared; the pouts, and rages, and tears all were washed away. Again she was Kitty Carr—Kitty Carr with yellow hair and great baby eyes. Ah, she had loved him, she had loved him.

After a while he perceived that something was amiss with him, something that had nothing to do with Kitty of Jeff, something of a different genre. Amazingly it burst on him at last; he was hungry. Simple enough! He would go into the kitchen in a moment and ask the colored cook for a sandwich. After that he must go back to the city.

He paused at the wall, jerked at something round, and, fingering it absently, put it to his mouth and tasted it as a baby tastes a bright toy. His teeth closed on it—Ah!

She'd left that damn kimono, that dirty pink kimono. She might have had the decency to take it with her, he thought. It would hang in the house like the corpse of their sick alliance. He would try to throw it away, but he would never be able to bring himself to move it. It would be like Kitty, soft and pliable, withal impervious. You couldn't move Kitty; you couldn't reach Kitty. There was nothing there to reach. He understood that perfectly—he had understood it all along.

He reached to the wall for another biscuit and with an effort pulled it out, nail and all. He carefully removed the nail from the centre, wondering idly if he had eaten the nail with the first biscuit. Preposterous! He would have remembered—it was a huge nail. He felt his stomach. He must be very hungry. He considered—remembered—yesterday he had had no dinner. It was the girl's day out and Kitty had lain in her room eating chocolate drops. She had said she felt "smothery" and couldn't bear having him near her. He had given George a bath and put him to bed, and then lain down on the couch intending to rest a minute before getting his own dinner. There he had fallen asleep and awakened about eleven, to find that there was nothing in the ice-box except a spoonful of potato salad. This he had eaten, together with some chocolate drops that he found on Kitty's bureau. This morning he had breakfasted hurriedly down town before going to the office. But at noon, beginning to worry about Kitty, he had decided to go home and take her out to lunch. After that there had been the note on his pillow. The pile of lingerie in the closet was gone—and she had left instructions for sending her trunk.

He had never been so hungry, he thought.

At five o'clock, when the visiting nurse tiptoed down-stairs, he was sitting on the sofa staring at the carpet.

"Mr. Cromwell?"

"Yes?"

"Oh, Mrs. Curtain won't be able to see you at dinner. She's not well. She told me to tell you that the cook will fix you something and that there's a spare bedroom."

"She's sick, you say?"

"She's lying down in her room. The consultation is just over."

"Did they—did they decide anything?"

"Yes," said the nurse softly. "Doctor Jewett says there's no hope. Mr. Curtain may live indefinitely, but he'll never see again or move again or think. He'll just breathe."

"Just breathe?"

"Yes."

For the first time the nurse noted that beside the writing-desk where she remembered that she had seen a line of a dozen curious round objects she had vaguely imagined to be some exotic form of decoration, there was now only one. Where the others had been, there was now a series of little nail-holes.

Harry followed her glance dazedly and then rose to his feet.

"I don't believe I'll stay. I believe there's a train."

She nodded. Harry picked up his hat.

"Good-by," she said pleasantly.

"Good-by," he answered, as though talking to himself and, evidently moved by some involuntary necessity, he paused on his way to the door and she saw him pluck the last object from the wall and drop it into his pocket.

Then he opened the screen door and, descending the porch steps, passed out of her sight.

V

After a while the coat of clean white paint on the Jeffrey Curtain house made a definite compromise with the suns of many Julys and showed its good faith by turning gray. It scaled—huge peelings of very brittle old paint leaned over backward like aged men practising grotesque gymnastics and finally dropped to a moldy death in the overgrown grass beneath. The paint on the front pillars became streaky; the white ball was knocked off the left-hand door-post; the green blinds darkened, then lost all pretense of color.

It began to be a house that was avoided by the tender-minded—some church bought a lot diagonally opposite for a graveyard, and this, combined with "the place where Mrs. Curtain stays with that living corpse," was enough to throw a ghostly aura over that quarter of the road. Not that she was left alone. Men and women came to see her, met her down town, where she went to do her marketing, brought her home in their cars—and came in for a moment to talk and to rest, in the glamour that still played in her smile. But men who did not know her no longer followed her with admiring glances in the street; a diaphanous veil had come down over her beauty, destroying its vividness, yet bringing neither wrinkles nor fat.

She acquired a character in the village—a group of little stories were told of her: how when the country was frozen over one winter so that no wagons nor automobiles could travel, she taught herself to skate so that she could make quick time to the grocer and druggist, and not leave Jeffrey alone for long. It was said that every night since his paralysis she slept in a small bed beside his bed, holding his hand.

Jeffrey Curtain was spoken of as though he were already dead. As the years dropped by those who had known him died or moved away—there were but half a dozen of the old crowd who had drunk cocktails together, called each other's wives by their first names, and thought that Jeff was about the wittiest and most talented fellow that Marlowe had ever known. Now, to the casual visitor, he was merely the reason that Mrs. Curtain excused herself sometimes and hurried up-stairs; he was a groan or a sharp cry borne to the silent parlor on the heavy air of a Sunday afternoon.

He could not move; he was stone blind, dumb, and totally unconscious. All day he lay in his bed, except for a shift to his wheelchair every morning while she straightened the room. His paralysis was creeping slowly toward his heart. At first—for the first year—Roxanne had received the faintest answering pressure sometimes when she held his hand—then it had gone, ceased one evening and never come back, and through two nights Roxanne lay wide-eyed, staring into the dark and wondering what had gone, what fraction of his soul had taken flight, what last grain of comprehension those shattered broken nerves still carried to the brain.

After that hope died. Had it not been for her unceasing care the last spark would have gone long before. Every morning she shaved and bathed him, shifted him with her own hands from bed to chair and back to bed. She was in his room constantly, bearing medicine, straightening a pillow, talking to him almost as one talks to a nearly human dog, without hope of response or appreciation, but with the dim persuasion of habit, a prayer when faith has gone.

Not a few people, one celebrated nerve specialist among them, gave her a plain impression that it was futile to exercise so much care, that if Jeffrey had been conscious he would have wished to die, that if his spirit were hovering in some wider air it would agree to no such sacrifice from her, it would fret only for the prison of its body to give it full release.

"But you see," she replied, shaking her head gently, "when I married Jeffrey it was—until I ceased to love him."

"But," was protested, in effect, "you can't love that."

"I can love what it once was. What else is there for me to do?"

The specialist shrugged his shoulders and went away to say that Mrs. Curtain was a remarkable woman and just about as sweet as an angel—but, he added, it was a terrible pity.

"There must be some man, or a dozen, just crazy to take care of her. . . ."

Casually—there were. Here and there some one began in hope—and ended in reverence. There was no love in the woman except, strangely enough, for life, for the people in the world, from the tramp to whom she gave food she could ill afford to the butcher who sold her a cheap cut of steak across the meaty board. The other phase was sealed up somewhere in that expressionless mummy who lay with his face turned ever toward the light as mechanically as a compass needle and waited dumbly for the last wave to wash over his heart.

After eleven years he died in the middle of a May night, when the scent of the syringa hung upon the window-sill and a breeze wafted in the shrillings of the frogs and cicadas outside. Roxanne awoke at two, and realized with a start she was alone in the house at last.

VI

After that she sat on her weather-beaten porch through many afternoons, gazing down across the fields that undulated in a slow descent to the white and green town. She was wondering what she would do with her life. She was thirty-six—handsome, strong, and free. The years had eaten up Jeffrey's insurance; she had reluctantly parted with the acres to right and left of her, and had even placed a small mortgage on the house.

With her husband's death had come a great physical restlessness. She missed having to care for him in the morning, she missed her rush to town, and the brief and therefore accentuated neighborly meetings in the butcher's and grocer's; she missed the cooking for two, the preparation of delicate liquid food for him. One day, consumed with energy, she went out and spaded up the whole garden, a thing that had not been done for years.

And she was alone at night in the room that had seen the glory of her marriage and then the pain. To meet Jeff again she went back in spirit to that wonderful year, that intense, passionate absorption and companionship, rather than looked forward to a problematical meeting hereafter; she awoke often to lie and wish for that presence beside her—inanimate yet breathing—still Jeff.

One afternoon six months after his death she was sitting on the porch, in a black dress which took away the faintest suggestion of plumpness from her figure. It was Indian summer—golden brown all about her; a hush broken by the sighing of leaves; westward a four o'clock sun dripping streaks of red and yellow over a flaming sky. Most of the birds had gone—only a sparrow that had built itself a nest on the cornice of a pillar kept up an intermittent cheeping varied by occasional fluttering sallies overhead. Roxanne moved her chair to where she could watch him and her mind idled drowsily on the bosom of the afternoon.

Harry Cromwell was coming out from Chicago to dinner. Since his divorce over eight years before he had been a frequent visitor. They had kept up what amounted to a tradition between them: when he arrived they would go to look at Jeff; Harry would sit down on the edge of the bed and in a hearty voice ask:

"Well, Jeff, old man, how do you feel to-day?"

Roxanne, standing beside, would look intently at Jeff, dreaming that some shadowy recognition of this former friend had passed across that broken mind—but the head, pale, carven, would only move slowly in its sole gesture toward the light as if something behind the blind eyes were groping for another light long since gone out.

These visits stretched over eight years—at Easter, Christmas, Thanksgiving, and on many a Sunday Harry had arrived, paid his call on Jeff, and then talked for a long while with Roxanne on the porch. He was devoted to her. He made no pretense of hiding, no attempt to deepen, this relation. She was his best friend as the mass of flesh on the bed there had been his best friend. She was peace, she was rest; she was the past. Of his own tragedy she alone knew.

He had been at the funeral, but since then the company for which he worked had shifted him to the East and only a business trip had brought him to the vicinity of Chicago. Roxanne had written him to come when he could—after a night in the city he had caught a train out.

They shook hands and he helped her move two rockers together.

"How's George?"

"He's fine, Roxanne. Seems to like school."

"Of course it was the only thing to do, to send him."

"Of course——"

"You miss him horribly, Harry?"

"Yes—I do miss him. He's a funny boy——"

He talked a lot about George. Roxanne was interested. Harry must bring him out on his next vacation. She had only seen him once in her life—a child in dirty rompers.

She left him with the newspaper while she prepared dinner—

she had four chops to-night and some late vegetables from her own garden. She put it all on and then called him, and sitting down together they continued their talk about George.

"If I had a child—" she would say.

Afterward, Harry having given her what slender advice he could about investments, they walked through the garden, pausing here and there to recognize what had once been a cement bench or where the tennis court had lain . . .

"Do you remember——"

Then they were off on a flood of reminiscences: the day they had taken all the snap-shots and Jeff had been photographed astride the calf; and the sketch Harry had made of Jeff and Roxanne, lying sprawled in the grass, their heads almost touching. There was to have been a covered lattice connecting the barn-studio with the house, so that Jeff could get there on wet days—the lattice had been started, but nothing remained except a broken triangular piece that still adhered to the house and resembled a battered chicken coop.

"And those mint juleps!"

"And Jeff's note-book! Do you remember how we'd laugh, Harry, when we'd get it out of his pocket and read aloud a page of material. And how frantic he used to get?"

"Wild! He was such a kid about his writing."

They were both silent a moment, and then Harry said:

"We were to have a place out here, too. Do you remember? We were to buy the adjoining twenty acres. And the parties we were going to have!"

Again there was a pause, broken this time by a low question from Roxanne.

"Do you ever hear of her, Harry?"

"Why—yes," he admitted placidly. "She's in Seattle. She's married again to a man named Horton, a sort of lumber king. He's a great deal older than she is, I believe."

"And she's behaving?"

"Yes—that is, I've heard so. She has everything, you see. Nothing much to do except dress up for this fellow at dinner-time."

"I see."

Without effort he changed the subject.

"Are you going to keep the house?"

"I think so," she said, nodding. "I've lived here so long, Harry, it'd seem terrible to move. I thought of trained nursing, but of course that'd mean leaving. I've about decided to be a boarding-house lady."

"Live in one?"

"No. Keep one. Is there such an anomaly as a boarding-house lady? Anyway I'd have a negress and keep about eight people in the summer and two or three, if I can get them, in the winter. Of course I'll have to have the house repainted and gone over inside."

Harry considered.

"Roxanne, why—naturally you know best what you can do, but it does seem a shock, Roxanne. You came here as a bride."

"Perhaps," she said, "that's why I don't mind remaining here as a boarding-house lady."

"I remember a certain batch of biscuits."

"Oh, those biscuits," she cried. "Still, from all I heard about the way you devoured them, they couldn't have been so bad. I was *so* low that day, yet somehow I laughed when the nurse told me about those biscuits."

"I noticed that the twelve nail-holes are still in the library wall where Jeff drove them."

"Yes."

It was getting very dark now, a crispness settled in the air; a little gust of wind sent down a last spray of leaves. Roxanne shivered slightly.

"We'd better go in."

He looked at his watch.

"It's late. I've got to be leaving. I go East to-morrow."

"Must you?"

They lingered for a moment just below the stoop, watching a moon that seemed full of snow float out of the distance where the lake lay. Summer was gone and now Indian summer. The grass was cold and there was no mist and no dew. After he left she would go in and light the gas and close the shutters, and he would go down the path and on to the village. To these two life had come quickly and gone, leaving not bitterness, but pity; not disillusion, but only pain. There was already enough moonlight when they shook hands for each to see the gathered kindness in the other's eyes.

THE ADJUSTER

At five o'clock the sombre egg-shaped room at the Ritz ripens to subtle melody—the light *clat-clat* of one lump, two lumps, into the cup, and the *ding* of the shining teapots and cream-pots as they kiss elegantly in transit upon a silver tray. There are those who cherish that amber hour above all other hours, for now the pale, pleasant toil of the lilies who inhabit the Ritz is over—the singing decorative part of the day remains.

Moving your eyes around the slightly raised horse-shoe balcony you might, one spring afternoon, have seen young Mrs. Alphonse Karr and young Mrs. Charles Hemple at a table for two. The one in the dress was Mrs. Hemple—when I say "the dress" I refer to that black immaculate affair with the big buttons and the red ghost of a cape at the shoulders, a gown suggesting with faint and fashionable irreverence the garb of a French cardinal, as it was meant to do when it was invented in the Rue de la Paix. Mrs. Karr and Mrs. Hemple were twenty-three years old, and their enemies said that they had done very well for themselves. Either might have had her limousine waiting at the hotel door, but both of them much preferred to walk home (up Park Avenue) through the April twilight.

Luella Hemple was tall, with the sort of flaxen hair that English country girls should have, but seldom do. Her skin was radiant, and there was no need of putting anything on it at all, but in deference to an antiquated fashion—this was the year 1920—she had powdered out its high roses and drawn on it a new mouth and new eyebrows—which were no more successful than such meddling deserves. This, of course, is said from the vantage-point of 1925. In those days the effect she gave was exactly right.

"I've been married three years," she was saying as she squashed out a cigarette in an exhausted lemon. "The baby will be two years old to-morrow. I must remember to get——"

She took a gold pencil from her case and wrote "Candles" and "Things you pull, with paper caps," on an ivory date-pad. Then, raising her eyes, she looked at Mrs. Karr and hesitated.

"Shall I tell you something outrageous?"

"Try," said Mrs. Kårr cheerfully.

"Even my baby bores me. That sounds unnatural, Ede, but it's true. He doesn't *begin* to fill my life. I love him with all my heart, but when I have him to take care of for an afternoon, I get so nervous that I want to scream. After two hours I begin praying for the moment the nurse'll walk in the door."

When she had made this confession, Luella breathed quickly and looked closely at her friend. She didn't really feel unnatural at all. This was the truth. There couldn't be anything vicious in the truth.

"It may be because you don't love Charles," ventured Mrs. Karr, unmoved.

"But I do! I hope I haven't given you that impression with all this talk." She decided that Ede Karr was stupid. "It's the very fact that I do love Charles that complicates matters. I cried myself to sleep last night because I know we're drifting slowly but surely toward a divorce. It's the baby that keeps us together."

Ede Karr, who had been married five years, looked at her critically to see if this was a pose, but Luella's lovely eyes were grave and sad.

"And what is the trouble?" Ede inquired.

"It's plural," said Luella, frowning. "First, there's food. I'm a vile housekeeper, and I have no intention of turning into a good one. I hate to order groceries, and I hate to go into the kitchen and poke around to see if the ice-box is clean, and I hate to pretend to the servants that I'm interested in their work, when really I never want to hear about food until it comes on the table. You see, I never learned to cook, and consequently a kitchen is about as interesting to me as a—as a boiler-room. It's simply a machine that I don't understand. It's easy to say, 'Go to cooking school,' the way people do in books—but, Ede, in real life does anybody ever change into a model *Hausfrau*—unless they have to?"

"Go on," said Ede non-committally. "Tell me more."

"Well, as a result, the house is always in a riot. The servants leave every week. If they're young and incompetent, I can't train them, so we have to let them go. If they're experienced, they hate a house where a woman doesn't take an intense interest in the price of asparagus. So they leave—and half the time we eat at restaurants and hotels."

"I don't suppose Charles likes that."

"Hates it. In fact, he hates about everything that I like. He's lukewarm about the theatre, hates the opera, hates dancing, hates cocktail parties—sometimes I think he hates everything pleasant in the world. I sat home for a year or so. While Chuck was on the way, and while I was nursing him, I didn't mind. But this year I told Charles frankly that I was still young enough to want some fun. And since then we've been going out whether he wants to or not." She paused, brooding. "I'm so sorry for him I don't know what to do, Ede—but if we sat home, I'd just be sorry for myself. And to tell you another true thing, I'd rather that he'd be unhappy than me."

Luella was not so much stating a case as thinking aloud. She considered that she was being very fair. Before her marriage men had always told her that she was "a good sport," and she had tried to carry this fairness into her married life. So she always saw Charley's point of view as clearly as she saw her own.

If she had been a pioneer wife, she would probably have fought the fight side by side with her husband. But here in New York there wasn't any fight. They weren't struggling together to obtain a far-off peace and leisure—she had more of either than she could use. Luella, like several thousand other young wives in New York, honestly wanted something to do. If she had had a little more money and a little less love, she could have gone in for horses or for vagarious amour. Or if they had had a little less money, her surplus energy would have been absorbed by hope and even by effort. But the Charles Hemples were in between. They were of that enormous American class who wander over Europe every summer, sneering rather pathetically and wistfully at the customs and traditions and pastimes of other countries, because they have no customs or tradition or pastimes of their own. It is a class sprung yesterday from fathers and mothers who might just as well have lived two hundred years ago.

The tea-hour had turned abruptly into the before-dinner hour. Most of the tables had emptied until the room was dotted rather than crowded with shrill isolated voices and remote, surprising laughter—in one corner the waiters were already covering the tables with white for dinner.

"Charles and I are on each other's nerves." In the new silence Luella's voice rang out with startling clearness, and she lowered it precipitately. "Little things. He keeps rubbing his face with his hand—all the time, at table, at the theatre—even when he's in bed.

It drives me wild, and when things like that begin to irritate you, it's nearly over." She broke off and, reaching backward, drew up a light fur around her neck. "I hope I haven't bored you, Ede. It's on my mind, because to-night tells the story. I made an engagement for to-night—an interesting engagement, a supper after the theatre to meet some Russians, singers or dancers or something, and Charles says he won't go. If he doesn't—then I'm going alone. And that's the end."

She put her elbows on the table suddenly and, bending her eyes down into her smooth gloves, began to cry, stubbornly and quietly. There was no one near to see, but Ede Karr wished that she had taken her gloves off. She would have reached out consolingly and touched her bare hand. But the gloves were a symbol of the difficulty of sympathizing with a woman to whom life had given so much. Ede wanted to say that it would "come out all right," that it wasn't "so bad as it seemed," but she said nothing. Her only reaction was impatience and distaste.

A waiter stepped near and laid a folded paper on the table, and Mrs. Karr reached for it.

"No, you mustn't," murmured Luella brokenly. "No, I invited *you!* I've got the money right here."

II

The Hemples' apartment—they owned it—was in one of those impersonal white palaces that are known by number instead of name. They had furnished it on their honeymoon, gone to England for the big pieces, to Florence for the bric-à-brac, and to Venice for the lace and sheer linen of the curtains and for the glass of many colors which littered the table when they entertained. Luella enjoyed choosing things on her honeymoon. It gave a purposeful air to the trip, and saved it from ever turning into the rather dismal wandering among big hotels and desolate ruins which European honeymoons are apt to be.

They returned, and life began. On the grand scale. Luella found herself a lady of substance. It amazed her sometimes that the specially created apartment and the specially created limousine were hers, just as indisputably as the mortgaged suburban bungalow out of *The Ladies' Home Journal* and the last year's car that fate might have given her instead. She was even more amazed when it all began to bore her. But it did. . . .

The evening was at seven when she turned out of the April dusk, let herself into the hall, and saw her husband waiting in the living-room before an open fire. She came in without a sound, closed the door noiselessly behind her, and stood watching him for a moment through the pleasant effective vista of the small *salon* which intervened. Charles Hemple was in the middle thirties, with a young serious face and distinguished iron-gray hair which would be white in ten years more. That and his deep-set, dark-gray eyes were his most noticeable features—women always thought his hair was romantic; most of the time Luella thought so too.

At this moment she found herself hating him a little, for she saw that he had raised his hand to his face and was rubbing it nervously over his chin and mouth. It gave him an air of unflattering abstraction, and sometimes even obscured his words, so that she was continually saying "What?" She had spoken about it several times, and he had apologized in a surprised way. But obviously he didn't realize how noticeable and how irritating it was, for he continued to do it. Things had now reached such a precarious state that Luella dreaded speaking of such matters any more—a certain sort of word might precipitate the imminent scene.

Luella tossed her gloves and purse abruptly on the table. Hearing the faint sound, her husband looked out toward the hall.

"Is that you, dear?"

"Yes, dear."

She went into the living-room, and walked into his arms and kissed him tensely. Charles Hemple responded with unusual formality, and then turned her slowly around so that she faced across the room.

"I've brought some one home to dinner."

She saw then that they were not alone, and her first feeling was of strong relief; the rigid expression on her face softened into a shy, charming smile as she held out her hand.

"This is Doctor Moon—this is my wife."

A man a little older than her husband, with a round, pale, slightly lined face, came forward to meet her.

"Good evening, Mrs. Hemple," he said. "I hope I'm not interfering with any arrangements of yours."

"Oh, no," Luella cried quickly. "I'm delighted that you're coming to dinner. We're quite alone."

Simultaneously she thought of her engagement to-night, and wondered if this could be a clumsy trap of Charles' to keep her at home. If it were, he had chosen his bait badly. This man—a tired placidity radiated from him, from his face, from his heavy, leisurely voice, even from the three-year-old shine of his clothes.

Nevertheless, she excused herself and went into the kitchen to see what was planned for dinner. As usual they were trying a new pair of servants, the luncheon had been ill-cooked and ill-served—she would let them go to-morrow. She hoped Charles would talk to them—she hated to get rid of servants. Sometimes they wept, and sometimes they were insolent, but Charles had a way with him. And they were always afraid of a man.

The cooking on the stove, however, had a soothing savor. Luella gave instructions about "which china," and unlocked a bottle of precious chianti from the buffet. Then she went in to kiss young Chuck good night.

"Has he been good?" she demanded as he crawled enthusiastically into her arms.

"Very good," said the governess. "We went for a long walk over by Central Park."

"Well, aren't you a smart boy!" She kissed him ecstatically.

"And he put his foot into the fountain, so we had to come home in a taxi right away and change his little shoe and stocking."

"That's right. Here, wait a minute, *Chuck!*" Luella unclasped the great yellow beads from around her neck and handed them to him. "You mustn't break mama's beads." She turned to the nurse. "Put them on my dresser, will you, after he's asleep?"

She felt a certain compassion for her son as she went away—the small enclosed life he led, that all children led, except in big families. He was a dear little rose, except on the days when she took care of him. His face was the same shape as hers; she was thrilled sometimes, and formed new resolves about life when his heart beat against her own.

In her own pink and lovely bedroom, she confined her attentions to her face, which she washed and restored. Doctor Moon didn't deserve a change of dress, and Luella found herself oddly tired, though she had done very little all day. She returned to the living-room, and they went in to dinner.

"Such a nice house, Mrs. Hemple," said Doctor Moon impersonally; "and let me congratulate you on your fine little boy."

"Thanks. Coming from a doctor, that's a nice compliment." She hesitated. "Do you specialize in children?"

"I'm not a specialist at all," he said. "I'm about the last of my kind—a general practitioner."

"The last in New York, anyhow," remarked Charles. He had begun rubbing his face nervously, and Luella fixed her eyes on Doctor Moon so that she wouldn't see. But at Charles's next words she looked back at him sharply.

"In fact," he said unexpectedly, "I've invited Doctor Moon here because I wanted you to have a talk with him to-night."

Luella sat up straight in her chair.

"A talk with *me?*"

"Doctor Moon's an old friend of mine, and I think he can tell you a few things, Luella, that you ought to know."

"Why—" She tried to laugh, but she was surprised and annoyed. "I don't see, exactly, what you mean. There's nothing the matter with me. I don't believe I've ever felt better in my life."

Doctor Moon looked at Charles, asking permission to speak. Charles nodded, and his hand went up automatically to his face.

"Your husband has told me a great deal about your unsatisfactory life together," said Doctor Moon, still impersonally. "He wonders if I can be of any help in smoothing things out."

Luella's face was burning.

"I have no particular faith in psychoanalysis," she said coldly, "and I scarcely consider myself a subject for it."

"Neither have I," answered Doctor Moon, apparently unconscious of the snub; "I have no particular faith in anything but myself. I told you I am not a specialist, nor, I may add, a faddist of any sort. I promise nothing."

For a moment Luella considered leaving the room. But the effrontery of the suggestion aroused her curiosity too.

"I can't imagine what Charles has told you," she said, controlling herself with difficulty, "much less why. But I assure you that our affairs are a matter entirely between my husband and me. If you have no objections, Doctor Moon, I'd much prefer to discuss something—less personal."

Doctor Moon nodded heavily and politely. He made no further attempt to open the subject, and dinner proceeded in what was little more than a defeated silence. Luella determined that, whatever happened, she would adhere to her plans for to-night. An hour ago her independence had demanded it, but now some gesture of defiance had become necessary to her self-respect. She would stay in the living-room for a short moment after dinner; then, when the coffee came, she would excuse herself and dress to go out.

But when they did leave the dining-room, it was Charles who, in a quick, unarguable way, vanished.

"I have a letter to write," he said; "I'll be back in a moment." Before Luella could make a diplomatic objection, he went quickly down the corridor to his room, and she heard him shut his door.

Angry and confused, Luella poured the coffee and sank into a corner of the couch, looking intently at the fire.

"Don't be afraid, Mrs. Hemple," said Doctor Moon suddenly. "This was forced upon me. I do not act as a free agent——"

"I'm not afraid of you," she interrupted. But she knew that she was lying. She was a little afraid of him, if only for his dull insensitiveness to her distaste.

"Tell me about your trouble," he said very naturally, as though she were not a free agent either. He wasn't even looking at her, and except that they were alone in the room, he scarcely seemed to be addressing her at all.

The words that were in Luella's mind, her will, on her lips, were: "I'll do no such thing." What she actually said amazed her. It came out of her spontaneously, with apparently no co-operation of her own.

"Didn't you see him rubbing his face at dinner?" she said despairingly. "Are you blind? He's become so irritating to me that I think I'll go mad."

"I see." Doctor Moon's round face nodded.

"Don't you see I've had enough of home?" Her breasts seemed to struggle for air under her dress. "Don't you see how bored I am with keeping house, with the baby—everything seems as if it's going on forever and ever? I want excitement; and I don't care what form it takes or what I pay for it, so long as it makes my heart beat."

"I see."

It infuriated Luella that he claimed to understand. Her feeling of defiance had reached such a pitch that she preferred that no one should understand. She was content to be justified by the impassioned sincerity of her desires.

"I've tried to be good, and I'm not going to try any more. If I'm one of those women who wreck their lives for nothing, then I'll do it now. You can call me selfish, or silly, and be quite right; but in five minutes I'm going out of this house and begin to be alive."

This time Doctor Moon didn't answer, but he raised his head as if he were listening to something that was taking place a little distance away.

"You're not going out," he said after a moment; "I'm quite sure you're not going out."

Luella laughed.

"I *am* going out."

He disregarded this.

"You see, Mrs. Hemple, your husband isn't well. He's been trying to live your kind of life, and the strain of it has been too much for him. When he rubs his mouth——"

Light steps came down the corridor, and the maid, with a frightened expression on her face, tiptoed into the room.

"Mrs. Hemple——"

Startled at the interruption, Luella turned quickly.

"Yes?"

"Can I speak to—?" Her fear broke precipitately through her slight training. "Mr. Hemple, he's sick! He came into the kitchen a while ago and began throwing all the food out of the ice-box, and now he's in his room, crying and singing——"

Suddenly Luella heard his voice.

III

Charles Hemple had had a nervous collapse. There were twenty years of almost uninterrupted toil upon his shoulders, and the recent pressure at home had been too much for him to bear. His attitude toward his wife was the weak point in what had otherwise been a strong-minded and well-organized career—he was aware of her intense selfishness, but it is one of the many flaws in the scheme of human relationships that selfishness in women has an irresistible appeal to many men. Luella's selfishness existed side by side with a childish beauty, and, in consequence, Charles Hemple had begun to take the blame upon himself for situations which she had obviously brought about. It was an unhealthy attitude, and his mind had sickened, at length, with his attempts to put himself in the wrong.

After the first shock and the momentary flush of pity that followed it, Luella looked at the situation with impatience. She was "a good sport"—she couldn't take advantage of Charles when he was sick. The question of her liberties had to be postponed until he was on his feet. Just when she had determined to be a wife no longer, Luella was compelled to be a nurse as well. She sat beside his bed while he talked about her in his delirium—about the days of their engagement, and how some friend had told him then that he was making a mistake, and about his happiness in the early months of their marriage, and his growing disquiet as the gap appeared. Evidently he had been more aware of it than she had thought—more than he ever said.

"Luella!" He would lurch up in bed. "Luella! Where *are* you?"

"I'm right here, Charles, beside you." She tried to make her voice cheerful and warm.

"If you want to go, Luella, you'd better go. I don't seem to be enough for you any more."

She denied this soothingly.

"I've thought it over, Luella, and I can't ruin my health on account of you—" Then quickly, and passionately: "Don't go, Luella, for God's sake, don't go away and leave me! Promise me you won't! I'll do anything you say if you won't go."

His humility annoyed her most; he was a reserved man, and she had never guessed at the extent of his devotion before.

"I'm only going for a minute. It's Doctor Moon, your friend, Charles. He came to-day to see how you were, don't you remember? And he wants to talk to me before he goes."

"You'll come back?" he persisted.

"In just a little while. There—lie quiet."

She raised his head and plumped his pillow into freshness. A new trained nurse would arrive to-morrow.

In the living-room Doctor Moon was waiting—his suit more worn and shabby in the afternoon light. She disliked him inordinately, with an illogical conviction that he was in some way to blame for her misfortune, but he was so deeply interested that she couldn't refuse to see him. She hadn't asked him to consult with the specialists, though—a doctor who was so down at the heel. . . .

"Mrs. Hemple." He came forward, holding out his hand, and Luella touched it, lightly and uneasily.

"You seem well," he said.

"I am well, thank you."

"I congratulate you on the way you've taken hold of things."

"But I haven't taken hold of things at all," she said coldly. "I do what I have to——"

"That's just it."

Her impatience mounted rapidly.

"I do what I have to, and nothing more," she continued; "and with no particular good-will."

Suddenly she opened up to him again, as she had the night of the catastrophe—realizing that she was putting herself on a footing of intimacy with him, yet unable to restrain her words.

"The house isn't going," she broke out bitterly. "I had to discharge the servants, and now I've got a woman in by the day. And the baby has a cold, and I've found out that his nurse doesn't know her business, and everything's just as messy and terrible as it can be!"

"Would you mind telling me how you found out the nurse didn't know her business?"

"You find out various unpleasant things when you're forced to stay around the house."

He nodded, his weary face turning here and there about the room.

"I feel somewhat encouraged," he said slowly. "As I told you, I promise nothing; I only do the best I can."

Luella looked up at him, startled.

"What do you mean?" she protested. "You've done nothing for me—nothing at all!"

"Nothing much—yet," he said heavily. "It takes time, Mrs. Hemple."

The words were said in a dry monotone that was somehow without offense, but Luella felt that he had gone too far. She got to her feet.

"I've met your type before," she said coldly. "For some reason you seem to think that you have a standing here as 'the old friend of the family.' But I don't make friends quickly, and I haven't given you the privilege of being so"—she wanted to say "insolent," but the word eluded her—"so personal with me."

When the front door had closed behind him, Luella went into the kitchen to see if the woman understood about the three different dinners—one for Charles, one for the baby, and one for herself. It was hard to do with only a single servant when things were so complicated. She must try another employment agency—this one had begun to sound bored.

To her surprise, she found the cook with hat and coat on, reading a newspaper at the kitchen table.

"Why"—Luella tried to think of the name—"why, what's the matter, Mrs.——"

"Mrs. Danski is my name."

"What's the matter?"

"I'm afraid I won't be able to accommodate you," said Mrs. Danski. "You see, I'm only a plain cook, and I'm not used to preparing invalid's food."

"But I've counted on you."

"I'm very sorry." She shook her head stubbornly. "I've got my own health to think of. I'm sure they didn't tell me what kind of a job it was when I came. And when you asked me to clean out your husband's room, I knew it was way beyond my powers."

"I won't ask you to clean anything," said Luella desperately. "If you'll just stay until to-morrow. I can't possibly get anybody else to-night."

Mrs. Danski smiled politely.

"I got my own children to think of, just like you."

It was on Luella's tongue to offer her more money, but suddenly her temper gave way.

"I've never heard of anything so selfish in my life!" she broke out. "To leave me at a time like this! You're an old fool!"

"If you'd pay me for my time, I'd go," said Mrs. Danski calmly.

"I won't pay you a cent unless you'll stay!"

She was immediately sorry she had said this, but she was too proud to withdraw the threat.

"You will so pay me!"

"You go out that door!"

"I'll go when I get my money," asserted Mrs. Danski indignantly. "I got my children to think of."

Luella drew in her breath sharply, and took a step forward. Intimidated by her intensity, Mrs. Danski turned and flounced, muttering, out of the door.

Luella went to the phone and, calling up the agency, explained that the woman had left.

"Can you send me some one right away? My husband is sick and the baby's sick——"

"I'm sorry, Mrs. Hemple; there's no one in the office now. It's after four o'clock."

Luella argued for a while. Finally she obtained a promise that they would telephone to an emergency woman they knew. That was the best they could do until to-morrow.

She called several other agencies, but the servant industry had apparently ceased to function for the day. After giving Charles his medicine, she tiptoed softly into the nursery.

"How's baby?" she asked abstractedly.

"Ninety-nine one," whispered the nurse, holding the thermometer to the light. "I just took it."

"Is that much?" asked Luella, frowning.

"It's just three-fifths of a degree. That isn't so much for the afternoon. They often run up a little with a cold."

Luella went over to the cot and laid her hand on her son's flushed cheek, thinking, in the midst of her anxiety, how much he resembled the incredible cherub of the "Lux" advertisement in the bus.

She turned to the nurse.

"Do you know how to cook?"

"Why—I'm not a good cook."

"Well, can you do the baby's food to-night? That old fool has left, and I can't get anyone, and I don't know what to do."

"Oh, yes, I can do the baby's food."

"That's all right, then. I'll try to fix something for Mr. Hemple. Please have your door open so you can hear the bell when the doctor comes. And let me know."

So many doctors! There had scarcely been an hour all day when there wasn't a doctor in the house. The specialist and their family physician every morning, then the baby doctor—and this afternoon there had been Doctor Moon, placid, persistent, unwelcome, in the parlor. Luella went into the kitchen. She could cook bacon and eggs for herself—she had often done that after the theatre. But the vegetables for Charles were a different matter—they must be left to boil or stew or something, and the stove had so many doors and ovens that she couldn't decide which to use. She chose a blue pan that looked new, sliced carrots into it, and covered them with a little water. As she put it on the stove and tried to remember what to do next, the phone rang, It was the agency.

"Yes, this is Mrs. Hemple speaking."

"Why, the woman we sent to you has returned here with the claim that you refused to pay her for her time."

"I explained to you that she refused to stay," said Luella hotly.

"She didn't keep her agreement, and I didn't feel I was under any obligation——"

"We have to see that our people are paid," the agency informed her; "otherwise we wouldn't be helping them at all, would we? I'm sorry, Mrs. Hemple, but we won't be able to furnish you with any one else until this little matter is arranged."

"Oh, I'll pay, I'll pay!" she cried.

"Of course we like to keep on good terms with our clients——"

"Yes—yes!"

"So if you'll send her money around to-morrow? It's seventy-five cents an hour."

"But how about to-night?" she exclaimed. "I've got to have some one to-night."

"Why—it's pretty late now. I was just going home myself."

"But I'm Mrs. Charles Hemple! Don't you understand? I'm perfectly good for what I say I'll do. I'm the wife of Charles Hemple, of 14 Broadway——"

Simultaneously she realized that Charles Hemple of 14 Broadway was a helpless invalid—he was neither a reference nor a refuge any more. In despair at the sudden callousness of the world, she hung up the receiver.

After another ten minutes of frantic muddling in the kitchen, she went to the baby's nurse, whom she disliked, and confessed that she was unable to cook her husband's dinner. The nurse announced that she had a splitting headache, and that with a sick child her hands were full already, but she consented, without enthusiasm, to show Luella what to do.

Swallowing her humiliation, Luella obeyed orders while the nurse experimented, grumbling, with the unfamiliar stove. Dinner was started after a fashion. Then it was time for the nurse to bathe Chuck, and Luella sat down alone at the kitchen table, and listened to the bubbling perfume that escaped from the pans.

"And women do this every day," she thought. "Thousands of women. Cook and take care of sick people—and go out to work too."

But she didn't think of those women as being like her, except in the superficial aspect of having two feet and two hands. She said it as she might have said "South Sea Islanders wear nose-rings." She was merely slumming to-day in her own home, and she wasn't enjoying it. For her, it was merely a ridiculous exception.

Suddenly she became aware of slow approaching steps in the

dining-room and then in the butler's pantry. Half afraid that it was Doctor Moon coming to pay another call, she looked up—and saw the nurse coming through the pantry door. It flashed through Luella's mind that the nurse was going to be sick too. And she was right —the nurse had hardly reached the kitchen door when she lurched and clutched at the handle as a winged bird clings to a branch. Then she receded wordlessly to the floor. Simultaneously the doorbell rang; and Luella, getting to her feet, gasped with relief that the baby doctor had come.

"Fainted, that's all," he said, taking the girl's head into his lap. The eyes fluttered. "Yep, she fainted, that's all."

"Everybody's sick!" cried Luella with a sort of despairing humor. "Everybody's sick but me, doctor."

"This one's not sick," he said after a moment. "Her heart is normal already. She just fainted."

When she had helped the doctor raise the quickening body to a chair, Luella hurried into the nursery and bent over the baby's bed. She let down one of the iron sides quietly. The fever seemed to be gone now—the flush had faded away. She bent over to touch the small cheek.

Suddenly Luella began to scream.

IV

Even after her baby's funeral, Luella still couldn't believe that she had lost him. She came back to the apartment and walked around the nursery in a circle, saying his name. Then, frightened by grief, she sat down and stared at his white rocker with the red chicken painted on the side.

"What will become of me now?" she whispered to herself. "Something awful is going to happen to me when I realize that I'll never see Chuck any more!"

She wasn't sure yet. If she waited here till twi-light, the nurse might still bring him in from his walk. She remembered a tragic confusion in the midst of which some one had told her that Chuck was dead, but if that was so, then why was his room waiting, with his small brush and comb still on the bureau, and why was she here at all?

"Mrs. Hemple."

She looked up. The weary, shabby figure of Doctor Moon stood in the door.

"You go away," Luella said dully.

"Your husband needs you."

"I don't care."

Doctor Moon came a little way into the room.

"I don't think you understand, Mrs. Hemple. He's been calling for you. You haven't any one now except him."

"I hate you," she said suddenly.

"If you like. I promised nothing, you know. I do the best I can. You'll be better when you realize that your baby is gone, that you're not going to see him any more."

Luella sprang to her feet.

"My baby isn't dead!" she cried. "You lie! You always lie!" Her flashing eyes looked into his and caught something there, at once brutal and kind, that awed her and made her impotent and acquiescent. She lowered her own eyes in tired despair.

"All right," she said wearily. "My baby is gone. What shall I do now?"

"Your husband is much better. All he needs is rest and kindness. But you must go to him and tell him what's happened."

"I suppose you think you made him better," said Luella bitterly.

"Perhaps. He's nearly well."

Nearly well—then the last link that held her to her home was broken. This part of her life was over—she could cut it off here, with its grief and oppression, and be off now, free as the wind.

"I'll go to him in a minute," Luella said in a far-away voice. "Please leave me alone."

Doctor Moon's unwelcome shadow melted into the darkness of the hall.

"I can go away," Luella whispered to herself. "Life has given me back freedom, in place of what it took away from me."

But she mustn't linger even a minute, or Life would bind her again and make her suffer once more. She called the apartment porter and asked that her trunk be brought up from the storeroom. Then she began taking things from the bureau and wardrobe, trying to approximate as nearly as possible the possessions that she had brought to her married life. She even found two old dresses that had formed part of her trousseau—out of style now, and a little tight in the hips—which she threw in with the rest. A new life. Charles was well again; and her baby, whom she had worshipped, and who had bored her a little, was dead.

When she had packed her trunk, she went into the kitchen automatically, to see about the preparations for dinner. She spoke to the cook about the special things for Charles and said that she herself was dining out. The sight of one of the small pans that had been used to cook Chuck's food caught her attention for a moment—but she stared at it unmoved. She looked into the ice-box and saw it was clean and fresh inside. Then she went into Charles's room. He was sitting up in bed, and the nurse was reading to him. His hair was almost white now, silvery white, and underneath it his eyes were huge and dark in his thin young face.

"The baby is sick?" he asked in his own natural voice.

She nodded.

He hesitated, closing his eyes for a moment. Then he asked:

"The baby is dead?"

"Yes."

For a long time he didn't speak. The nurse came over and put her hand on his forehead. Two large, strange tears welled from his eyes.

"I knew the baby was dead."

After another long wait, the nurse spoke:

"The doctor said he could be taken out for a drive to-day while there was still sunshine. He needs a little change."

"Yes."

"I thought"—the nurse hesitated—"I thought perhaps it would do you both good, Mrs. Hemple, if you took him instead of me."

Luella shook her head hastily.

"Oh, no," she said. "I don't feel able to, to-day."

The nurse looked at her oddly. With a sudden feeling of pity for Charles, Luella bent down gently and kissed his cheek. Then, without a word, she went to her own room, put on her hat and coat, and with her suitcase started for the front door.

Immediately she saw that there was a shadow in the hall. If she could get past that shadow, she was free. If she could go to the right or left of it, or order it out of her way! But, stubbornly, it refused to move, and with a little cry she sank down into a hall chair.

"I thought you'd gone," she wailed. "I told you to go away."

"I'm going soon," said Doctor Moon, "but I don't want you to make an old mistake."

"I'm not making a mistake—I'm leaving my mistakes behind."

"You're trying to leave yourself behind, but you can't. The more you try to run away from yourself, the more you'll have yourself with you."

"But I've got to go away," she insisted wildly. "Out of this house of death and failure!"

"You haven't failed yet. You've only begun."

She stood up.

"Let me pass."

"No."

Abruptly she gave way, as she always did when he talked to her. She covered her face with her hands and burst into tears.

"Go back into that room and tell the nurse you'll take your husband for a drive," he suggested.

"I can't."

"Oh, yes."

Once more Luella looked at him, and knew that she would obey. With the conviction that her spirit was broken at last, she took up her suitcase and walked back through the hall.

V

The nature of the curious influence that Doctor Moon exerted upon her, Louella could not guess. But as the days passed, she found herself doing many things that had been repugnant to her before. She stayed at home with Charles; and when he grew better, she went out with him sometimes to dinner, or the theatre, but only when he expressed a wish. She visited the kitchen every day, and kept an unwilling eye on the house, at first with a horror that it would go wrong again, then from habit. And she felt that it was all somehow mixed up with Doctor Moon—it was something he kept telling her about life, or almost telling her, and yet concealing from her, as though he were afraid to have her know.

With the resumption of their normal life, she found that Charles was less nervous. His habit of rubbing his face had left him, and if the world seemed less gay and happy to her than it had before, she experienced a certain peace, sometimes, that she had never known.

Then, one afternoon, Doctor Moon told her suddenly that he was going away.

"Do you mean for good?" she demanded with a touch of panic.

"For good."

For a strange moment she wasn't sure whether she was glad or sorry.

"You don't need me any more," he said quietly. "You don't realize it, but you've grown up."

He came over and, sitting on the couch beside her, took her hand. Luella sat silent and tense—listening.

"We make an agreement with children that they can sit in the audience without helping to make the play," he said, "but if they still sit in the audience after they're grown, somebody's got to work double time for them, so that they can enjoy the light and glitter of the world."

"But I want the light and glitter," she protested. "That's all there is in life. There can't be anything wrong in wanting to have things warm."

"Things will still be warm."

"How?"

"Things will warm themselves from you."

Luella looked at him, startled.

"It's your turn to be the centre, to give others what was given to you for so long. You've got to give security to young people and peace to your husband, and a sort of charity to the old. You've got to let the people who work for you depend on you. You've got to cover up a few more troubles than you show, and be a little more patient than the average person, and do a little more instead of a little less than your share. The light and glitter of the world is in your hands."

He broke off suddenly.

"Get up," he said, "and go to that mirror and tell me what you see."

Obediently Luella got up and went close to a purchase of her honeymoon, a Venetian pier-glass on the wall.

"I see new lines in my face here," she said, raising her finger and placing it between her eyes, "and a few shadows at the sides that might be—that are little wrinkles."

"Do you care?"

She turned quickly. "No," she said.

"Do you realize that Chuck is gone? That you'll never see him any more?"

"Yes." She passed her hands slowly over her eyes. "But that all seems so vague and far away."

"Vague and far away," he repeated; and then: "And are you afraid of me now?"

"Not any longer," she said, and she added frankly, "now that you're going away."

He moved toward the door. He seemed particularly weary tonight, as though he could hardly move about at all.

"The household here is in your keeping," he said in a tired whisper. "If there is any light and warmth in it, it will be your light and warmth; if it is happy, it will be because you've made it so. Happy things may come to you in life, but you must never go seeking them any more. It is your turn to make the fire."

"Won't you sit down a moment longer?" Luella ventured.

"There isn't time." His voice was so low now that she could scarcely hear the words. "But remember that whatever suffering comes to you, I can always help you—if it is something that can be helped. I promise nothing."

He opened the door. She must find out now what she most wanted to know, before it was too late.

"What have you done to me?" she cried. "Why have I no sorrow left for Chuck—for anything at all? Tell me; I almost see, yet I can't see. Before you go—tell me who you are!"

"Who am I?—" His worn suit paused in the doorway. His round, pale face seemed to dissolve into two faces, a dozen faces, a score, each one different yet the same—sad, happy, tragic, indifferent, resigned—until threescore Doctor Moons were ranged like an infinite series of reflections, like months stretching into the vista of the past.

"Who am I?" he repeated; "I am five years."

The door closed.

At six o'clock Charles Hemple came home, and as usual Luella met him in the hall. Except that now his hair was dead white, his long illness of two years had left no mark upon him. Luella herself was more noticeably changed—she was a little stouter, and there were those lines around her eyes that had come when Chuck died one evening back in 1921. But she was still lovely, and there was a mature kindness about her face at twenty-eight, as if suffering had touched her only reluctantly and then hurried away.

"Ede and her husband are coming to dinner," she said. "I've got theatre tickets, but if you're tired, I don't care whether we go or not."

"I'd like to go."

She looked at him.

"You wouldn't."

"I really would."

"We'll see how you feel after dinner."

He put his arm around her waist. Together they walked into the nursery where the two children were waiting up to say good night.

HOT AND COLD BLOOD

One day when the young Mathers had been married for about a year, Jaqueline walked into the rooms of the hardware brokerage which her husband carried on with more than average success. At the open door of the inner office she stopped and said: "Oh, excuse me—" She had interrupted an apparently trivial yet somehow intriguing scene. A young man named Bronson whom she knew slightly was standing with her husband; the latter had risen from his desk. Bronson seized her husband's hand and shook it earnestly—something more than earnestly. When they heard Jaqueline's step in the doorway both men turned and Jaqueline saw that Bronson's eyes were red.

A moment later he came out, passing her with a somewhat embarrassed "How do you do?" She walked into her husband's office.

"What was Ed Bronson doing here?" she demanded curiously, and at once.

Jim Mather smiled at her, half shutting his gray eyes, and drew her quietly to a sitting position on his desk.

"He just dropped in for a minute," he answered easily. "How's everything at home?"

"All right." She looked at him with curiosity. "What did he want?" she insisted.

"Oh, he just wanted to see me about something."

"What?"

"Oh, just something. Business."

"Why were his eyes red?"

"Were they?" He looked at her innocently, and then suddenly they both began to laugh. Jaqueline rose and walked around the desk and plumped down into his swivel chair.

"You might as well tell me," she announced cheerfully, "because I'm going to stay right here till you do."

"Well—" he hesitated, frowning. "He wanted me to do him a little favor."

Then Jaqueline understood, or rather her mind leaped half accidentally to the truth.

"Oh." Her voice tightened a little. "You've been lending him some money."

"Only a little."

"How much?"

"Only three hundred."

"*Only* three hundred." The voice was of the texture of Bessemer cooled. "How much do we spend a month, Jim?"

"Why—why, about five or six hundred, I guess." He shifted uneasily. "Listen, Jack. Bronson'll pay that back. He's in a little trouble. He's made a mistake about a girl out in Woodmere——"

"And he knows you're famous for being an easy mark, so he comes to you," interrupted Jaqueline.

"No." He denied this formally.

"Don't you suppose I could use that three hundred dollars?" she demanded. "How about that trip to New York we couldn't afford last November?"

The lingering smile faded from Mather's face. He went over and shut the door to the outer office.

"Listen, Jack," he began, "you don't understand this. Bronson's one of the men I eat lunch with almost every day. We used to play together when we were kids, we went to school together. Don't you see that I'm just the person he'd be right to come to in trouble? And that's just why I couldn't refuse."

Jaqueline gave her shoulders a twist as if to shake off this reasoning.

"Well," she answered decidedly, "all I know is that he's no good. He's always lit and if he doesn't choose to work he has no business living off the work you do."

They were sitting now on either side of the desk, each having adopted the attitude of one talking to a child. They began their sentences with "Listen!" and their faces wore expressions of rather tried patience.

"If you can't understand, I can't tell you," Mather concluded, at the end of fifteen minutes, on what was, for him, an irritated key. "Such obligations do happen to exist sometimes among men and they have to be met. It's more complicated than just refusing to lend money, especially in a business like mine where so much depends on the good-will of men down-town."

Mather was putting on his coat as he said this. He was going home with her on the street-car to lunch. They were between automobiles—they had sold their old one and were going to get a new one in the spring.

Now the street-car, on this particular day, was distinctly unfortunate. The argument in the office might have been forgotten under other circumstances, but what followed irritated the scratch until it became a serious temperamental infection.

They found a seat near the front of the car. It was late February and an eager, unpunctilious sun was turning the scrawny street snow into dirty, cheerful rivulets that echoed in the gutters. Because of this the car was less full than usual—there was no one standing. The motorman had even opened his window and a yellow breeze was blowing the late breath of winter from the car.

It occurred pleasurably to Jaqueline that her husband sitting beside her was handsome and kind above other men. It was silly to try to change him. Perhaps Bronson might return the money after all, and anyhow three hundred dollars wasn't a fortune. Of course he had no business doing it—but then——

Her musings were interrupted as an eddy of passengers pushed up the aisle. Jaqueline wished they'd put their hands over their mouths when they coughed, and she hoped that Jim would get a new machine pretty soon. You couldn't tell what disease you'd run into in these trolleys.

She turned to Jim to discuss the subject—but Jim had stood up and was offering his seat to a woman who had been standing beside him in the aisle. The woman, without so much as a grunt, sat down. Jaqueline frowned.

The woman was about fifty and enormous. When she first sat down she was content merely to fill the unoccupied part of the seat, but after a moment she began to expand and to spread her great rolls of fat over a larger and larger area until the process took on the aspect of violent trespassing. When the car rocked in Jaqueline's direction the woman slid with it, but when it rocked back she managed by some exercise of ingenuity to dig in and hold the ground won.

Jaqueline caught her husband's eye—he was swaying on a strap—and in an angry glance conveyed to him her entire disapproval of his action. He apologized mutely and became urgently engrossed in a row of car cards. The fat woman moved once more against Jaqueline—she was now practically overlapping her. Then she turned puffy, disagreeable eyes full on Mrs. James Mather, and coughed rousingly in her face.

With a smothered exclamation Jaqueline got to her feet, squeezed with brisk violence past the fleshy knees, and made her way, pink with rage, toward the rear of the car. There she seized a strap, and there she was presently joined by her husband in a state of considerable alarm.

They exchanged no word, but stood silently side by side for ten minutes while a row of men sitting in front of them crackled their newspapers and kept their eyes fixed virtuously upon the day's cartoons.

When they left the car at last Jaqueline exploded.

"You big *fool!*" she cried wildly. "Did you see that horrible woman you gave your seat to? Why don't you consider *me* occasionally instead of every fat selfish washwoman you meet?"

"How should I know——"

But Jaqueline was as angy at him as she had ever been—it was unusual for anyone to get angry at him.

"You didn't see any of those men getting up for *me,* did you? No wonder you were too tired to go out last Monday night. You'd probably given your seat to some—to some horrible, Polish *wash*woman that's strong as an ox and *likes* to stand up!"

They were walking along the slushy street stepping wildly into great pools of water. Confused and distressed, Mather could utter neither apology nor defense.

Jaqueline broke off and then turned to him with a curious light in her eyes. The words in which she couched her summary of the situation were probably the most disagreeable that had ever been addressed to him in his life.

"The trouble with you, Jim, the reason you're such an easy mark, is that you've got the ideas of a college freshman—you're a professional nice fellow."

II

The incident and the unpleasantness were forgotten. Mather's vast good nature had smoothed over the roughness within an hour. References to it fell with a dying cadence throughout several days—then ceased and tumbled into the limbo of oblivion. I say "limbo," for oblivion is, unfortunately, never quite oblivious. The subject was drowned out by the fact that Jaqueline with her customary spirit and coolness began the long, arduous, up-hill business of bearing a child. Her natural traits and prejudices became intensified and she was less inclined to let things pass.

It was April now, and as yet they had not bought a car. Mather had discovered that he was saving practically nothing and that in another half-year he would have a family on his hands. It worried him. A wrinkle—small, tentative, undisturbing—appeared for the first time as a shadow around his honest, friendly eyes. He worked far into the spring twilight now, and frequently brought home with him the overflow from his office day. The new car would have to be postponed for a while.

April afternoon, and all the city shopping on Washington Street. Jaqueline walked slowly past the shops, brooding without fear or depression on the shape into which her life was now being arbitrarily forced. Dry summer dust was in the wind; the sun bounded cheerily from the plate-glass windows and made radiant gasoline rainbows where automobile drippings had formed pools on the street.

Jaqueline stopped. Not six feet from her a bright new sport roadster was parked at the curb. Beside it stood two men in conversation, and at the moment when she identified one of them as young Bronson she heard him say to the other in a casual tone:

"What do you think of it? Just got it this morning."

Jaqueline turned abruptly and walked with quick tapping steps to her husband's office. With her usual curt nod to the stenographer she strode by her to the inner room. Mather looked up from his desk in surprise at her brusque entry.

"Jim," she began breathlessly, "did Bronson ever pay you that three hundred?"

"Why—no," he answered hesitantly, "not yet. He was in here last week and he explained that he was a little bit hard up."

Her eyes gleamed with angry triumph.

"Oh, he did?" she snapped. "Well, he's just bought a new sport roadster that must have cost anyhow twenty-five hundred dollars."

He shook his head, unbelieving.

"I saw it," she insisted. "I heard him say he'd just bought it."

"He *told* me he was hard up," repeated Mather helplessly.

Jaqueline audibly gave up by heaving a profound noise, a sort of groanish sigh.

"He was *us*ing you! He knew you were easy and he was *us*ing you. Can't you see? He wanted *you* to buy him the car and you *did!*" She laughed bitterly. "He's probably roaring his sides out to think how easily he worked you."

"Oh, no," protested Mather with a shocked expression, "you must have mistaken somebody for him——"

"We walk—and he rides on our money," she interrupted excitedly. "Oh, it's rich—it's rich. If it wasn't so maddening, it'd be just absurd. Look here—!" Her voice grew sharper, more restrained—there was a touch of contempt in it now. "You spend half your time doing things for people who don't give a damn about you or what becomes of you. You give up your seat on the street-car to *hogs,* and come home too dead tired to even *move.* You're on all sorts of committees that take at least an hour a day out of your business and you don't get a cent out of them. You're—eternally—being *used!* I won't stand it! I thought I married a man—not a professional Samaritan who's going to fetch and carry for the world!"

As she finished her invective Jaqueline reeled suddenly and sank into a chair—nervously exhausted.

"Just at this time," she went on brokenly, "I need you. I need your strength and your health and your arms around me. And if you—if you just give it to *every* one, it's spread *so* thin when it reaches me——"

He knelt by her side, moving her tired young head until it lay against his shoulder.

"I'm sorry, Jaqueline," he said humbly, "I'll be more careful. I didn't realize what I was doing."

"You're the dearest person in the world," murmured Jaqueline huskily, "but I want all of you and the best of you for me."

He smoothed her hair over and over. For a few minutes they rested there silently, having attained a sort of Nirvana of peace and understanding. Then Jaqueline reluctantly raised her head as they were interrupted by the voice of Miss Clancy in the doorway.

"Oh, I beg your pardon."

"What is it?"

"A boy's here with some boxes. It's C. O. D."

Mather rose and followed Miss Clancy into the outer office.

"It's fifty dollars."

He searched his wallet—he had omitted to go to the bank that morning.

"Just a minute," he said abstractedly. His mind was on Jaqueline, Jaqueline who seemed forlorn in her trouble, waiting for him in the other room. He walked into the corridor, and opening the door of "Clayton and Drake, Brokers" across the way, swung wide a low gate and went up to a man seated at a desk.

"Morning, Fred," said Mather.

Drake, a little man of thirty with pince-nez and bald head, rose and shook hands.

"Morning, Jim. What can I do for you?"

"Why, a boy's in my office with some stuff C. O. D. and I haven't a cent. Can you let me have fifty till this afternoon?"

Drake looked closely at Mather. Then, slowly and startlingly, he shook his head—not up and down but from side to side.

"Sorry, Jim," he answered stiffly, "I've made a rule never to make a personal loan to anybody on any conditions. I've seen it break up too many friendships."

"What?"

Mather had come out of his abstraction now, and the monosyllable held an undisguised quality of shock. Then his natural tact acted automatically, springing to his aid and dictating his words though his brain was suddenly numb. His immediate instinct was to put Drake at ease in his refusal.

"Oh, I see." He nodded his head as if in full agreement, as if he himself had often considered adopting just such a rule. "Oh, I see how you feel. Well—I just—I wouldn't have you break a rule like that for anything. It's probably a good thing."

They talked for a minute longer. Drake justified his position easily; he had evidently rehearsed the part a great deal. He treated Mather to an exquisitely frank smile.

Mather went politely back to his office leaving Drake under the impression that the latter was the most tactful man in the city. Mather knew how to leave people with that impression. But when he entered his own office and saw his wife staring dismally out the window into the sunshine he clinched his hands, and his mouth moved in an unfamiliar shape.

"All right, Jack," he said slowly, "I guess you're right about most things, and I'm wrong as hell."

III

During the next three months Mather thought back through many years. He had had an unusually happy life. Those frictions between man and man, between man and society, which harden most of us into a rough and cynical quarrelling trim, had been conspicuous by their infrequency in his life. It had never occurred to him before that he had paid a price for this immunity, but now he perceived how here and there, and constantly, he had taken the rough side of the road to avoid enmity or argument, or even question.

There was, for instance, much money that he had lent privately, about thirteen hundred dollars in all, which he realized, in his new enlightenment, he would never see again. It had taken Jaqueline's harder, feminine intelligence to know this. It was only now when he owed it to Jaqueline to have money in the bank that he missed these loans at all.

He realized too the truth of her assertions that he was continually doing favors—a little something here, a little something there; the sum total, in time and energy expended, was appalling. It had pleased him to do the favors. He reacted warmly to being thought well of, but he wondered now if he had not been merely indulging a selfish vanity of his own. In suspecting this, he was, as usual, not quite fair to himself. The truth was that Mather was essentially and enormously romantic.

He decided that these expenditures of himself made him tired at night, less efficient in his work, and less of a prop to Jaqueline, who, as the months passed, grew more heavy and bored, and sat through the long summer afternoons on the screened veranda waiting for his step at the end of the walk.

Lest that step falter, Mather gave up many things—among them the presidency of his college alumni association. He let slip other labors less prized. When he was put on a committee, men had a habit of electing him chairman and retiring into a dim background, where they were inconveniently hard to find. He was done with such things now. Also he avoided those who were prone to ask favors—fleeing a certain eager look that would be turned on him from some group at his club.

The change in him came slowly. He was not exceptionally unworldly—under other circumstances Drake's refusal of money would not have surprised him. Had it come to him as a story he would scarcely have given it a thought. But it had broken in with harsh abruptness upon a situation existing in his own mind, and the shock had given it a powerful and literal significance.

It was mid-August now, and the last of a baking week. The curtains of his wide-open office windows had scarcely rippled all the day, but lay like sails becalmed in warm juxtaposition with the smothering screens. Mather was worried—Jaqueline had over-tired herself, and was paying for it by violent sick headaches, and business seemed to have come to an apathetic standstill. That morning he had been so irritable with Miss Clancy that she had looked at him in surprise. He had immediately apologized, wishing afterward that he hadn't. He was working at high speed through this heat—why shouldn't she?

She came to his door now, and he looked up faintly frowning.

"Mr. Edward Lacy."

"All right," he answered listlessly. Old man Lacy—he knew him slightly. A melancholy figure—a brilliant start back in the eighties, and now one of the city's failures. He couldn't imagine what Lacy wanted unless he were soliciting.

"Good afternoon, Mr. Mather."

A little, solemn, gray-haired man stood on the threshold. Mather rose and greeted him politely.

"Are you busy, Mr. Mather?"

"Well, not so *very*." He stressed the qualifying word slightly.

Mr. Lacy sat down, obviously ill at ease. He kept his hat in his hands, and clung to it tightly as he began to speak.

"Mr. Mather, if you've got five minutes to spare, I'm going to tell you something that—that I find at present it's necessary for me to tell you."

Mather nodded. His instinct warned him that there was a favor to be asked, but he was tired, and with a sort of lassitude he let his chin sink into his hand, welcoming any distraction from his more immediate cares.

"You see," went on Mr. Lacy—Mather noticed that the hands which fingered at the hat were trembling—"back in eighty-four your father and I were very good friends. You've heard him speak of me no doubt."

Mather nodded.

"I was asked to be one of the pallbearers. Once we were—very close. It's because of that that I come to you now. Never before in my life have I ever had to come to any one as I've come to you now, Mr. Mather—come to a stranger. But as you grow older your friends die or move away or some misunderstanding separates you. And your children die unless you're fortunate enough to go first—and pretty soon you get to be alone, so that you don't have any friends at all. You're isolated." He smiled faintly. His hands were trembling violently now.

"Once upon a time almost forty years ago your father came to me and asked me for a thousand dollars. I was a few years older than he was, and though I knew him only slightly, I had a high opinion of him. That was a lot of money in those days, and he had no security—he had nothing but a plan in his head—but I liked the way he had of looking out of his eyes—you'll pardon me if I say you look not unlike him—so I gave it to him without security."

Mr. Lacy paused.

"Without security," he repeated. "I could afford it then. I didn't lose by it. He paid it back with interest at six per cent before the year was up."

Mather was looking down at his blotter, tapping out a series of triangles with his pencil. He knew what was coming now, and his muscles physically tightened as he mustered his forces for the refusal he would have to make.

"I'm now an old man, Mr. Mather," the cracked voice went on. "I've made a failure—I *am* a failure—only we needn't go into that now. I have a daughter, an unmarried daughter who lives with me. She does stenographic work and has been very kind to me. We live together, you know, on Selby Avenue—we have an apartment, quite a nice apartment."

The old man sighed quaveringly. He was trying—and at the same time was afraid—to get to his request. It was insurance, it seemed. He had a ten-thousand-dollar policy, he had borrowed on it up to the limit, and he stood to lose the whole amount unless he could raise four hundred and fifty dollars. He and his daughter had about seventy-five dollars between them. They had no friends—he had explained that—and they had found it impossible to raise the money. . . .

Mather could stand the miserable story no longer. He could not spare the money, but he could at least relieve the old man of the blistered agony of asking for it.

"I'm sorry, Mr. Lacy," he interrupted as gently as possible, "but I can't lend you that money."

"No?" The old man looked at him with faded, blinking eyes that were beyond all shock, almost, it seemed, beyond any human emotion except ceaseless care. The only change in his expression was that his mouth dropped slowly ajar.

Mather fixed his eyes determinedly upon his blotter.

"We're going to have a baby in a few months, and I've been saving for that. It wouldn't be fair to my wife to take anything from her—or the child—right now."

His voice sank to a sort of mumble. He found himself saying platitudinously that business was bad—saying it with revolting facility.

Mr. Lacy made no argument. He rose without visible signs of disappointment. Only his hands were still trembling and they worried Mather. The old man was apologetic—he was sorry to have bothered him at a time like this. Perhaps something would turn up. He had thought that if Mr. Mather did happen to have a good deal extra—why, he might be the person to go to because he was the son of an old friend.

As he left the office he had trouble opening the outer door. Miss Clancy helped him. He went shabbily and unhappily down the corridor with his faded eyes blinking and his mouth still faintly ajar.

Jim Mather stood by his desk, and put his hand over his face and shivered suddenly as if he were cold. But the five-o'clock air outside was hot as a tropic noon.

IV

The twilight was hotter still an hour later as he stood at the corner waiting for his car. The trolley-ride to his house was twenty-five minutes, and he bought a pink-jacketed newspaper to appetize his listless mind. Life had seemed less happy, less glamorous of late. Perhaps he had learned more of the world's ways—perhaps its glamour was evaporating little by little with the hurried years.

Nothing like this afternoon, for instance, had ever happend to him before. He could not dismiss the old man from his mind. He pictured him plodding home in the weary heat—on foot, probably, to save carfare—opening the door of a hot little flat, and confessing to his daughter that the son of his friend had not been able to help him out. All evening they would plan helplessly until they said good night to each other—father and daughter, isolated by chance in this world—and went to lie awake with a pathetic loneliness in their two beds.

Mather's street-car came along, and he found a seat near the front, next to an old lady who looked at him grudgingly as she moved over. At the next block a crowd of girls from the department-store district flowed up the aisle, and Mather unfolded his paper. Of late he had not indulged in his habit of giving up his seat. Jaqueline was right—the average young girl was able to stand as well as he was. Giving up his seat was silly, a mere gesture. Nowadays not one woman in a dozen even bothered to thank him.

It was stifling hot in the car, and he wiped the heavy damp from his forehead. The aisle was thickly packed now, and a woman standing beside his seat was thrown momentarily against his shoulder as the car turned a corner. Mather took a long breath of the hot foul air, which persistently refused to circulate, and tried to centre his mind on a cartoon at the top of the sporting page.

"Move for'ard ina car, please!" The conductor's voice pierced the opaque column of humanity with raucous irritation. "Plen'y of room for'ard!"

The crowd made a feeble attempt to shove forward, but the unfortunate fact that there was no space into which to move precluded any marked success. The car turned another corner, and again the woman next to Mather swayed against his shoulder. Ordinarily he would have given up his seat if only to avoid this reminder that she was there. It made him feel unpleasantly cold-blooded. And the car was horrible—horrible. They ought to put more of them on the line these sweltering days.

For the fifth time he looked at the pictures in the comic strip. There was a beggar in the second picture, and the wavering image of Mr. Lacy persistently inserted itself in the beggar's place. God! Suppose the old man really did starve to death—suppose he threw himself into the river.

"Once," thought Mather, "he helped my father. Perhaps, if it hadn't, my own life would have been different than it has been. But Lacy could afford it then—and I can't."

To force out the picture of Mr. Lacy, Mather tried to think of Jaqueline. He said to himself over and over that he would have been sacrificing Jaqueline to a played-out man who had had his chance and failed. Jaqueline needed her chance now as never before.

Mather looked at his watch. He had been on the car ten minutes. Fifteen minutes still to ride, and the heat increasing with breathless intensity. The woman swayed against him once more, and looking out the window he saw that they were turning the last down-town corner.

It occurred to him that perhaps he ought, after all, to give the woman his seat—her last sway toward him had been a particularly tired sway. If he were sure she was an older woman—but the texture of her dress as it brushed his hand gave somehow the impression that she was a young girl. He did not dare look up to see. He was afraid of the appeal that might look out of her eyes if they were old eyes or the sharp contempt if they were young.

For the next five minutes his mind worked in a vague suffocated way on what now seemed to him the enormous problem of whether or not to give her the seat. He felt dimly that doing so would partially atone for his refusal to Mr. Lacy that afteroon. It would be rather terrible to have done those two cold-blooded things in succession—and on such a day.

He tried the cartoon again, but in vain. He must concentrate on Jaqueline. He was dead tired now, and if he stood up he would be more tired. Jaqueline would be waiting for him, needing him. She would be depressed and she would want him to hold her quietly in his arms for an hour after dinner. When he was tired this was rather a strain. And afterward when they went to bed she would ask him from time to time to get her medicine or a glass of ice-water. He hated to show any weariness in doing these things. She might notice and, needing something, refrain from asking for it.

The girl in the aisle swayed against him once more—this time it was more like a sag. She was tired, too. Well, it was weary to work. The ends of many proverbs that had to do with toil and the long day floated fragmentarily through his mind. Everybody in the world was tired—this woman, for instance, whose body was sagging so wearily, so strangely against his. But his home came first and his girl that he loved was waiting for him there. He must keep his strength for her, and he said to himself over and over that he would not give up his seat.

Then he heard a long sigh, followed by a sudden exclamation, and he realized that the girl was no longer leaning against him. The exclamation multiplied into a clatter of voices—then came a pause—then a renewed clatter that travelled down the car in calls and little staccato cries to the conductor. The bell clanged violently, and the hot car jolted to a sudden stop.

"Girl fainted up here!"

"Too hot for her!"

"Just keeled right over!"

"Get back there! Gangway, you!"

The crowd eddied apart. The passengers in front squeezed back and those on the rear platform temporarily disembarked. Curiosity and pity bubbled out of suddenly conversing groups. People tried to help, got in the way. Then the bell rang and voices rose stridently again.

"Get her out all right?"

"Say, did you see that?"

"This damn' company ought to——"

"Did you see the man that carried her out? He was pale as a ghost, too."

"Yes, but did you hear——?"

"What?"

"That fella. That pale fella that carried her out. He was sittin' beside her—he says she's his wife!"

The house was quiet. A breeze pressed back the dark vine leaves of the veranda. letting in thin yellow rods of moonlight on the wicker chairs. Jaqueline rested placidly on the long settee with her head in his arms. After a while she stirred lazily; her hand reaching up patted his cheek.

"I think I'll go to bed now. I'm so tired. Will you help me up?"

He lifted her and then laid her back among the pillows.

"I'll be with you in a minute," he said gently. "Can you wait for just a minute?"

He passed into the lighted living-room, and she heard him thumbing the pages of a telephone directory; then she listened as he called a number.

"Hello, is Mr. Lacy there? Why—yes, it *is* pretty important—if he hasn't gone to sleep."

A pause. Jaqueline could hear restless sparrows splattering through the leaves of the magnolia over the way. Then her husband at the telephone:

"Is this Mr. Lacy? Oh, this is Mather. Why— why, in regard to that matter we talked about this afternoon, I think I'll be able to fix that up after all." He raised his voice a little as though some one at the other end found it difficult to hear. "James Mather's son, I said— About that little matter this afternoon——"

GRETCHEN'S FORTY WINKS

THE sidewalks were scratched with brittle leaves, and the bad little boy next door froze his tongue to the iron mail-box. Snow before night, sure. Autumn was over. This, of course, raised the coal question and the Christmas question; but Roger Halsey, standing on his own front porch, assured the dead suburban sky that he hadn't time for worrying about the weather. Then he let himself hurriedly into the house, and shut the subject out into the cold twilight.

The hall was dark, but from above he heard the voices of his wife and the nursemaid and the baby in one of their interminable conversations, which consisted chiefly of "Don't!" and "Look out, Maxy!" and "Oh, there he *goes!*" punctuated by wild threats and vague bumpings and the recurrent sound of small, venturing feet.

Roger turned on the hall-light and walked into the living-room and turned on the red silk lamp. He put his bulging portfolio on the table, and sitting down rested his intense young face in his hand for a few minutes, shading his eyes carefully from the light. Then he lit a cigarette, squashed it out, and going to the foot of the stairs called for his wife.

"Gretchen!"

"Hello, dear." Her voice was full of laughter. "Come see baby."

He swore softly.

"I can't see baby now," he said aloud. "How long 'fore you'll be down?"

There was a mysterious pause, and then a succession of "Don'ts" and "Look outs, Maxy" evidently meant to avert some threatened catastrophe.

"How long 'fore you'll be down?" repeated Roger, slightly irritated.

"Oh, I'll be right down."

"How soon?" he shouted.

He had trouble every day at this hour in adapting his voice from the urgent key of the city to the proper casualness for a model home. But to-night he was deliberately impatient. It almost disappointed him when Gretchen came running down the stairs, three at a time, crying "What is it?" in a rather surprised voice.

They kissed—lingered over it some moments. They had been married three years, and they were much more in love than that implies. It was seldom that they hated each other with that violent hate of which only young couples are capable, for Roger was still actively sensitive to her beauty.

"Come in here," he said abruptly. "I want to talk to you."

His wife, a bright-colored, Titian-haired girl, vivid as a French rag doll, followed him into the living-room.

"Listen, Gretchen"—he sat down at the end of the sofa—"beginning with to-night I'm going to—What's the matter?"

"Nothing. I'm just looking for a cigarette. Go on."

She tiptoed breathlessly back to the sofa and settled at the other end.

"Gretchen—" Again he broke off. Her hand, palm upward, was extended toward him. "Well, what is it?" he asked wildly.

"Matches."

"What?"

In his impatience it seemed incredible that she should ask for matches, but he fumbled automatically in his pocket.

"Thank you," she whispered. "I didn't mean to interrupt you. Go on."

"Gretch——"

Scratch! The match flared. They exchanged a tense look.

Her fawn's eyes apologized mutely this time, and he laughed. After all, she had done no more than light a cigarette; but when he was in this mood her slightest positive action irritated him beyond measure.

"When you've got time to listen," he said crossly, "you might be interested in discussing the poorhouse question with me."

"What poorhouse?" Her eyes were wide, startled; she sat quiet as a mouse.

"That was just to get your attention. But, beginning to-night, I start on what'll probably be the most important six weeks of my life—the six weeks that'll decide wheher we're going on forever in this rotten little house in this rotten little suburban town."

Boredom replaced alarm in Gretchen's black eyes. She was a Southern girl, and any question that had to do with getting ahead in the world always tended to give her a headache.

"Six months ago I left the New York Lithographic Company," announced Roger, "and went in the advertising business for myself."

"I know," interrupted Gretchen resentfully; "and now instead of getting six hundred a month sure, we're living on a risky five hundred."

"Gretchen," said Roger sharply, "if you'll just believe in me as hard as you can for six weeks more we'll be rich. I've got a chance now to get some of the biggest accounts in the country." He hesitated. "And for these six weeks we won't go out at all, and we won't have any one here. I'm going to bring home work every night, and we'll pull down all the blinds and if any one rings the door-bell we won't answer."

He smiled airily as if it were a new game they were going to play. Then, as Gretchen was silent, his smile faded, and he looked at her uncertainly.

"Well, what's the matter?" she broke out finally. "Do you expect me to jump up and sing? You do enough work as it is. If you try to do any more you'll end up with a nervous breakdown. I read about a——"

"Don't worry about me," he interrupted; "I'm all right. But you're going to be bored to death sitting here every evening."

"No, I won't," she said without conviction—"except to-night."

"What about to-night?"

"George Tompkins asked us to dinner."

"Did you accept?"

"Of course I did," she said impatiently. "Why not? You're always talking about what a terrible neighborhood this is, and I thought maybe you'd like to go to a nicer one for a change."

"When I go to a nicer neighborhood I want to go for good," he said grimly.

"Well, can we go?"

"I suppose we'll have to if you've accepted."

Somewhat to his annoyance the conversation abruptly ended. Gretchen jumped up and kissed him sketchily and rushed into the kitchen to light the hot water for a bath. With a sigh he carefully deposited his portfolio behind the bookcase—it contained only sketches and layouts for display advertising, but it seemed to him the first thing a burglar would look for. Then he went abstractedly up-stairs, dropping into the baby's room for a casual moist kiss, and began dressing for dinner.

They had no automobile, so George Tompkins called for them at 6:30. Tompkins was a successful interior decorator, a broad, rosy man with a handsome mustache and a strong odor of jasmine. He and Roger had once roomed side by side in a boarding-house in New York, but they had met only intermittently in the past five years.

"We ought to see each other more," he told Roger to-night. "You ought to go out more often, old boy. Cocktail?"

"No, thanks."

"No? Well, your fair wife will—won't you, Gretchen?"

"I love this house," she exclaimed, taking the glass and looking admiringly at ship models, Colonial whiskey bottles, and other fashionable débris of 1925.

"I like it," said Tompkins with satisfaction. "I did it to please myself, and I succeeded."

Roger stared moodily around the stiff, plain room, wondering if they could have blundered into the kitchen by mistake.

"You look like the devil, Roger," said his host. "Have a cocktail and cheer up."

"Have one," urged Gretchen.

"What?" Roger turned around absently. "Oh, no, thanks. I've got to work after I get home."

"Work!" Tompkins smiled. "Listen, Roger, you'll kill yourself with work. Why don't you bring a little balance into your life—work a little, then play a little?"

"That's what I tell them," said Gretchen.

"Do you know an average business man's day?" demanded Tompkins as they went in to dinner. "Coffee in the morning, eight hours' work interrupted by a bolted luncheon, and then home again with dyspepsia and a bad temper to give the wife a pleasant evening."

Roger laughed shortly.

"You've been going to the movies too much," he said dryly.

"What?" Tompkins looked at him with some irritation. "Movies? I've hardly ever been to the movies in my life. I think the movies are atrocious. My opinions on life are drawn from my own observations. I believe in a balanced life."

"What's that?" demanded Roger.

"Well"—he hesitated—"probably the best way to tell you would be to describe my own day. Would that seem horribly egotistic?"

"Oh, no!" Gretchen looked at him with interest. "I'd love to hear about it."

"Well, in the morning I get up and go through a series of exercises. I've got one room fitted up as a little gymnasium, and I punch the bag and do shadow-boxing and weight-pulling for an hour. Then after a cold bath— There's a thing now! Do you take a daily cold bath?"

"No," admitted Roger, "I take a hot bath in the evening three or four times a week."

A horrified silence fell. Tompkins and Gretchen exchanged a glance as if something obscene had been said.

"What's the matter?" broke out Roger, glancing from one to the other in some irritation. "You know I don't take a bath every day— I haven't got the time."

Tompkins gave a prolonged sigh.

"After my bath," he continued, drawing a merciful veil of silence over the matter, "I have breakfast and drive to my office in New York, where I work until four. Then I lay off, and if it's summer I hurry out here for nine holes of golf, or if it's winter I play squash for an hour at my club. Then a good snappy game of bridge until dinner. Dinner is liable to have something to do with business, but in a pleasant way. Perhaps I've just finished a house for some customer, and he wants me to be on hand for his first party to see that the lighting is soft enough and all that sort of thing. Or maybe I sit down with a good book of poetry and spend the evening alone. At any rate, I do something every night to get me out of myself."

"It must be wonderful," said Gretchen enthusiastically. "I wish we lived like that."

Tompkins bent forward earnestly over the table.

"You can," he said impressively. "There's no reason why you shouldn't. Look here, if Roger'll play nine holes of golf every day it'll do wonders for him. He won't know himself. He'll do his work better, never get that tired, nervous feeling— What's the matter?"

He broke off. Roger had perceptibly yawned.

"Roger," cried Gretchen sharply, "there's no need to be so rude. If you did what George said, you'd be a lot better off." She turned indignantly to their host. "The latest is that he's going to work at night for the next six weeks. He says he's going to pull down the blinds and shut us up like hermits in a cave. He's been doing it every Sunday for the last year; now he's going to do it every night for six weeks."

Tompkins shook his head sadly.

"At the end of six weeks," he remarked, "he'll be starting for the sanitarium. Let me tell you, every private hospital in New York is full of cases like yours. You just strain the human nervous system a little too far, and bang!—you've broken something. And in order to save sixty hours you're laid up sixty weeks for repairs." He broke off, changed his tone, and turned to Gretchen with a smile. "Not to mention what happens to you. It seems to me it's the wife rather than the husband who bears the brunt of these insane periods of overwork."

"I don't mind," protested Gretchen loyally.

"Yes, she does," said Roger grimly; "she minds like the devil. She's a shortsighted little egg, and she thinks it's going to be forever until I get started and she can have some new clothes. But it can't be helped. The saddest thing about women is that, after all, their best trick is to sit down and fold their hands."

"Your ideas on women are about twenty years out of date," said Tompkins pityingly. "Women won't sit down and wait any more."

"Then they'd better marry men of forty," insisted Roger stubbornly. "If a girl marries a young man for love she ought to be willing to make any sacrifice within reason, so long as her husband keeps going ahead."

"Let's not talk about it," said Gretchen impatiently. "Please, Roger, let's have a good time just this once."

When Tompkins dropped them in front of their house at eleven Roger and Gretchen stood for a moment on the sidewalk looking at the winter moon. There was a fine, damp, dusty snow in the air, and Roger drew a long breath of it and put his arm around Gretchen exultantly.

"I can make more money than he can," he said tensely. "And I'll be doing it in just forty days."

"Forty days," she sighed. "It seems such a long time—when everybody else is always having fun. If I could only sleep for forty days."

"Why don't you, honey? Just take forty winks, and when you wake up everything'll be fine."

She was silent for a moment.

"Roger," she asked thoughtfully, "do you think George meant what he said about taking me horseback riding on Sunday?"

Roger frowned.

"I don't know. Probably not—I hope to Heaven he didn't." He hesitated. "As a matter of fact, he made me sort of sore to-night—all that junk about his cold bath."

With their arms about each other, they started up the walk to the house.

"I'll bet he doesn't take a cold bath every morning," continued Roger ruminatively; "or three times a week, either." He fumbled in his pocket for the key and inserted it in the lock with savage precision. Then he turned around defiantly. "I'll bet he hasn't had a bath for a month."

II

After a fortnight of intensive work, Roger Halsey's days blurred into each other and passed by in blocks of twos and threes and fours. From eight until 5.30 he was in his office. Then a half-hour on the commuting train, where he scrawled notes on the backs of envelopes under the dull yellow light. By 7.30 his crayons, shears, and sheets of white cardboard were spread over the living-room table, and he labored there with much grunting and sighing until midnight, while Gretchen lay on the sofa with a book, and the door-bell tinkled occasionally behind the drawn blinds. At twelve there was always an argument as to whether he would come to bed. He would agree to come after he had cleared up evrything; but as he was invariably sidetracked by half a dozen new ideas, he usually found Gretchen sound asleep when he tiptoed up-stairs.

Sometimes it was three o'clock before Roger squashed his last cigarette into the overloaded ash-tray, and he would undress in the dark, disembodied with fatigue, but with a sense of triumph that he had lasted out another day.

Christmas came and went and he scarcely noticed that it was gone. He remembered it afterward as the day he completed the window-cards for Garrod's shoes. This was one of the eight large accounts for which he was pointing in January—if he got half of them he was assured a quarter of a million dollars' worth of business during the year.

But the world outside his business became a chaotic dream. He was aware that on two cool December Sundays George Tompkins had taken Gretchen horseback riding, and that another time she had gone out with him in his automobile to spend the afternoon skiing on the country-club hill. A picture of Tompkins, in an expensive frame, had appeared one morning on their bedroom wall. And one night he was shocked into a startled protest when Gretchen went to the theatre with Tompkins in town.

But his work was almost done. Daily now his layouts arrived from the printers until seven of them were piled and docketed in his office safe. He knew how good they were. Money alone couldn't buy such work; more than he realized himself, it had been a labor of love.

December tumbled like a dead leaf from the calendar. There was an agonizing week when he had to give up coffee because it made his heart pound so. If he could hold on now for four days—three days——

On Thursday afternoon H. G. Garrod was to arrive in New York. On Wednesday evening Roger came home at seven to find Gretchen poring over the December bills with a strange expression in her eyes.

"What's the matter?"

She nodded at the bills. He ran through them, his brow wrinkling in a frown.

"Gosh!"

"I can't help it," she burst out suddenly. "They're terrible."

"Well, I didn't marry you because you were a wonderful housekeeper. I'll manage about the bills some way. Don't worry your little head over it."

She regarded him coldly.

"You talk as if I were a child."

"I have to," he said with sudden irritation.

"Well, at least I'm not a piece of bric-à-brac that you can just put somewhere and forget."

He knelt down by her quickly, and took her arms in his hands.

"Gretchen, listen!" he said breathlessly. "For God's sake, don't go to pieces now! We're both all stored up with malice and reproach, and if we had a quarrel it'd be terrible. I love you, Gretchen. Say you love me—quick!"

"You know I love you."

The quarrel was averted, but there was an unnatural tenseness all through dinner. It came to a climax afterward when he began to spread his working materials on the table.

"Oh, Roger," she protested, "I thought you didn't have to work to-night."

"I didn't think I'd have to, but something came up."

"I've invited George Tompkins over."

"Oh, gosh!" he exclaimed. "Well, I'm sorry, honey, but you'll have to phone him not to come."

"He's left," she said. "He's coming straight from town. He'll be here any minute now."

Roger groaned. It occurred to him to send them both to the movies, but somehow the suggestion stuck on his lips. He did not want her at the movies; he wanted her here, where he could look up and know she was by his side.

George Tompkins arrived breezily at eight o'clock. "Aha!" he cried reprovingly, coming into the room. "Still at it."

Roger agreed coolly that he was.

"Better quit—better quit before you have to." He sat down with a long sigh of physical comfort and lit a cigarette. "Take it from a fellow who's looked into the question scientifically. We can stand so much, and then—bang!"

"If you'll excuse me"—Roger made his voice as polite as possible—"I'm going up-stairs and finish this work."

"Just as you like, Roger." George waved his hand carelessly. "It isn't that I mind. I'm the friend of the family and I'd just as soon see the missus as the mister." He smiled playfully. "But if I were you, old boy, I'd put away my work and get a good night's sleep."

When Roger had spread out his materials on the bed up-stairs he found that he could still hear the rumble and murmur of their voices through the thin floor. He began wondering what they found to talk about. As he plunged deeper into his work his mind had a tendency to revert sharply to his question, and several times he arose and paced nervously up and down the room.

The bed was ill adapted to his work. Several times the paper slipped from the board on which it rested, and the pencil punched through. Everything was wrong to-night. Letters and figures blurred before his eyes, and as an accompaniment to the beating of his temples came those persistent murmuring voices.

At ten he realized that he had done nothing for more than an hour, and with a sudden exclamation he gathered together his papers, replaced them in his portfolio, and went down-stairs. They were sitting together on the sofa when he came in.

"Oh, hello!" cried Gretchen, rather unnecessarily, he thought. "We were just discussing you."

"Thank you," he answered ironically. "What particular part of my anatomy was under the scalpel?"

"Your health," said Tompkins jovially.

"My health's all right," answered Roger shortly.

"But you look at it so selfishly, old fella," cried Tompkins. "You only consider yourself in the matter. Don't you think Gretchen has any rights? If you were working on a wonderful sonnet or a—a portrait of some madonna or something"—he glanced at Gretchen's Titian hair—"why, then I'd say go ahead. But you're not. It's just some silly advertisement about how to sell Nobald's hair tonic, and if all the hair tonic ever made was dumped into the ocean to-morrow the world wouldn't be one bit the worse for it."

"Wait a minute," said Roger angrily; "that's not quite fair. I'm not kidding myself about the importance of my work—it's just as useless as the stuff you do. But to Gretchen and me it's just about the most important thing in the world."

"Are you implying that my work is useless?" demanded Tompkins incredulously.

"No; not if it brings happiness to some poor sucker of a pants manufacturer who doesn't know how to spend his money."

Tompkins and Gretchen exchanged a glance.

"Oh-h-h!" exclaimed Tompkins ironically. "I didn't realize that all these years I've just been wasting my time."

"You're a loafer," said Roger rudely.

"Me?" cried Tompkins angrily. "You call me a loafer because I have a little balance in my life and find time to do interesting things? Because I play hard as well as work hard and don't let myself get to be a dull, tiresome drudge?"

Both men were angry now, and their voices had risen, though on Tompkin's face there still remained the semblance of a smile.

"What I object to," said Roger steadily, "is that for the last six weeks you seem to have done all your playing around here."

"Roger!" cried Gretchen. "What do you mean by talking like that?"

"Just what I said."

"You've just lost your temper." Tompkins lit a cigarette with ostentatious coolness. "You're so nervous from overwork you don't know what you're saying. You're on the verge of a nervous break——"

"You get out of here!" cried Roger fiercely. "You get out of here right now—before I throw you out!"

Tompkins got angrily to his feet.

"You—you throw me out?" he cried incredulously.

They were actually moving toward each other when Gretchen stepped between them, and grabbing Tompkin's arm urged him toward the door.

"He's acting like a fool, George, but you better get out," she cried, groping in the hall for his hat.

"He insulted me!" shouted Tompkins. "He threatened to throw me out!"

"Never mind, George," pleaded Gretchen. "He doesn't know what he's saying. Please go! I'll see you at ten o'clock to-morrow."

She opened the door.

"You won't see him at ten o'clock to-morrow," said Roger steadily. "He's not coming to this house any more."

Tompkins turned to Gretchen.

"It's his house," he suggested. "Perhaps we'd better meet at mine."

Then he was gone, and Gretchen had shut the door behind him. Her eyes were full of angry tears.

"See what you've done!" she sobbed. "The only friend I had, the only person in the world who liked me enough to treat me decently, is insulted by my husband in my own house."

She threw herself on the sofa and began to cry passionately into the pillows.

"He brought it on himself," said Roger stubbornly. "I've stood as much as my self-respect will allow. I don't want you going out with him any more."

"I will go out with him!" cried Gretchen wildly. "I'll go out with him all I want! Do you think it's any fun living here with you?"

"Gretchen," he said coldly, "get up and put on your hat and coat and go out that door and never come back!"

Her mouth fell slightly ajar.

"But I don't want to get out," she said dazedly.

"Well, then, behave yourself." And he added in a gentler voice: "I thought you were going to sleep for this forty days."

"Oh, yes," she cried bitterly, "easy enough to say! But I'm tired of sleeping." She got up, faced him defiantly. "And what's more, I'm going riding with George Tompkins to-morrow."

"You won't go out with him if I have to take you to New York and sit you down in my office until I get through."

She looked at him with rage in her eyes.

"I hate you," she said slowly. "And I'd like to take all the work you've done and tear it up and throw it in the fire. And just to give you something to worry about to-morrow, I probably won't be here when you get back."

She got up from the sofa, and very deliberately looked at her flushed, tear-stained face in the mirror. Then she ran up-stairs and slammed herself into the bedroom.

Automatically Roger spread out his work on the living-room table. The bright colors of the designs, the vivid ladies—Gretchen had posed for one of them—holding orange ginger ale or glistening silk hosiery, dazzled his mind into a sort of coma. His restless crayon moved here and there over the pictures, shifting a block of letters half an inch to the right, trying a dozen blues for a cool blue, and eliminating the word that made a phrase anæmic and pale. Half an hour passed—he was deep in the work now; there was no sound in the room but the velvety scratch of the crayon over the glossy board.

After a long while he looked at his watch—it was after three. The wind had come up outside and was rushing by the house corners in loud, alarming swoops, like a heavy body falling through space. He stopped his work and listened. He was not tired now, but his head felt as if it was covered with bulging veins like those pictures that hang in doctors' offices showing a body stripped of decent skin. He put his hands to his head and felt it all over. It seemed to him that on his temple the veins were knotty and brittle around an old scar.

Suddenly he began to be afraid. A hundred warnings he had heard swept into his mind. People did wreck themselves with overwork, and his body and brain were of the same vulnerable and perishable stuff. For the first time he found himself envying George Tompkin's calm nerves and healthy routine. He arose and began pacing the room in a panic.

"I've got to sleep," he whispered to himself tensely. "Otherwise I'm going crazy."

He rubbed his hand over his eyes, and returned to the table to put up his work, but his fingers were shaking so that he could scarcely grasp the board. The sway of a bare branch against the window made him start and cry out. He sat down on the sofa and tried to think.

"Stop! Stop! Stop!" the clock said. "Stop! Stop! Stop!"

"I can't stop," he answered aloud. "I can't afford to stop."

Listen! Why, there was the wolf at the door now! He could hear its sharp claws scrape along the varnished woodwork. He jumped up, and running to the front door flung it open; then started back with a ghastly cry. An enormous wolf was standing on the porch, glaring at him with red, malignant eyes. As he watched it the hair bristled on its neck; it gave a low growl and disappeared in the darkness. Then Roger realized with a silent, mirthless laugh that it was the police dog from over the way.

Dragging his limbs wearily into the kitchen, he brought the alarm-clock into the living-room and set it for seven. Then he wrapped himself in his overcoat, lay down on the sofa and fell immediately into a heavy, dreamless sleep.

When he awoke the light was still shining feebly, but the room was the gray color of a winter morning. He got up, and looking anxiously at his hands found to his relief that they no longer trembled. He felt much better. Then he began to remember in detail the events of the night before, and his brow drew up again in three shallow wrinkles. There was work ahead of him, twenty-four hours of work; and Gretchen, whether she wanted to or not, must sleep for one more day.

Roger's mind glowed suddenly as if he had just thought of a new advertising idea. A few minutes later he was hurrying through the sharp morning air to Kingsley's drug-store.

"Is Mr. Kingsley down yet?"

The druggist's head appeared around the corner of the prescription-room.

"I wonder if I can talk to you alone."

At 7.30, back home again, Roger walked into his own kitchen. The general housework girl had just arrived and was taking off her hat.

"Bebé"—he was not on familiar terms with her; this was her name—"I want you to cook Mrs. Halsey's breakfast right away. I'll take it up myself."

It struck Bebé that this was an unusual service for so busy a man to render his wife, but if she had seen his conduct when he had carried the tray from the kitchen she would have been even more surprised. For he set it down on the dining-room table and put into the coffee half a teaspoonful of a white substance that was not powdered sugar. Then he mounted the stairs and opened the door of the bedroom.

Gretchen woke up with a start, glanced at the twin bed which had not been slept in, and bent on Roger a glance of astonishment, which changed to contempt when she saw the breakfast in his hand. She thought he was bringing it as a capitulation.

"I don't want any breakfast," she said coldly, and his heart sank, "except some coffee."

"No breakfast?" Roger's voice expressed disappointment.

"I said I'd take some coffee."

Roger discreetly deposited the tray on a table beside the bed and returned quickly to the kitchen.

"We're going away until to-morrow afternoon," he told Bebé, "and I want to close up the house right now. So you just put on your hat and go home."

He looked at his watch. It was ten minutes to eight, and he wanted to catch the 8.10 train. He waited five minutes and then tiptoed softly up-stairs and into Gretchen's room. She was sound asleep. The coffee cup was empty save for black dregs and a film of thin brown paste on the bottom. He looked at her rather anxiously, but her breathing was regular and clear.

From the closet he took a suitcase and very quickly began filling it with her shoes—street shoes, evening slippers, rubber-soled oxfords —he had not realized that she owned so many pairs. When he closed the suitcase it was bulging.

He hesitated a minute, took a pair of sewing scissors from a box, and following the telephone-wire until it went out of sight behind the dresser, severed it in one neat clip. He jumped as there was a soft knock at the door. It was the nursemaid. He had forgotten her existence.

"Mrs. Halsey and I are going up to the city till to-morrow," he said glibly. "Take Maxy to the beach and have lunch there. Stay all day."

Back in the room, a wave of pity passed over him. Gretchen seemed suddenly lovely and helpless, sleeping there. It was somehow terrible to rob her young life of a day. He touched her hair with his fingers, and as she murmured something in her dream he leaned over and kissed her bright cheek. Then he picked up the suitcase full of shoes, locked the door, and ran briskly down the stairs.

III

By five o'clock that afternoon the last package of cards for Garrod's shoes had been sent by messenger to H. G. Garrod at the Biltmore Hotel. He was to give a decision next morning. At 5.30 Roger's stenographer tapped him on the shoulder.

"Mr. Golden, the superintendent of the building, to see you."

Roger turned around dazedly.

"Oh, how do?"

Mr. Golden came directly to the point. If Mr. Halsey intended to keep the office any longer, the little oversight about the rent had better be remedied right away.

"Mr. Golden," said Roger wearily, "everything'll be all right to-morrow. If you worry me now maybe you'll never get your money. After to-morrow nothing'll matter."

Mr. Golden looked at the tenant uneasily. Young men sometimes did away with themselves when business went wrong. Then his eye fell unpleasantly on the initialled suitcase beside the desk.

"Going on a trip?" he asked pointedly.

"What? Oh, no. That's just some clothes."

"Clothes, eh? Well, Mr. Halsey, just to prove that you mean what you say, suppose you let me keep that suitcase until to-morrow noon."

"Help yourself."

Mr. Golden picked it up with a deprecatory gesture.

"Just a matter of form," he remarked.

"I understand," said Roger, swinging around to his desk. "Good afternoon."

Mr. Golden seemed to feel that the conversation should close on a softer key.

"And don't work too hard, Mr. Halsey. You don't want to have a nervous break——"

"No," shouted Roger, "I don't. But I will if you don't leave me alone."

As the door closed behind Mr. Golden, Roger's stenographer turned sympathetically around.

"You shouldn't have let him get away with that," she said. "What's in there? Clothes?"

"No," answered Roger absently. "Just all my wife's shoes."

He slept in the office that night on a sofa beside his desk. At dawn he awoke with a nervous start, rushed out into the street for coffee, and returned in ten minutes in a panic—afraid that he might have missed Mr. Garrod's telephone call. It was then 6.30.

By eight o'clock his whole body seemed to be on fire. When his two artists arrived he was stretched on the couch in almost physical pain. The phone rang imperatively at 9.30, and he picked up the receiver with trembling hands.

"Hello."

"Is this the Halsey agency?"

"Yes, this is Mr. Halsey speaking."

"This is Mr. H. G. Garrod."

Roger's heart stopped beating.

"I called up, young fellow, to say that this is wonderful work you've given us here. We want all of it and as much more as your office can do."

"Oh, God!" cried Roger into the transmitter.

"What?" Mr. H. G. Garrod was considerably startled. "Say, wait a minute there!"

But he was talking to nobody. The phone had clattered to the floor, and Roger, stretched full length on the couch, was sobbing as if his heart would break.

IV

Three hours later, his face somewhat pale, but his eyes calm as a child's, Roger opened the door of his wife's bedroom with the morning paper under his arm. At the sound of his footsteps she started awake.

"What time is it?" she demanded.

He looked at his watch.

"Twelve o'clock."

Suddenly she began to cry.

"Roger," she said brokenly, "I'm sorry I was so bad last night."

He nodded coolly.

"Everything's all right now," he answered. Then, after a pause: "I've got the account—the biggest one."

She turned toward him quickly.

"You have?" Then, after a minute's silence: "Can I get a new dress?"

"Dress?" He laughed shortly. "You can get a dozen. This account alone will bring us in forty thousand a year. It's one of the biggest in the West."

She looked at him, startled.

"Forty thousand a year!"

"Yes."

"Gosh"—and then faintly—"I didn't know it'd really be anything like that." Again she thought a minute. "We can have a house like George Tompkins'."

"I don't want an interior-decoration shop."

"Forty thousand a year!" she repeated again, and then added softly: "Oh, Roger——"

"Yes?"

"I'm not going out with George Tompkins."

"I wouldn't let you, even if you wanted to," he said shortly.

She made a show of indignation.

"Why, I've had a date with him for this Thursday for weeks.

"It isn't Thursday."

"It is."

"It's Friday."

"Why, Roger, you must be crazy! Don't you think I know what day it is?"

"It isn't Thursday," he said stubbornly. "Look!" And he held out the morning paper.

"Friday!" she exclaimed. "Why, this is a mistake! This must be last's week's paper. To-day's Thursday."

She closed her eyes and thought for a moment.

"Yesterday was Wednesday," she said decisively. "The laundress came yesterday. I guess I know."

"Well," he said smugly, "look at the paper. There isn't any question about it."

With a bewildered look on her face she got out of bed and began searching for her clothes. Roger went into the bathroom to shave. A minute later he heard the springs creak again. Gretchen was getting back into bed.

"What's the matter?" he inquired, putting his head around the corner of the bathroom.

"I'm scared," she said in a trembling voice. "I think my nerves are giving away. I can't find any of my shoes."

"You shoes? Why, the closet's full of them."

"I know, but I can't see one." Her face was pale with fear. "Oh, Roger!"

Roger came to her bedside and put his arm around her.

"Oh, Roger," she cried, "what's the matter with me? First that newspaper, and now all my shoes. Take care of me, Roger."

"I'll get the doctor," he said.

He walked remorselessly to the telephone and took up the receiver.

"Phone seems to be out of order," he remarked after a minute; "I'll send Bebé."

The doctor arrived in ten minutes.

"I think I'm on the verge of a collapse," Gretchen told him in a strained voice.

Doctor Gregory sat down on the edge of the bed and took her wrist in his hand.

"It seems to be in the air this morning."

"I got up," said Gretchen in an awed voice, "and I found that I'd lost a whole day. I had an engagement to go riding with George Tompkins——"

"What?" exclaimed the doctor in surprise. Then he laughed. "George Tompkins won't go riding with any one for many days to come."

"Has he gone away?" asked Gretchen curiously.

"He's going West."

"Why?" demanded Roger. "Is he running away with somebody's wife?"

"No," said Doctor Gregory. "He's had a nervous breakdown."

"What?" they exclaimed in unison.

"He just collapsed like an opera-hat in his cold shower."

"But he was always talking about his—his balanced life," gasped Gretchen. "He had it on his mind."

"I know," said the doctor. "He's been babbling about it all morning. I think it's driven him a little mad. He worked pretty hard at it, you know."

"At what?" demanded Roger in bewilderment.

"At keeping his life balanced." He turned to Gretchen. "Now all I'll prescribe for this lady here is a good rest. If she'll just stay around the house for a few days and take forty winks of sleep she'll be as fit as ever. She's been under some strain."

"Doctor," exclaimed Roger hoarsely, "don't you think I'd better have a rest or something? I've been working pretty hard lately."

"You!" Doctor Gregory laughed, slapped him violently on the back. "My boy, I never saw you looking better in your life."

Roger turned away quickly to conceal his smile—winked forty times, or almost forty times, at the autographed picture of Mr. George Tompkins, which hung slightly askew on the bedroom wall.